WIRED GHOST

PARADISE CRIME THRILLERS BOOK 11

TOBY NEAL

The course of true love never did run smooth.
~William Shakespeare

CHAPTER ONE

Sophie
Day one, two weeks after the end of Wired Truth

LOOKING for a runaway teen living with meth cookers, especially during a massive volcanic eruption, was probably not a good idea. But it was too late now. They were committed.

Sophie Smithson grabbed the sissy strap to stabilize herself as the Security Solutions SUV, driven by her partner, Jake Dunn, bumped across a black rock plain on the Big Island. Their client, Ki Ayabe, an import business owner, had hired Security Solutions to locate and retrieve his seventeen-year-old daughter Lia, who'd supposedly run off with a meth cooker named Finn O'Brien "to shame and anger me," Ayabe had declared. Sophie hadn't liked the pompous, sharp-tempered Japanese man, but his tale of an out-of-control teen being taken advantage of by an older drug dealer was compelling.

"Weird set of directions," Jake frowned, peering through the windshield to scan the empty black plain, made mysterious by a heavy mist of volcanic emissions. "Not much out here."

Sophie tapped the navigation app on her phone. "There are no road signs to the *kipuka* where the meth lab is located. Natural formations and GPS coordinates were the best our informant could do. Thankfully, there's a track we can follow." *Kipukas,* small, raised "islands" of old growth trees, bushes, and wildlife, surrounded by fields of raw, new lava, were a phenomenon unique to the Big Island.

Jake flexed his large hands on the wheel. "We've got a big chuckhole ahead."

The white Ford Escape wasn't really built for the terrain of their current route, and Sophie clung to the dash, as well as the strap, as the vehicle bucked through the stony rut. She glanced at Jake. "You sure you aren't missing your easy California life installing alarm systems?"

"You know I hated that," Jake grinned, a flash of white teeth. "Thanks for getting me back on the Security Solutions payroll. It was a relief to let Felicia buy me out of the business." Jake had recently gone through a breakup with his girlfriend/business partner, and relocated to Oahu to be with Sophie. They were taking it slow, just beginning to date again, and this was their first job together in more than two years.

"The case looked interesting. A chance to get away from Oahu with my boyfriend." They hit a particularly deep hole, and Sophie yelped as her head banged the door frame, swearing in Thai. *"Daughter of a rabid jackal!"*

"Sorry." Jake wrestled the wheel, slowing them further. "This is a bit rugged, but it's an adventure. And the end of your month with Momi is always a good time to be distracted."

"Exactly what I was thinking." Sophie stabilized herself with a hand on the dash. "Ginger and Anubis love all the socialization they'll get with other dogs at the boarding kennel while we're gone. And I always try to fill my schedule when I have to send Momi back to Kaua`i." Sophie's two-year-old daughter was currently with her biological father, Alika Wolcott, and nanny, Armita, in their unusual custody arrangement of one month on, one month off. While always a hard adjustment for Sophie when Momi and Armita left, the situation gave her time to work active cases in the field. When her daughter and Armita were with her, Sophie did administrative tasks in the office. Her child seemed to take the changes of venue in stride, with the consistency of care that Armita maintained by accompanying Momi back and forth between homes.

Jake slowed the SUV further and crawled the vehicle over a mound of rock. "I don't like the seismic reports we've been seeing the last few days for Kilauea Volcano."

"There *have* been a lot of micro-earthquakes reported lately. But the eruption at Kilauea has been steady since the 1980's. There is no reason to assume there's going to be any new lava flows in this area," Sophie said. "The main danger we have to watch out for is the emissions. The gases can be quite toxic, but they're only present around the areas with fresh activity. According to my source, this *kipuka* is where the meth lab is hidden. I had to call in a favor to get this intel, but hopefully it's here, and saves us a lot of time."

"Still. It's too bad the wind is coming from the south and pushing in all this vog," Jake said. "Visibility is so much better when it's blowing out to sea."

The vog blanketed the plain in a soft, gray shroud. The sun glared acid yellow through the particulate gases and hurt Sophie's eyes, adding to a spooky feeling as they moved through the rough terrain. She slid on a pair of mirrored sunglasses as they reached a flat area marked by several rusted out vehicles.

"I think this is the end of the road," Sophie said.

Jake already had his hand on his weapon as he guided the SUV into a turn. "I'm positioning us for a quick getaway."

"Good idea." Sophie jumped out of the Ford and covered them visually with her Glock, as Jake maneuvered the vehicle into position pointed back the way they'd come. She saw no one, but that didn't mean they weren't being watched.

Jake checked his weapon, ejecting the magazine and then ramming it back into the grip. Sophie had gotten used to her Glock 19 police issue pistol during her FBI years. They both wore body armor under camo fatigues done in a gray, brownish-black and slate blue pattern that Sophie hoped would help blend with the surroundings.

Sophie headed for a rough path visible between the junked cars and checked her GPS again. "This track is heading in the direction of the coordinates. We're on the right path."

They moved out, Sophie in front, Jake at her back.

"What's the plan? Arrive, guns blazing, grab the girl, and haul her back to her father, tucked under my arm?" Jake asked.

"Like I told you back at the office, I don't really know. You're the extraction specialist." Sophie slanted a glance over her shoulder at Jake. "I still remember that from your business card when I first met you."

"And I remember being sandbagged by how gorgeous you were in that skimpy red top when you first met me at your door," Jake said.

"That was my sleep outfit. I wasn't expecting you."

"All the more unforgettable."

Sophie smiled, but kept scanning the barren lava for hostiles.

Yes, she and Jake were reconnecting and taking it slow, but that didn't mean they didn't have a history—an intense one that had been blossoming until Momi's kidnapping as a newborn, when the circumstances around that devastating event had torn them apart.

Sophie continued to watch carefully as they trekked through the vog along the stony, uneven trail worn onto the raw lava surface. "All we really know about the case is that Lia is supposed to be with this guy Finn O'Brien. He's an undocumented Irishman who supposedly came to the Big Island on vacation, and outstayed his visa. The man found a way to make an illegal living out here, and has gathered a close team of scoundrels and rogues to help him with that."

"Scoundrels and rogues?"

"If the adjective fits . . ."

"I think we should be prepared for resistance, beginning with our target. Lia's a minor, but she's not likely to want to come back to daddy because, although Ayabe won't admit it, she basically ran

4

away. O'Brien's a meth cooker and dealer with a record and not much to lose. Let's recon their camp first, then pull back and figure out a plan. We might need reinforcements."

"Just what I was going to suggest." Sophie flashed her smile at him. The last wisps of her depression, easily activated when her daughter was gone, had been dispelled by the upcoming action.

"Would you mind if I moved out in front?" Jake raised his brows, steel-gray eyes serious.

"Not at all. I was wondering how long you'd be able to hang back," Sophie said. "I wasn't joking when I said I relied on your Special Ops background in situations like this."

"Thanks." He kissed her as he passed by, a quick touch on the lips that lit her nerve endings.

Yes, she had a boyfriend in Jake—but the jury was still out on whether they would make it. So much had happened between them, and others. . . *like Connor*. Now the de facto leader of a clandestine spy organization with its roots in guarding Thailand's royal family, her former lover known as the Ghost continued to practice his unique brand of cyber justice, and through that organization he now commanded an army of ninjas. He wanted her to help him with his "mission," and though Sophie had dabbled in equalizing the scales of justice, she wasn't ready to commit to anything more.

Maybe this time with Jake would show her a new direction—and meanwhile, his rear view wasn't hard to look at. She suppressed a grin.

They reached a fork in the trail. Jake stopped. "You've got the GPS. Which way do we go?"

CHAPTER TWO

Jake

Sᴏᴘʜɪᴇ ʀᴇᴍᴏᴠᴇᴅ her phone from her pocket while Jake scanned the spooky, vog-shrouded plain. "I don't like this," he said.

"I don't, either." She frowned down at the device, and when she did, the gunshot scar bisecting her cheekbone pulled up like the cord on a window shade. "We're within a half mile. Take the left fork."

Sometimes he forgot how close Sophie'd come to death that time, but the scar would always be there to remind him. The terrible experience of carrying her unconscious, blood-soaked body out of a grave-like pit, as he tried to keep her alive, would always be etched on his memory.

Along with their camo fatigues, they carried small backpacks that, instead of snacks, contained extra weapons, ammo, supplies for a quick shelter, and even a dose of sleepy drugs to hit the target with if Lia Ayabe proved too belligerent.

But Jake hated going into a potential conflict situation with so little information.

All they really knew was that the girl was underage, that she was shacked up with a dangerous meth cooker and his crew, and that the drug gang was holed up in an extremely remote and volatile lava area. *Not good.*

"Let's go off comm," Jake said. "No more talking. We don't know how far out they might have countermeasures." They didn't need the GPS anymore now that he'd gotten a look at the distance, and taken the trail leading to the coordinates.

Sophie nodded and fell in behind him. Her trust in his leadership warmed him.

Jake palmed his weapon and kept his eyes moving and ears tuned, walking light on the balls of his feet to minimize the crunch of the gravel—and still, he almost hit the tripwire.

He stopped so suddenly, leaning over, that Sophie collided with his back.

Jake held up a fist. Sophie moved back and out of the way as Jake bent carefully, taking a penlight out of his pocket and lighting up the thin wire strung across the path. Sophie sucked in a breath and went very still.

The only thing that had clued him in to the line was the slightly different shade of a rock on the side of the trail to which an IED had been attached. Jake followed the wire from the rock to the other side of the trail. A grenade's pin had been connected to the line.

Tripping on the wire would have pulled the pin, and the grenade would've gone off—a simple but effective trap for the unwary.

Jake disconnected the pin and picked up the grenade. He tucked it into his leg pouch, turning to Sophie with a wink and a smile, hoping to reassure her. "Might be able to use this later."

Sophie nodded, but her eyes were wide and her tawny skin had paled.

Jake kept his pen light on and they walked slower—but he saw nothing further as they approached the *kipuka.*

Untouched, old growth giant koa and ohia trees forming a uniquely Hawaiian forest rose out of the barren lava like a fantasy scene set on a knoll, wreathed in drifting skeins of vog and mist. Formed by lava flowing around a raised hill or ridge, *kipukas* were relics of a previous time. As they approached, the air sweetened with the twittering song of endangered, seldom seen endemic birds that lived in these isolated, high elevation remnant forests, drinking the nectar of flowers and feasting on bugs that lived only in the bark of rare trees.

Jake crouched to inspect the ground as the trail disappeared into bushy growth at the base of the *kipuka*'s slight elevation. He flashed the high intensity penlight around, and spotted another nearly invisible trip line, tied between two large *hapu`u* tree ferns.

"Be careful, Jake." Sophie touched his back, her voice husky.

They hadn't made love since reconnecting a couple of weeks ago; they still had a lot of talks to have, a lot of ground to cover, a lot of mistakes to forgive; and most of those were Jake's.

But even in this moment of danger, her touch affected him more than he wanted it to. Jake gritted his teeth and focused on the task at hand.

He traced the fishing line to another grenade, and this time he detected a wireless camera node on another tree, pointed in their direction. He cursed under his breath, and gestured Sophie out of the way.

He moved up on the surveillance device from the side, knocking it off the fern tree. He crunched it under a boot, and then pushed at the tree and dug at its roots with a heel, kicking it askew and disturbing the earth at the base. "Hopefully no one's monitoring the camera closely and it's just set to a motion sensor alarm. I'm trying to make it look like a pig knocked the camera off the tree and destroyed it—worth a shot that they didn't see us."

Sophie helped in scuffing up the ground as if one of the many wild boar in the area had gone after the tree's roots.

"Let's get off this trail and see if we've been made." Jake gestured for Sophie to follow him, glad that they had chosen clothing that would meld with the forest floor, foliage, and the dark shades of the lava.

They moved away from the path into the brush and bushes as

quietly as they could, and finally Jake tugged Sophie down beside him in the shadow of a large ohia tree. "We need to work our way closer to the camp. See if we can move in and grab our target, or at least verify her location and come back with a better strike team."

Sophie nodded. "That's the plan." Jake led them forward slowly through virgin forest, paralleling the path the meth cookers had made.

Hearing the crunching of leaves underfoot and the sound of voices, Jake stopped Sophie with a hand on her arm, and they hunkered down behind a fallen tree. Jake peeked up long enough to spot two men coming along the trail.

"That damn camera," one of them grumbled. "Stupid thing is always making the alarm go off." He was wearing a red ball cap, a bright target in the dim jungle.

"Probably just another wild pig or a battery that needs changing," the other man agreed. He wore a Primo Beer hoodie over drop-waisted jeans like an urban gangsta dropped into the Hawaii wilderness.

These guys weren't pros, but the weapons they packed were plenty deadly: Red Cap carried an AK, loosely hanging by a chest strap, and Primo Beer carried a couple of Desert Eagle chrome magnums, one in his hand and the other tucked into his belt.

Jake and Sophie held absolutely still as the men passed them, loud and oblivious.

"Now's a good time to get some distance toward the camp," Jake whispered. He grabbed Sophie's hand, guiding her up onto the well-maintained trail. They broke into a run, both holding their weapons at the ready, and soon reached a fence topped with razor wire, and a locked gate.

"We're at ground zero," Jake whispered. He led Sophie into the shelter of a large, fallen log off to the side of the path. "Let's move in closer and see what we can see."

CHAPTER THREE

Connor

CONNOR WALKED among the rows of drilling trainee ninjas in the main courtyard of the Yām Khûmkạn's temple stronghold. The recruits practiced all around him, their black robes anonymous, their shaved heads rendering them almost indistinguishable. And yet, Connor could sense each man's energy, and registered them in his mind's eye in all the shades of the rainbow.

He could already tell which men would struggle. He could see the ones that would fail. And he knew which ones would betray the code. A perception of the energy field around each person had been becoming clearer and clearer to him in the time since he'd been promoted to Number One leader in the Master's absence.

But Connor had no one to discuss his perceptions with, now that the Master had gone.

Was this how the Master knew which number to ink onto the back of the recruits' shaved scalps when they first arrived? Why then, did the Master allow things to play out, and the recruits to go through their training? Was there a chance for someone to change the ugly color of their aura to something cleaner, clearer?

Connor glanced towards the dais at the front of the orderly rows, where his second-in-command, Pi, lead them by example.

Pi's movements were crisp. His form was impeccable, perfect. His stance was strong. The color of his aura was a fine bright blue, but there was a sickly quality wavering through it, a bruised edge that revealed corruption.

Connor knew, when he had defeated Pi in combat and allowed him to live, that he'd potentially only delayed a problem that would have to be resolved.

But still he didn't want conflict. He wanted a partnership with Pi, an equal sharing of the responsibility of leadership. He didn't feel ready to run everything at the compound indefinitely, alone. *How long would it go on?*

He already missed Sophie and her precious daughter Momi, the daughter of his heart. Not only that, but he also had many possible cases awaiting his brand of justice. Running the compound and the management of the recruits was time-consuming. With no idea of the time frame of the Master's absence, he couldn't make any forward movement in the ways that would make sense to him: namely, handing over more and more of the responsibility for the day-to-day running of the compound to Pi, and spending more time on the overall mission of the Yām Khûmkạn and his vigilante justice activities.

Jake was back with Sophie, and sometime in the future, there would be a reckoning between him and his onetime friend. Jake still carried anger toward Connor for a perceived deception involved with his ongoing friendship with Sophie, and Connor didn't look forward to when Jake delivered the beatdown he'd promised—*but he'd endure it, for Sophie's sake.*

Connor adjusted a recruit's stance near him with a touch of the ivory baton he carried. Moving on, he corrected another man's kick, falling in beside him to model the proper form. He moved to the end of the row, and then, when all of the fight choreography had been completed, and Pi had given the signal to fall back into stillness, Connor raised his hands and gave the daily blessing.

The men dispersed to their various tasks, leaving Connor and Pi alone in the courtyard.

It was time.

Connor nodded to Nine, his closest friend and ally in the organization. Nine trotted off. They'd discussed this plan in advance, and Connor approached Pi. "Come. Take breakfast with me in the garden, and we will discuss the progress of the men."

Pi was a harshly handsome man, bulkier than Connor, with dark eyes and expressive black brows. His hair, too, was growing out and was already longer than the blond fuzz covering Connor's scalp now that he no longer had to shave it.

Connor led the man through the maze of aisles and stairs to the Master's garden. This sanctuary was the antithesis of the Spartan environment of the compound, with its ancient stone and lack of ornamentation. The garden was surrounded by high walls to protect it from the jungle and the elements. Beautiful flowering and fruit trees lined those walls. A koi pond, thick with water lilies, was the centerpiece. The grass around the pond was smooth as velvet, and a table waited under one of the trees, already laid with two places and their meal dishes.

He felt Pi wondering at the beauty of the place, at Connor's motives for bringing him there. This wasn't telepathy, but an odd kind of knowing, a sense of the emotions of those around him. Connor's new ability to slow and manipulate time was evolving in new directions. He had to speak to the Master about it as soon as possible. *But that time was not now.*

Connor brought his attention back to the moment. Facing the pond was a six-foot high, one-foot diameter, column of tiger's eye gemstone. That plinth had been the site of Connor's first exposure to the Master's incredible abilities, powers he was beginning to share.

"I have a test for you," Connor told Pi. "Something the Master showed me."

Pi glanced around the garden, but his gaze came back to the column as he stood beside Connor. Early morning sun struck the stone and seemingly lit it from within. Light flared over the polished surface in mesmerizing patterns.

"What is this test, Number One?" As always, Pi's words were outwardly respectful but vibrated with challenge.

"Leap up on top of that pillar, seat yourself in lotus position, and engage in meditation. When you feel ready, dismount and land standing." Connor well-remembered the Master, one of the first times he had met with him privately, seated cross-legged atop the column. The first rays of the morning sun had struck the gem, turning the column to fire. Connor would never forget standing there, wondering how the Master had gotten to the top, let alone seated himself in that position.

And then the Master had dismounted with a flip, landing on his feet in the grass, perfectly serene.

"Looks easy enough," Pi said.

Connor did not reply.

Pi approached the column. He had clearly never seen the Master at meditation there, or he would not have done what he did—he grasped the column with his hands and thighs, gripping on with tree trunk legs and powerful arms, attempting to shinny up the pillar. He almost made it to the top, but then slid down the length of the pole to land in a disgruntled heap on the grass.

Pi immediately began another assault on the stone column.

Connor might as well get comfortable. He walked over to the table, sat down, and uncovered the dishes, poured himself tea and began a breakfast of eggs, fried rice, and fresh vegetables from the compound's garden.

Pi continued to attempt to climb the plinth, but every time he neared the top, he slid back down. Connor was reminded of watching greased pole climbing contests on YouTube, in another life before this one.

Finally, Pi was able to hook his fingers over the top of the plinth, and, using pure arm strength, drag his body up onto the circular, flat top. The diameter was too narrow for Pi to get his feet under him to stand, or even sit. He hung, draped over the pillar's crown, on his belly.

He glared over at Connor, who was nearly finished with his breakfast. "I will have to work up to this task."

"So it appears. Come have some breakfast before it gets cold." Connor picked up his teacup and took a sip.

Pi shoved back off of the top of the tiger's eye and slid to the ground, frustration in his abrupt movements. Connor, watching the man's energy field, frowned as it darkened from dark blue to almost black around the edges.

That was all the warning he had, as Pi reached into the pocket of his *gi*. A flash of metal—and something was flying toward Connor.

Connor stretched time, slowing it down—and he saw a steel ninja star spinning gently, end over end, moving through the air like a child's whirligig and headed straight for Connor's head.

Connor got up from his seat, moving at normal speed, and plucked the six-bladed *shuriken* out of the air, absorbing its momentum with a whirl of his own. He sandwiched it between his palms and walked over to Pi. The man's face was mottled with rage and his energy had gone black with hate.

Connor would have to find someone else to be his leadership partner. He shut his eyes; he felt nothing but compassion and sorrow for Pi. The man could have had all that he wanted, but he'd let jealousy control him.

Connor positioned himself directly in front of his rival, and allowed time to move forward normally again.

Pi crashed into him, carried forward by the momentum of his throw. Connor steadied him with a hand on his shoulder and held out the star, glinting on his palm. "This is yours."

Pi's eyes widened. He staggered back and away from Connor's touch, sputtering. "How did you . . ."

Connor gathered energy from within, centered himself, and

leaped from the ground, performing a neat twist to land on top of the pillar. "You failed, Pi. You are not fit to lead the Yām Khûmkạn. Witnesses?"

Nine, and three more of the senior brethren, were stationed around the walls of the garden, watching through secret peepholes on ledges outside the walls. They rose to stand in their positions, and their heads appeared at the four compass points of the circular garden. They then ascended to stand on the parapet and look down into the sheltered bower.

"We witness, Number One," Nine called out in a loud, ringing voice. "Pi is not fit to lead."

Connor stood on one leg and, carefully using balance and the strength of his feet, eased down into lotus position on the top of the plinth. Seated with his legs folded on the narrow circle of the column, he shut his eyes. "Escort him from the compound," he said quietly.

From behind his closed lids, Connor could still see Pi below him, emitting dark vibrations of hate and despair. The warm, bright energy signatures of Connor's loyal followers on the wall moved as they walked to escort Pi to the outer wall of the compound, where he would be sent out onto the jungle road and into exile.

Pi darted suddenly toward the breakfast table.

Connor opened his eyes as his rival grabbed a knife off of the table, reversing the handle and pointing it toward his own throat.

Connor slowed time again. He floated down off the plinth and plucked the knife out of Pi's fingers. Once more he stood in front of the man, close enough to touch him, this time grasping the means of Pi's intended suicide.

Connor set the knife back down on the breakfast table as time snapped back into normal speed. Pi gasped and his empty hands touched his throat. His eyes fastened on Connor, filled with despair and rage. "How are you doing this?"

"I don't really know. But time obeys my will. And I sense that it is not your time to go from this mortal plane."

"I don't want to live if I am not a part of the Yām."

"I understand. And yet, live you must."

A glimmer of hope in the man's dark eyes. "But why, master?"

Connor didn't correct him; the title of respect was merited. "I can't see the future. Maybe I will be able to someday. I just know it's not your time to die."

The elders from the top of the wall had finally reached them, and they took Pi's arms to escort him away.

"I will never forget what I've seen here," Pi said.

Connor inclined his head. There was nothing more to say. The senior men escorted him away.

Connor sat and gestured to Nine. "Why don't you join me for breakfast instead?"

Nine sat across from him. The man's square, solid shoulders hunched forward, and his unreadable eyes met Connor's. "Your powers are increasing, Number One."

"Yes. But I don't yet know what it means. I can now see the energy fields around people, and read their feelings. This was one of the Master's gifts, although he did not explain that. Now that I have this gift, too, I realize that's how he did so many of the things that seemed impossible to us."

"A divine mystery." Nine uncovered a dish and began eating.

Connor poured some more tea. His thoughts returned to Sophie and her daughter. What did it mean that his powers were increasing? Would they affect his ability to spend time with the only people he considered family?

His private island, Phi Ni, off the coast of Thailand, continued to be an open secret from the Yām Khûmkạn, and the place where he could meet Sophie and her entourage.

"I think you should reach out to the Master," Nine said. "It's time to find out what his plans are, why he has left you in charge, and update him on the situation with Pi. It would also be good to have news of your beloved Sophie's mother, and her health."

"We are not together like that. Sophie has another man in her life." Connor needed at least one person he trusted like a brother. Nine had been that person.

"And yet she is your beloved." Nine poured himself some more tea.

Connor paused to think that over. He and Sophie had had no physical chemistry when they'd last kissed, even filled with expectation and excitement at being together. And still, he had no doubt that she was the only woman he would ever love. "I guess you're right, after all. There are many kinds of love."

"And we explore none of them here at the Yām Khûmkạn," Nine said. "Unfortunately."

"That's another question I have for the Master. Why the celibacy? What does it do for us? How does that aspect affect us as guardians and agents of Thailand? And yet, the Master himself is not celibate." Pim Wat, Sophie's deadly mother, had long shared the Master's bed.

"My assumption has always been that focusing our sexual energy towards the work increases our power."

Connor shook his head. "Perhaps. As my powers have increased, sexual desire and interest have waned."

"We can see that in the older men, in their discipline. The younger ones still suffer. There is much changing of the sheets," Nine grumbled.

"If I stay here permanently, I will want to understand more clearly why we do things the way we do, and how it helps our mission. If it doesn't, I am not opposed to the men having lovers and families."

Nine raised his head, his eyes wide. "That would require a complete overhaul of all protocols."

Connor smiled. "Then perhaps it's time for me to get in touch with the Master, before I change things so much here that he can't recognize this place when he returns."

CHAPTER FOUR

Sophie

SOPHIE CROUCHED beside Jake in the lee of the fallen log. The smell of damp and rotten wood, a pleasantly earthy scent, filled her nostrils. Her ears were tuned for any sound from the trail or the camp, but all she could hear were her own elevated respiration, the twitter of the birds in the trees overhead, and the deep sound of Jake's controlled breathing. She could feel his warmth too, without even touching him; the man threw off heat like a stove.

She scanned around them one more time, still feeling vulnerable and barely hidden, but saw nothing out of the ordinary. She refocused on Jake.

Her partner had his phone out. Using his fingertips, he expanded an image. "This satellite pic of the camp just came in from Bix. This is the intel I was hoping for, going in."

Sophie leaned in close to see.

The image was surprisingly clear for a satellite picture; it made her shiver a little to think of how much of anyone's life could be tracked easily using the cameras circling the planet.

The photograph showed a perimeter of forest inside the fence line, providing some cover for the camp. A central metal barn, whose roof was painted in camouflage colors, squatted beneath the trees, surrounded by smaller outbuildings.

Jake pointed a finger at the closest hut. "Drawing a line from the front gate to this shack, I can estimate where we are relative to the main building. Let's wait here until nightfall. Then make a cut in the fence and go into the sheds that look like they house people; see if we can identify our target. Dark will be a better potential opportunity to extract her, given that they have so many countermeasures."

Sophie looked up into the canopy of trees. "What time is nightfall?"

"Three hours."

She raised her brows. "That's a long time to sit behind a log and wait."

"We could find somewhere with more cover." Jake's smile flickered. "I can think of some ways to pass the time."

Sophie wanted to smile, but shook her head instead. "I think we should go in now. The longer we're hanging out here, the more chance of discovery."

As if to underline her words, they heard the two men coming back. Both ducked lower behind the log. "Gonna have to replace that camera," Red Cap's voice grumbled. "Freakin' pigs."

"At least with our fence, they can't get inside the compound," Primo Beer said.

"O'Brien is going to be pissed."

Jake and Sophie exchanged a glance. "The boyfriend," Jake mouthed.

Sophie risked a glance up and over the log. Red Cap was undoing the padlock on the simple gate made of a square panel of fencing wire. He pulled it open with a creak, and he and Primo Beer went through.

The man was turning back around to re-lock it, when the earth shuddered violently. Red Cap fell to his knees, clinging to the fence.

It took Sophie several seconds to understand what was happening as the quiet forest erupted in sounds of disturbance: the trees shrieked and moaned as they lashed back and forth, rubbing against each other. A sound like wind rushed through their branches, raining twigs and leaves on the heaving ground. Everything jerked around Sophie, as if being in a movie that was glitching. Sophie covered her mouth with a hand to keep from crying out.

"Earthquake!" Jake hissed from behind her.

Sophie's gaze had been on the meth gang. Red Cap stayed on his knees, holding onto the fence, while Primo Beer howled in fright as he lay spread-eagled on the ground.

Jake surged up and over the log, running toward the men and the still open gate, only staggering a little as the uneven bucking of the ground continued—he'd apparently decided to take advantage of the distraction to make a move.

Sophie fumbled her weapon out and pushed up on the log, relieved to find that the earthquake was subsiding into a series of uneven shudders, even as she heard a tremendous rending crash of a tree falling in the distance. She couldn't seem to steady her legs, but forced them to work anyway, jogging toward the gate.

Jake was already through the aperture. He'd punched Red Cap in the head, knocking the man into a sprawl of unconscious arms and legs, and now had Primo Beer in a chokehold in the crook of his elbow.

The man soon went limp.

Sophie slid her backpack off and took out a couple of zip ties, securing Red Cap's feet and hands. Following Jake's example, she tugged the man out through the gate and down, hauling him under the armpits into the depression behind the log where they'd so recently sheltered.

Jake was panting with exertion as he secured his captive, and Sophie was a little relieved to hear it as she was severely out of breath from dragging a couple of hundred pounds of human more than fifty feet into cover.

"Got the tape?" Jake asked.

Sophie nodded, pulling out a roll of heavy silver duct tape from her pack. She tore off a strip and covered Red Cap's mouth with it, as Jake taped Primo Beer's.

Jake looked at his heavy metal watch. "Five minutes. Thank you, earthquake."

"It was a very handy diversion, but I'm worried what it means for an eruption in this area," Sophie said.

"Agree. We need to get in, grab our girl, and get out. Let's move."

CHAPTER FIVE

Jake

JAKE LED THE WAY FORWARD, and paused behind a tree outside the cluster of buildings to assess the situation. He could feel the heat of Sophie's body close behind him as he scanned the area.

The earthquake had acted like kicking an anthill would do.

The crew burst out of the buildings. Jake quickly counted them, looking for and taking note of a petite Asian girl with long black hair: *the target.*

"We have two options. We can wait until they go back in to whatever they're doing, or we can rush them now. Grab her while chaos reigns."

Sophie took a moment to watch the scene before them. He could almost hear her busy brain working. "Rush them now. They aren't going to expect it."

"I'll handle the dealers, you get the girl, since you're carrying the tranq."

"Copy that." Sophie fumbled the tranquilizer dart gun out of her backpack and slipped it into her pocket, leaving her hands free. "She might want to come with us."

"Don't hold your breath." Jake pulled both of his pistols, and strode forward into the clearing. His voice cracked like a whip over the chaotic group. "Drop your weapons and no one gets hurt."

He didn't see any weapons, but the assumption had to be that everyone was armed.

Two of the men complied, their eyes wide with surprise as they dropped pistols and a knife on the ground, and raised their hands. One man, taller than the rest, bearded with handsome features, grabbed the target in his arms.

"Back the hell away!" O'Brien shouted, holding a pistol against the girl's temple.

Lia Ayabe shrieked like a singed cat and writhed in her captor's arms. "What the hell are you doing?"

"Some boyfriend," Jake muttered, trying to get a shot at the asshole's head.

Sophie, meanwhile, circled around behind the duo. She stepped up and placed the bore of her Glock on the back of the boyfriend's head. "Drop it now." If Jake's voice had been a whip, Sophie's was an icy stiletto.

O'Brien raised his arms slowly, letting go of the girl, and dropped his pistol.

Lia tore out of her boyfriend's arms and whirled on him, ignoring Jake and Sophie. "What the hell was that about?"

The man pursed his lips and shook his head. "Just an act. Trying to get them to let us go."

"I don't care what you were trying to do! Don't touch me!"

Sophie grabbed the target by the arm, keeping her weapon pointed at the boyfriend. "It's okay, Lia. We're getting you out of here."

"Everybody on your knees." Jake was already pulling zip ties out of a handy side pocket to secure the dealers. The men complied, grumbling, and he advanced toward them.

"Hey there, cowboy." A deep voice with an Irish accent cut

across the clearing. "I've got a shotgun aimed at your woman, and I'm hoping you don't want her to die."

Jake's gaze flew to the doorway of the largest shed.

A tall man with a shaved head and a neat red beard stood in the doorway, holding a Remington Tac-13 semi-auto comfortably across his tight midsection. His eyes were on Jake, but that killer gun was on Sophie. "Drop your weapons and let go of my girl, or the lady gets it."

The guy who'd grabbed the target wasn't the boyfriend.

Sophie slowly raised her hands. The girl tore away from her, running to plaster herself against O'Brien. She looked tiny beside his bulk, and way too young, but the vicious tone of her voice gave Jake a chill. "Shoot 'em, baby."

"On your knees," O'Brien said, his flat blue eyes expressionless. *Who was this guy?* Clearly, they'd underestimated him—Finn O'Brien was no stranger to violence.

Sophie glanced over at Jake. He held her gaze and gave a slight nod as he dropped to his knees, lacing his fingers on the back of his head. *No contract was worth dying for.*

Sophie knelt as well. "We were hired by Lia's father to bring her home," she said. "We're not cops. Let us leave, and you'll have no further trouble."

"That's not going to happen," O'Brien said.

The other gang members scrambled to their feet. Eager to prove his worth, the one who'd grabbed the girl reached Jake first. He kicked him in the legs, cursing ripely. Jake went down and curled into a ball, his arms around his head. Pain detonated like explosions in his body as the bastards rained kicks and blows on him.

"Stop it!" Sophie screamed, but they didn't stop, and there was nothing for Jake to do but take it and live to fight another day.

A blow to his head brought welcome darkness.

THE ONLY WAY Jake knew he was awake was the pain, because the darkness was as thick as it had been when he'd been knocked out.

He groaned, and his voice sounded funny—echoey and hollow.

"Jake. Are you okay?" Sophie's voice came from right beside him, pressured with stress.

"Not sure." Jake ran his tongue around the inside of his mouth, testing for broken teeth. He tasted blood and he'd bitten his tongue rather badly, but nothing else had been lost, thank the good Lord. He liked his teeth and his mom had paid good money for orthodontia in his teens. He breathed shallowly against sharp stabs of soreness from his ribs and abdomen. His thighs were one big mess of bruises, but when he stretched his legs out gently, he could move them. "Nothing's broken. I think. Maybe a few ribs—those are the worst." He rubbed his eyes, but nothing. Still couldn't see. "What the crap happened to the lights? Am I blind?" He tried to keep his breathing even and calm, though he was blinking rapidly in rising panic at the total blackness.

"No, you're not. They pitched us into a lava tube. There's no light down here." Sophie's hands touched his face, his head, and he hissed a sharp breath as she encountered the goose egg on the back of his skull. "I'm feeling for wounds."

"Don't bother." Jake twitched away from her touch. "Let's focus on getting out of here before you worry about first aid. How long was I out?"

"Not long. Fifteen minutes or so."

Now that his eyes had been open a while, Jake could perceive a slight gray circle in the space above him. "That the way we came in? They covered the hole."

"Yes. A plywood circle."

A rank odor had been penetrating Jake's awareness; a fruity but foul scent that felt like a slimy substance being rubbed all over his abraded skin. "What the hell is that smell?"

"I think this is their refuse pit." He could tell Sophie was breathing through her mouth. "There's human waste down here. Kitchen scraps. And, I think, some decomp."

"Decomp? As in . . . a body?"

"Maybe it's a dead animal," Sophie said, but she didn't sound hopeful.

A wave of nausea swamped Jake. He shut his eyes. He was light-headed, disoriented by the totally black environment, and that smell . . . "Gah! I think I'm going to puke."

"It would be better on your ribs if you didn't," Sophie said evenly. "Not to mention the odors we are currently subjected to. Though I expect in a few hours they will no longer seem so acute."

Jake breathed slowly through his nose, counting to five on each inhale and exhale, and spitting out the taste of bile until the nausea receded.

"What have you been able to determine about this chamber?" He finally asked.

"They stripped us of everything in our pockets, so I don't have anything to use for light. I didn't want to start exploring because I have a sense that this is a roomy cavern, and I didn't want to lose track of you while you were unconscious." Sophie's voice continued to be eerily calm. "I've established a five-foot perimeter around our drop site."

Jake craned his neck to look up overhead. "How far up is that?"

"You're wondering how we got in here."

"Yeah. And how high we have to climb to get out."

"I don't think climbing out is going to be possible. The overhead hole is at the top of a sort of stone bubble. They threw you in first; I took a minute to look around while I had some illumination and could see that the walls were out of reach of the hole at the top. So there's no way to climb back up to the opening from below."

Jake swore; Sophie stayed silent, maybe because she'd had fifteen more minutes than he had to assess their situation.

"How are you staying so calm?"

"I was trapped in a lava tube for days on Kaua'i, remember? I mastered my fear and disorientation then."

"I'm feeling really dizzy." Jake lay back down. "I need a minute."

"The disorientation goes away eventually," Sophie said. "You come to trust that what you think are the edges of your body, really are what you think they are. But it's a weird feeling, kind of like you're floating in space or something. No one tells you how crazy it makes you to completely lose your sight." Sophie patted Jake gently, establishing the position of his body, and then hooked an arm under his. "Let's get out of the filth of the trash pile. They chucked everything in here; fortunately, it was a big enough heap to break our fall into the pit. But no reason for us to wallow any longer in their shit. Literally."

Jake couldn't control the nausea rolling through him this time. He dry-heaved into the slime, muck, and garbage as they crawled through it onto a dry, rough area.

The tiny, faint circle of light above them got even further away.

CHAPTER SIX

Sophie

SOPHIE WISHED she weren't so familiar with the bizarre subterranean environment of the lava tube, but she'd been involved with finding a boy who'd fallen into one of the tubes formed by underground rivers of lava, and been trapped there with him for a time until their rescue.

All of the disorientation from sensory deprivation that Jake was feeling was something she'd already experienced and, eventually, bested.

She helped her groaning partner out of the immediate area of the rubbish pile and into the darker edges of their prison as her mind ticked over their situation.

They had been chucked down here to die, and to judge by the smell at the edge of the pile, they weren't the first. The feral grin on Lia Ayabe's narrow little face as she supervised the disposal of Jake's beaten, unconscious body into the hole, and then did the honors for Sophie herself, was not something Sophie would easily forget.

Sophie had fought to get away. No sense, anymore, in meekly letting them throw her in the pit when their only possible hope might be escaping to fetch help. She'd gotten in some good licks on the hired hands, but with Jake out of commission and possibly badly injured, she hadn't wanted to make the situation worse. She'd been dragged to the edge and pushed in to fall twenty feet to land on the refuse pile by that evil little bitch, Lia, herself. Once they'd been searched and all weapons or useful tools removed, and their identities verified, O'Brien had cheered Lia on.

"These two aren't even real cops," he'd said. "Collateral damage in the game of love, my dear." His lilting Irish brogue made his foul words even more repulsive. "We're moving out, anyway. The lava's unstable and I don't like the look of the news reports out of Kilauea's seismic monitoring center."

The girl was only seventeen years old, but if she'd ever had a conscience, it had been wiped out by using meth and her relationship with a sociopath.

And now they had to find a way to stay alive and get out of here.

Kendall Bix, their President of Operations, had the coordinates of the camp. If they didn't check in by tomorrow, he'd mobilize a rescue team. By the time he did, the meth gang would be long gone. They just had to hang in there and wait for help to arrive and find them.

Sophie no longer cared what happened to their target. That kid had made her bed.

"We need to stay alive until tomorrow, when Bix checks in and we're not responding," Sophie told Jake. The cavern was surprisingly large, but she finally reached the rocky wall and settled her injured partner against it. "We're going to be fine in here until then."

"Speak for yourself. I've definitely got some cracked ribs, maybe worse," Jake said. "My nose is bleeding again." He sounded stuffed up.

Sophie sighed. "They sure enjoyed kicking the shit out of you. But I didn't go into the pit without a fight. I wanted to escape and get help, but that evil little girl shoved me in here herself." The picture kept playing in her mind over and over: Sophie held up at the edge of the pit by two of the flunkies as Lia Ayabe, little and cute and young, had charged at her and slammed two hands into her chest, knocking her backward with only pinwheeling arms to break her fall.

She'd been very lucky that Jake had rolled part of the way down the trash pile, because she'd landed so heavily the trash still bore the imprint of her body. "I'm not exactly in great shape, either."

They commiserated over each other's injuries, but in this filthy dark cave there was simply nothing to be done about them.

"So. Let's review. Tell me what I missed while I was knocked out. Did you pick up any actionable intel?" Jake asked.

"Not much. O'Brien told his men they were going to evacuate from the site due to our discovery of them and the troubling volcanic reports coming in from Kilauea's monitoring station. Apparently, that earthquake was indicative of an imminent eruption."

"Just what we need. A volcano going off while we're trapped underground in a lava tube," Jake groaned.

As if in agreement, the walls shuddered and the ground bucked. Sophie cried out as rocks crumbled from the ceiling and thundered as they hit the ground around them. She threw herself over Jake, but he was already trying to shelter her. So they clung together, their heads hidden down below their shoulders, as a hailstorm of pebbles and dirt rained down on them.

At last the earthquake stopped.

Sophie raised her head. The gray circle of light was bright because the piece of plywood the gang had used to cover the pit had fallen in, along with some of the edges of the hole they'd been forced into. A haze of dirt and dust made both of them cough, and Sophie lifted her filthy shirt to breathe through it. "One good thing from the earthquake—some of the smell from the trash pile has been buried," Sophie said, and coughed.

"We have to find a way out of here. Another one of these quakes, and this whole cavern could collapse." Jake heaved himself up onto his hands and knees. In the dim gray light, covered with slime from the garbage pile, which the fall of dust and dirt had adhered to, he looked and smelled like he'd crawled up out of the primordial ooze.

"Now that there's a little more light in here, let's do a recon of this cave and see if we can find anything that we can use to get out. I'll go right, you go left."

"Okay." Sophie hated to leave his side, but there was no help for it. She staggered to her feet and navigated along the wall, one hand trailing over the rough stone. She was glad she'd kept her shirt up over her mouth and nose as the cavern continued thick with disturbed sediment; or *was it new volcanic emissions, blowing in from somewhere?*

She suppressed a surge of panic at the thought.

"This haze isn't really clearing," Jake hacked and choked from where he'd disappeared from her view. His voice didn't sound as echoey as it had before; the part of the ceiling that had collapsed had introduced a muffling layer of debris, as well as the toxic air they were trying to breathe.

"Make a filter from your shirt," Sophie said. "Tie it over your nose and mouth like I did." She'd finally reached the roughly circular wall of the cavern and begun curving back around when she encountered another opening. This was roughly six feet in diameter and led away from their cavern. "I found a hole. Looks like it might lead somewhere, and the air's slightly fresher here," she called to Jake.

"Yeah? Well I found some old crap they pitched in here that might be useful," Jake said. "Work your way over to my side and let's take a little inventory."

Sophie's eyes were gritty from the haze, which seemed to be dissipating at last. She continued on, looking for any further openings or cracks in the walls or ceiling, and seeing none. Nothing but rock, dirt, and fallen piles of ashy soil that had detached from the ceiling. She eventually made her way back to her partner, who was squatting outside of a circle of dim sunlight that looked bright in contrast to the thick darkness. "What did you find?"

"A body," Jake said, and held up a human skull.

CHAPTER SEVEN

Jake

SOPHIE'S short hair was gray and thick with the ashy sediment from overhead; her honey-brown eyes gleamed in the filth that coated her face. "We landed in a crime scene."

"Who knows? The guy might have died of natural causes and they didn't bother to bury him." Jake waggled the skull back and forth, and the bits of hair clinging to the scalp swayed in a macabre way. "If only these bones could talk."

Sophie tightened her jaw, clearly not interested in the body. "You said you found something useful."

"Yeah. They didn't clear the body. I found some very old smokes in his pocket, and this." Jake flicked a good quality stainless steel lighter triumphantly. "He was also wearing a belt with a knife on it." He held up the item in question, a wicked looking combat blade. "We're armed. We have a source of light. It's all good now."

As if to mock them, the ground shuddered again, a feeling like being on an animal shaking its coat. Jake threw himself on Sophie instinctively as more debris rained down on them from around the opening above.

The quake was short this time and ended almost as soon as it started. Sophie cursed in Thai, and wriggled beneath him. "I appreciate you trying to protect me, Jake, but right now you smell like the devil's armpit. Get off!"

Everything still hurt. Every breath stabbed like a thousand ice picks. Jake groaned as he rolled off Sophie onto the rough stone floor of the cavern. "Why did I have to land in a pile of crap after getting the shit beat out of me?"

"I don't know. Life's not fair?" Sophie pointed to the litter of bones that marked the body. "I'm sure that guy agrees." She put her hands on her hips and looked toward their light source, the crumbling hole far above. "I worry that the ceiling will collapse further. I think we should figure out a way to use your lighter. We could make a torch and explore the tunnel I found. At least the air and stink are better there, and if it's a dead end, we can always come back. Eventually, Bix will be looking for us at the coordinates I sent."

"Sounds like a plan." Even though breathing hurt, Jake would rather be on the move than trying to keep his mind off their circumstances and waiting for help. "Let's find some kind of stick. We need something that can burn—ideally, a fuel source."

"Ugh. I guess we have to get back into the trash." Sophie pulled her shirt back up over her nose and mouth again, and approached the foul-smelling heap that had mercifully broken their twenty-foot fall.

Jake breathed shallowly through his mouth and focused on the fact that, once they were able to make some torches, they'd be able to get away from the stench—at least for a little while.

He pulled aside several branches and a palm frond or two. With the knife, he'd be able to fashion them into some kind of handle—but nothing would last long if they didn't find something that could fuel the torch. Perhaps the clothing on the corpse could be useful. Technically, they should have left the body undisturbed, but the necessity of survival outweighed corruption of a possible crime scene.

"Eureka!" Sophie shouted.

Jake spun to see her, halfway up the refuse pile, brandishing several spherical items. The light was too dim to see exactly what they were, but he turned eagerly away from the grisly prospect of stripping the clothing from a corpse whose body had rotted inside of the garments.

"Eureka? That's a new one for you. What you got there?"

"Coconuts." Sophie tossed one of them down to him. "The husks are great fuel, and these are old coconuts. Hopefully the meat inside the nut is nice and dried out—coconut is very oily. We can put the coconut meat in something and burn it."

Jake eyed the gray, roughly football-sized coconut. He'd seen local men open them in a matter of minutes with a machete or an axe, but they had nothing down here but a knife. The dense husk covering the outside was hard to get through, not to mention the tremendously hard inner nut. "Could take us hours to deal with this thing."

Sophie frowned and put her hands on her hips. Silhouetted on top of the pile, even covered with grime she was a magnificent sight. "What, are you in a hurry to go into a completely dark lava tube with a torch that'll go out in minutes?"

Jake stepped up, handed her back the coconut, and presented the knife in its scabbard. "You go, girl. I'm off to look for something easier to deal with."

Sophie snorted. "Good luck."

She squished down off the pile and sat on the rocky ground. She took off her shoes, gripped the coconut with her feet, and jabbed the knife into the tough fibrous exterior.

Jake twitched in reaction. Watching her do that was too nerve-wracking; she could so easily slip with that knife and cut herself. But he couldn't offer to help after making a fuss, so he bit his tongue, turned away, and went back to searching the refuse pile.

An hour or so later of digging and sifting, Jake found a can filled with used Crisco frying oil. "Eureka!" he yelled, holding the lidded tin aloft.

He was rewarded by hearing Sophie laugh.

Down here in the cesspit with a dead body, trapped, literally covered with shit, she was laughing.

He loved her so freakin' much.

Jake made his way back to her, his eyes widening to see that she'd stripped the tough, fibrous husk off the coconut, and had begun smashing the fist-sized nut itself between two rocks. "We can still use this meat inside. For fuel, or to eat if we get hungry enough."

"I'd have to be pretty damn hungry." Jake squatted beside her and held up his prize. "Exhibit A. Fuel oil."

The coconut gave way to Sophie's pounding with a crunch. She held up one of its large brown shards, lined with shriveled white coconut gone translucent with age. "Exhibit B. Even more fuel."

"Excellent. Now we need something that can hold the flame and wick the fuel." Jake pointed to the corpse. "I was going to pull that guy's clothes off him. He doesn't need them anymore."

"But the smell. Burning, it will be even worse." Sophie shuddered. "Plus, it's a crime scene. They might be able to tell something about his death from the clothes."

"I'm pretty grossed out by the body fluids and fats that are soaked into the cloth," Jake said. "And you're right. But maybe we could cut off the lower legs of his jeans . . ."

"Ugh. Why don't we just dip some of this coconut husk in the oil and try that?"

Jake cocked his head, considering. "Okay. We can give that a go."

Sophie dipped a finger-wide shred of coconut husk into the oil in the tin. It had thickened up, so it adhered to the fibrous husk like a blob of mayonnaise. "If the husk can hold the fuel without burning up, we could plant a few pieces in the oil as wicks, and carry your whole tin."

Jake flicked the lighter. "The moment of truth." He held the flame to the coconut husk.

It promptly flared high, emitting black smoke, and burned down until Sophie had to drop it. She swore.

"I wish you'd tell me what you're saying in English."

"*Rat guts vomited from the mouth of a cat.* It doesn't translate well."

Jake chuckled. "Fair enough. I don't like the idea of carrying a sloshing can of hot oil with a flaming wick through uncertain terrain, anyway. Here's what I think we should do. Let's use the knife to cut the edge of the dead guy's jeans off, just that rolled bit of fabric at the bottom. We can dip it into the oil and use it as a wick. I think the jeans material will hold the flame better. We can experiment first, but my idea is to soak that in the oil, wrap it around a stick, and light it. When the flame starts to go out, we can dip it in the oil again. Keep one torch going all the time, but have two to work with."

"Sounds good to me."

They both turned to eye the dead man. Decomp had come and gone, leaving darkly-stained garments surrounding bones that still held remnants of skin and hair that hadn't been eaten by the bugs that flew freely around the trash pile.

"I bet he was a lot worse a few months ago," Jake said. "The bugs and maggots have had time to clean up a lot of it."

Sophie grimaced. "Good thing I have a strong stomach. I'll cut the jeans off at the knees. That should be enough." She was still holding the knife, and she pulled her shirt mask up over her nose and mouth, and advanced to kneel next to the corpse.

Sophie never hesitated to wade right in and do what needed to be done—another reason Jake loved her. Kneeling beside her and helping her free the cloth from the clinging remnants of skin and bone, he glimpsed the empowering tattoos on her inner arms—the ones on the outsides of her thighs were hidden by her pants. But she had other ones he'd seen in their private times together, a mandala of Thai writing around her navel that spelled out *love, joy, bliss.*

He'd see that tattoo again. Trace it with kisses. But when they were out of danger, out of this foul and filthy environment, and a whole lot cleaner.

They cut the jeans material into narrow strips and carefully soaked it in the oil. Sophie lit a test strip on a twig. The oil smelled of fried chicken, a macabre twist to the whole bizarre and disgusting experience. "Colonel Sanders is here with us in this cave," Jake said, waving the test torch carefully. "Who knew we'd have him for company. The good news is, the jeans material is holding the flame. It's not burning up."

"No idea who Colonel Sanders is, but this oil smell is making me hungry," Sophie said, wrapping another soaked strip carefully around one of the sticks whose leaves and branches he'd already stripped. "I wish that weren't true, but all I ate today was a protein bar."

"Thanks for saying that, because I was thinking the same thing. Maybe we'll end up eating that old coconut before we get out of here."

"I already packed it in one of my pockets," Sophie said, patting it.

"I think water might be more of a problem before this adventure is over." Jake finished making his torch, tucking the ends of the fabric carefully into a tightly wrapped bundle at one end of the stick. He put the plastic lid back on the oil tin. "I have a cargo pocket big enough to carry this." He slid it into the pocket and snapped the flap closed. "The moment of truth, take two."

Jake flicked the lighter and lit his torch. It flared bright, and the smell of fried chicken masked the other reeks around them momentarily. "I believe we're ready to venture into the lava tube, Sophie. Lead on."

The earth trembled, just a tiny shudder—but enough to make more dirt and debris fall in from the fragile opening. Sophie took one last look at the bit of open sky above the hole, prompting Jake to look at it too.

"I guess we better go," Sophie grimaced. "We'll never be stronger than right now."

"Depressing thought." Jake elbowed her, trying for a smile. "We can always come back if it's a dead end."

"I don't like the sound of dead end. I prefer blocked tunnel," Sophie said with dignity.

"I have to agree with you on that one." Jake held the torch high to light their way as they moved away from the cave's overhead opening, saying goodbye to the light one last time.

CHAPTER EIGHT

Sophie

SHE WAS FALLING in love with Jake again.

Who else could make her laugh by bouncing her own words back to her? Who else could get up from a beating like he'd taken and, with nothing more than a moan and groan or two, get on with solving the problems they found themselves in? Who else did she have confidence in, as they tried to cheat death yet another time?

Only Jake.

Okay, maybe Connor, too. And Raveaux was amazingly capable.

But only Jake could deal with a situation like this with real *attitude*.

Sophie had taken the lit torch to lead them to the exit she'd found. She stopped at the opening into the lava tube that led away from the central cavern, hesitating as she stared into the narrow black tunnel. It looked so black, so impossibly small. "I don't know. Maybe we should wait in here for Bix to send help."

"It could take days for them to find us, and I don't think this cavern is that stable." Jake moved up beside her. She held the flickering torch aloft and they peered into the much narrower tunnel ahead. "Hard to tell how far this tube goes. We don't have to commit to it. We're just checking out our options."

"There's some air coming through here, so it must vent out somewhere." Sophie pointed to the way the flame of the torch bent in a slight breeze. "I've studied the way lava moves underground since I got stuck in a tube like this the last time. Lava flows like water in its liquid state; it heads downhill, it pools around obstacles. A bigger cavern like the one we're leaving was sort of like a puddle of lava at the time it was created. Since we didn't find an exit point other than this one, and the terrain goes slightly downhill toward the coast, my guess is that the lava came up from below the cavern, pooled in that main chamber, and this is where it ran down toward the ocean. Hopefully, we will find an opening where it exited."

"Unless it emptied out underwater in the ocean." Jake shivered theatrically.

"We'll know if it did. The water would have backfilled the tunnel until it found equilibrium once the lava cooled; we'd have to stop when we come to that point."

Jake's eyes were slate-colored in the gleam of the torch. "You're so sexy when you talk geology to me."

"You're so sexy, period." She couldn't help what popped out of her mouth—and she wasn't sorry when his gaze seemed to heat.

"I freakin' love you so much. I'd kiss you if I wasn't so filthy."

"You can kiss me anyway. Our lips probably only have the usual trillions of bacteria," she said primly.

He laughed.

Jake's laugh still made her toes curl.

And then he kissed her.

What started out playful soon wasn't.

"I'd give a million dollars for a shower and a bed right now," Jake eventually said.

Sophie chuckled breathlessly. "Anticipation is the spice of life, to paraphrase the American saying."

"You're getting downright good at those truisms. Let's move, so we can get out of this shithole and get busy." Jake waggled his brows. "As they say." He took the lead this time, taking the torch from her, and holding it high to light their way.

The makeshift light, which burned steadily, if smokily, wasn't really adequate to illuminate Sophie's footing. She stumbled over a rough protrusion on the floor. *"Twin sons of a conjoined snake!"*

"You're sexy when you talk dirty, babe, but I don't want you to keep stubbing your toes. Grab onto my belt."

Sophie grasped Jake's belt with both hands and focused on not catching her feet, mercifully covered with good quality hiking boots, on the rough, jagged floor. But even with the flickering flame, making their way through the lava tube reminded her of the case on Kaua`i where she'd gone into a similar setting, without a light, to rescue a young boy who'd been trapped down there for days.

Sound was muffled by the porous stone without a large space to amplify it like the cavern they'd originally entered. The walls were smooth as jet in some areas, prickly and porous in others, with needle-like protrusions stabbing down from the ceiling, the remains of lava dripping.

The tube-like tunnel went steadily downward, curving to and fro. Sophie frowned. They weren't moving that fast, but she felt warmer. *Maybe she was getting her heart rate up . . .*

She refused to think it was nearby lava, warming the walls.

"I think we should talk," Jake said.

"About what?" Sophie carefully navigated a large rock blocking their path.

"About our future."

"We don't have a future unless we get out of here."

"Let's assume we will."

"I think it's better to focus on right now."

"See, this is why we're a good partnership." Jake tugged on Sophie's belt, bringing her to a halt. "Do you hear something?" he whispered.

Sophie shut her eyes. Touch, hearing, and smell were amplified, where vision was next to useless. "I do hear something. It's water dripping."

"Good. I'm thirsty. Wasn't going to mention it since there was no point."

"Maybe there's an underground pool ahead. These tubes often fill with water from the soil above. The good news is, the water's usually pure and drinkable, because it's been naturally filtered through the stone."

Jake's torch chose that moment to begin to sputter. Sophie quickly lifted hers to catch the last of his flame, and she stepped forward. "Now you can hold onto my belt."

"Sure I can't hold onto . . . right here?" He patted the part in question.

"Jake. Focus. Think—if there's a pool up ahead, we might be able to wash up."

"Get moving, woman!" He slapped her behind.

Sophie snorted a laugh.

Incredibly, she was having fun. She flicked a glance over her shoulder as she walked toward the sound of water. "I'm enjoying this, Jake. How strange is that?"

"Adventure is the best kind of fun in the world, and it's not a real adventure if there isn't some risk involved. Remember when we rescued those kids from the cult on the Big Island? And you asked me if it was always like that?"

"And you said, 'only the best days.' I remember that. I was getting used to being out of the office." Sophie lifted the torch high. "Well. I think our water shortage is over."

The lava tube had opened up to another cavern. Sophie's torch gleamed on the still, black surface of an underground pool that stretched from one side of it to the other, and off into a distance that the torch's light couldn't pierce.

CHAPTER NINE

Jake

JAKE DROPPED to a squat and dipped his fingers into the water, licking them tentatively. He glanced up at Sophie as she held the torch aloft. "Not salty. This is fresh water." He scooped a double handful and brought it to his mouth. "And it's delicious. Also freeze-your-ass cold. What the hell? I thought we were in Hawaii."

"That's strange," Sophie murmured. "Because a little while ago I thought I felt warmer."

"I don't know about you, but cold or not, I want to rinse off this shit we're covered in. What do you say to a refreshing bath?"

Sophie frowned. "I know we're both sexually frustrated, Jake, but we should continue to make survival a priority. If we bathe in the water, we'll pollute it. We should see if we can find a way around this pond or whatever it is, and once we've determined we've gone as far as we want to go today, we can assess getting clean in a non-essential water source. Hydration is the priority right now."

Jake emitted a gusty sigh. "You're right of course, boss."

This time Sophie was the one to wiggle her brows. "You make me so hot when you call me 'boss.'"

"Oh ho. The way to your heart is through your ego, eh? I knew it." Jake couldn't resist the jab, and immediately regretted it, as Sophie's playful expression stiffened into that familiar mask she hid behind.

"Let's drink as much as we need, and go this way." She pointed to a narrow, rocky parapet that appeared to lead around one side of the water source. "Perhaps there's another area we can bathe in on the other side. I don't even want to put my hands in the water and corrupt it." Sophie wedged her torch between a couple of rocks. She extended herself to lean down to drink the water directly, by planting her chin in it.

Jake moved to copy her. They both drank as much as they could hold.

Jake stood up, his stomach sloshing and full. Water had never tasted so good. "I'm sorry I said that. About your ego."

Sophie shrugged. "Doesn't matter. It's true." She picked up the torch and headed for the narrow ledge against the wall. "We're going to have to go slow. It would be a disaster to fall in and have the torch go out, or the lighter or oil be lost."

"It does matter," Jake said, following her. "I don't want to say hurtful things to you. Have you close up on me."

"We've both said a lot of hurtful things. It seems to be part of relationships." Sophie turned sideways, apparently the only way she could fit onto the ledge. She sidled onto the narrow outcrop, holding the torch aloft with one hand and clinging to the rocks with the other. "You're going to have some trouble here, Jake—you're wider than me. Let's not talk about this now."

"When else will we talk about it? I'm an ass. Please forgive me." Jake stepped up onto the ledge with his back to the wall. He was so much thicker than Sophie. She was right—his boot toes protruded out over the water. He stepped back off and tucked the unlit torch into the back of his pants, then checked that the oil can was tightly closed. He refastened the snap on his leg pocket, and turned to face the ledge, clinging with both hands. "I'm going to tackle this like I'm bouldering."

"Whatever works." Sophie turned to face forward, pressing against the stone wall, as well. "It's hard to hold the torch up and hang onto the rock, too."

"You have to forgive me. For what I said." It felt important that he win this argument.

"Like I have to forgive you for leaving me for Felicia? Taking her and starting your own company? Living with her for two years and leaving me to raise my child alone?" Sophie's voice was sharp.

Jake's neck went hot. He chose each finger-and toehold carefully, sidling after her. "I apologized for all of that. And in fairness, I thought you were with another guy all the time you were with me. I had evidence of it!"

"I never lied that I had other relationships, of other kinds, with other men than you. You knew about Alika. Maybe you didn't know the full truth about Connor, but you told me you chose to believe me when I told you that we were only friends." Sophie was panting a bit, her voice uneven with emotion. "You were my only lover when we were together. And you really don't know me very well if you think I'd cheat—nor did you trust me, for that matter. That became abundantly clear."

Sophie got wordier when she was upset. Finding a place to wash up and make love was beginning to seem like a mirage dancing out of reach; clearly, they still had a lot of issues to work out.

"Trust goes both ways, lady." The heat of defensive anger made Jake's fingers sweaty on the rock. "I told you how I felt about cheaters. And why."

"And yet you cheated on me with those hookers in Thailand. And then left me for Felicia." Her sad, husky tone pierced him, all the way to the heart.

"I was wrong." Jake shut his eyes, clinging to the rock. Shame washed over him. "I'm so freakin' sorry, Sophie. I was hurting. I thought you'd betrayed me, and I'd almost died by torture. I wasn't thinking straight."

But Sophie kept going. She edged her way around a boulder. The light of the torch disappeared, leaving Jake stranded in darkness, with nothing but a dim reflection of the flame, flickering and bouncing off the black water below, to navigate by.

Hell if he was going to ask her to stop, or call out for help.

Jake tried to let his eyes adjust as much as possible, but the torch was getting farther away. He had to try to catch up. He put out a boot, felt for a foothold, reached sideways for a handhold, and gently eased over, placing his other foot carefully.

Reach out, feel for toehold, stretch arm, grab a handhold, ease over, set down foot, re-grip . . . *Was she just going to leave him in the dark?*

The torch reappeared just as he was reaching the boulder that Sophie'd disappeared around. Her face peered around the protrusion, backlit so that he couldn't see her expression.

Jake steadied himself as best he could. He focused on her dimly-lit face. "Sophie, I'm sorry about all that. But I can't keep apologizing and groveling. Not that I mind, it just doesn't accomplish anything. You have to decide to let that shit go, or we can't move forward."

"And you have to trust me. No reservations. No conditions." She lowered the torch to illuminate his feet. "Or we can't move forward." The torchlight finally reflected up on Sophie's face enough for him to see her expression. Her lips were trembling, her eyes full of tears. "I want to let it go. I'm trying to."

"And I want to trust you. I'm doing it." He sidled around the boulder and came up flush against her body.

They leaned their foreheads together, breathing each other's air for a long moment.

"You came back for me," he said. "I trust you. With my life. With my heart."

"Then I forgive you. I choose to let that shit go."

Jake angled his face a little, hoping—but the next move had to come from her.

Sophie seemed to know it too, and she kissed him, a soft but thorough joining that stole his breath. "I want to be with you, Jake. Let's put the past behind us."

"I—" but Jake had let go of the boulder too soon.

His foot slipped into the water, and he was falling—until Sophie grabbed the front of his shirt with her free hand and yanked forcefully, hauling him back enough that he could grab the rock wall and regain his footing. He shook out his soaked boot and pant leg. "You're my badass babe, Soph," he panted.

"Good. And you're my *kun dii.*" She began her crabwise sidle again. "That was refreshing, but I think we should stick to priorities for now."

"Cootie?" Jake followed, resuming his careful movements along the edge. "Never heard that before as a term of endearment."

"*Kun dii.*" Sophie pronounced the Thai phrase slowly. "It means 'my dear' or 'my love.' What does 'cootie' mean in American?"

"It's slang for a bug, a pest." He smirked. "Cootie. Kind of apropos."

Sophie's eyes gleamed with laughter over her shoulder. "Perfect. You are my cootie from now on. Ha!"

"*Phom rak khun khrup,*" Jake enunciated carefully. Sophie stopped to look back at him, her eyes wide. "I love you, Sophie."

"Your accent is terrible." She blinked rapidly. "Let's get off this ledge and continue this conversation on stable ground."

"Preferably naked," Jake said.

"That's my cootie."

Jake laughed, and finally, Sophie did too.

CHAPTER TEN

Raveaux

PIERRE RAVEAUX SMOOTHED the front of his button-down shirt, a silky cotton that his wife Gita had bought him more than five years ago. He stared unseeing out the window of the plane, allowing his mind to rest on her briefly. The stroke of his fingertips down the row of genuine pearl shell buttons, then across to the small pocket inset over his heart, reminded him of touching her—skin pure golden satin, warm and smooth under his hands.

He didn't often allow himself to remember his wife, let alone those details.

Gita had been dead for close to five years now, along with his four-year-old daughter Lucie. Everyone said it was time to move on. And when he'd finally opened his heart a tiny crack, entertained the idea of another woman in his life—Sophie had turned away from the tender bud of possibility to her former lover.

And now, both of them were missing.

"Would you like something to drink, sir?" The flight attendant stood at his elbow holding a tray of liquids—that awful syrupy pineapple-orange-guava drink that everyone seemed to love, and water.

"I prefer water, please."

She handed the sealed plastic cup to him with a smile that told him she found him attractive, even more so now that he'd opened his mouth and uttered a couple of words in a French accent.

Raveaux did not smile back. Smiling was a habit he'd lost since the death of his family. He looked across the empty seat beside him to gaze out the window at the sea below, flecked with whitecaps like bits of lint on a crinkled blue blanket. The flight was short from Oahu to Hilo on the Big Island of Hawaii, and soon they'd be on the ground—but Sophie had told him to look for whales, even on these short flights, and now he never forgot to.

Raveaux peeled the aluminum lid back, regretting the wasteful use of resources in all these disposables. Europeans had had to live with high costs and crowding so much longer that they were more careful in their use of these kinds of conveniences. Though he'd been in the United States for a year now, he was still surprised by the wanton waste he often saw around him—even in the Islands, with their finite space and high cost of living.

He drank the water in a couple of sips and set the container aside, glancing down at his phone. He'd woken very early to the chime of an incoming text at his apartment in Waikiki. The device was in airplane mode, but he was still able to scroll to the terse directive he'd received from Kendall Bix, president of operations for Security Solutions, the company he contracted for.

"Raveaux: I need you to go to the Big Island and follow up on the case Sophie and her partner, Jake Dunn, are pursuing. The volcanic activity in the area they were last heard from has increased, and they are not responding. Find where they are, what's going on with their case, and liaise with law enforcement. Call me ASAP to confirm and get details."

He'd called Bix immediately, his pulse elevated with alarm—and his heart rate hadn't calmed as he learned more about the dangerous escalation in volcanic activity on the Big Island, and more details about the case Jake and Sophie were on.

Raveaux scrolled a little further down, locating the contact number for the client who'd hired Security Solutions to recover his errant daughter, and a set of GPS coordinates which showed where Sophie's phone had last been pinged. Bix had also sent over a satellite photo of that area. Raveaux looked at the image again, blowing it up wider on his phone to study the topography of the unique formation.

Sophie and Jake had disappeared on a *kipuka*, and what was now most alarming were glowing rivers of fresh lava that forked, flowing around the raised area where they had last been heard from. If they were still on that *kipuka,* they weren't getting off of it without help.

Thankfully, he'd been given a directive to contact the local police department and work with them and any rescue teams dealing with victims stranded in the emergency currently generated by the volcano's eruption—because he had no real idea of how to proceed. He was a stranger in a strange land, and contacting law enforcement first, given the challenges of the unique situation, made sense.

The minute the plane touched down, Raveaux called the Hilo police station nearest the area off of Saddle Road where Sophie and Jake had disappeared. "I'd like to report two missing persons in need of assistance. They may be trapped by lava flows," Raveaux told the intake officer he was routed to.

Explaining who he was, who Sophie and Jake were, what they were doing out on the lava, who they were pursuing and why, took the rest of the time getting off the plane and down and out of the Hilo Airport building as he headed for the car rental kiosk.

"I'll come to you," Raveaux told the officer taking his information. "I was told to ask for Captain Ohale. Sophie Smithson is known to him from past cases, and socially. I'll be at your station soon to meet with your chief." He hit the End button on his phone.

Raveaux was going to have to establish his bona fides in person; his law enforcement background as an elite detective on the French

Riviera had taught him that who you knew was important at any police station the world over.

"CAPTAIN BRUCE OHALE. I'm in charge at this station." The big Hawaiian man's hand engulfed Raveaux's as they shook. Ohale gestured to one of two plastic chairs drawn up in front of his battered metal desk. "Have a seat, and run this situation by me again. From the beginning."

"Of course." Raveaux tugged his tailored trousers down and sat, crossing one leg over the other as he took Ohale's measure. The station leader had a large, square head whose shape was emphasized by a military-style buzz cut.

Ohale's dark brown eyes gleamed with intelligence and candor as the man took in Raveaux's trim build, fine clothing, and salt-and-pepper hair with a similar assessing glance. "We don't often get someone with your kind of background in our area."

"Sophie Smithson is the CEO of Security Solutions. Her disappearance in the midst of a natural disaster has us all very worried," Raveaux said carefully. "I'm an investigation contractor with Security Solutions, and one of our most mobile members. I was available to get on a plane and come as soon as our president of operations, Kendall Bix, asked me to." Raveaux smoothed the buttoned placket of his shirt. "We're not sure if Ms. Smithson and her partner Jake Dunn, whom I'm given to understand you are acquainted with, have gone off the grid as a result of the persons they were pursuing for a case, or due to the recent eruption emergency. In any event, we'd like to work with you on their rescue due to the criminal nature of the people they were confronting."

"And who are those people, exactly?"

"Sophie and Jake were hired by Ki Ayabe, the parent of a minor daughter, Lia Ayabe, who's supposedly run away to live with a methamphetamine producer. The suspect's name is Finn O'Brien."

Raveaux took out his phone and scrolled to the case file, showing Ohale the picture they had of the client's daughter and her boyfriend. "Security Solutions would like to formally ask for support in a rescue mission to find Sophie and Jake."

Ohale sat back in his chair, which squeaked in protest. He steepled thick fingers and glanced out the window, which featured a view of the parking lot, mostly empty of police cruisers. "We've been after this meth cooker, O'Brien, for a while now, but couldn't find where he was holed up. Our staff is spread thin dealing with all that's going on with the eruption, but we can't miss this chance, both to rescue your people, and grab up O'Brien and his men. They're bad news, a cancer on our community."

Raveaux flicked to the satellite picture with its coordinates and held up his phone for Ohale to see. "Don't ask how we have this information, but we know right where they are. I'll forward this to you. When can we get a team together?"

CHAPTER ELEVEN

Raveaux

RAVEAUX CLUNG to a ceiling strap as he sat in the front seat of a Humvee driven by a National Guardsman. The rear of the vehicle was bristling with troops seated on benches, gripping weapons. The vehicle crawled over and through deep potholes, traversing the lava plain toward the *kipuka* where Sophie's and Jake's phone signals had been lost.

Raveaux shut his eyes—there wasn't much to see in the feature-less gray "vog" that covered the plain, and he was feeling decidedly out of his element. He worked on lowering his heart rate by slowing his breathing, counting down from five with every inhale and exhale, his mind quieting inside the chamber of his helmet. His body, encased in a heavy bulletproof vest, sweated with tension in the humidity.

It had been a long time since he'd gone into an unknown hostile situation, in strange terrain, surrounded by this much firepower.

A tap on his shoulder. He turned his head toward Captain Ohale, seated beside him on the wide bench seat. "We're almost there." Ohale's dark brown eyes gleamed with excitement. Raveaux had a feeling the man didn't get out from behind his desk very often, and relished this adventure.

Raveaux and Ohale were the only two from the Hilo station—Ohale's staff was tied up with emergency response efforts, and the burly station chief had been the only one able to come on the rescue raid—because that's what it was, a combination of *rescue* and *raid*.

Six National Guardsmen sat in back, strapped and ready, loaded with tear gas canisters and plenty of ammo to take down any resistance from the meth factory—and prepared to bring everyone in, out of danger of the lava flow.

Hopefully the gang surrendered without a fight, if they were at all aware of how desperate their situation was. Though they could likely survive the immediate crisis on the *kipuka*, thanks to its elevation above the flow, poisonous gases emitted by the volcano could still kill them, and food and water would become a problem if they were isolated there for long.

Raveaux checked his phone, hoping for a text from Sophie.

He needed to stop doing that.

Sophie would have reached out to someone other than him if she'd been able to. He was just a colleague who'd worked a case with her, when he got honest with himself. But now that he was within range of her signal, he couldn't seem to keep from checking the damn phone every five minutes. "Give it up," he muttered to himself. "She's with her boyfriend now."

"What?" Ohale yelled over the bouncing roar of their transport.

"Nothing." Raveaux shook his head.

They reached an open area where a large, open-doored chopper painted in camouflage colors waited for them. Raveaux jumped out of the transport vehicle along with the other men. They trotted in an orderly line over to the chopper and got in. Raveaux and Ohale were last, taking seats that had been left unoccupied next to the pilot.

They rose once everyone was strapped in, the heavy bird weaving from side to side in a gust of foul-smelling wind. The open doors at the sides of the helicopter allowed unlimited visibility as they lifted up into and above the belt of ashy smoke layering the ground and spun ponderously to head in the direction of their destination.

Safe in the cradle of his five-point harness, Raveaux leaned out as far as he could to scan the ground. The range of visibility was limited by the vog, but the pilot was following Sophie and Jake's last known coordinates. Something was bound to pop up soon.

"There!" Raveaux pointed, his voice tinny in the comm built into the helmet. "I see their vehicle. White SUV, six o'clock."

The pilot circled a crude parking area where Sophie and Jake had parked the Security Solutions vehicle, along with a few rusted-out hulks of dead cars.

"There's a path over the lava." Ohale pointed. "That must lead to the suspects' encampment." He told the pilot to follow the trail.

Raveaux lifted a pair of binoculars to his eyes, trying to ignore the thudding of his heart amplified by the vest and helmet as he scanned the rough black surface of the lava plain for any sign of Sophie or Jake.

There were none—and suddenly, the faint path across the rough black stone was obliterated by a lava river.

Nothing could have prepared Raveaux for the awesome sight of that natural phenomenon.

The lava glowed in an unearthly way, like the hottest heart of a fire, streaked by black crusts of hardening stone carried along on its surface. Though the river wasn't moving particularly fast, there was an inexorable quality to it—nothing could stop this particular flow, or block its path for long. The lava engulfed and consumed everything in front of it, emitting little bursts of fire and smoke as it did so.

The hairs rose on Raveaux's arms, as his scarred skin shuddered with the remembered sensation of extreme heat. *The car exploding. His wife and daughter, burning. Reaching into the flames toward Lucie, his arms engulfed in fire . . .*

Raveaux shut his eyes as the chopper lifted higher to clear a flaming tree surrounded by the lava below.

That was then. This is now. He opened his eyes again. *Shake it off, Pierre!*

The transport chopper reached the elevated, heavily wooded edge of the *kipuka*. Raveaux and Ohale scanned the edge of the forest, where the faint trail disappeared into trees.

"How are we going to set down with all this tree cover?" Raveaux asked through the comm.

"We aren't. You'll be rappelling in," the pilot replied. Raveaux could hear the National Guardsmen in the back already preparing their ropes and belts. "You're not trained for this, so I'll be using a winch to lower you and Ohale," the pilot clarified.

"We'll hold back and wait for the Guardsmen to secure the area," Ohale chimed in.

"Copy that," Raveaux replied, relieved. He'd served two years in France's armed forces right out of high school, but those rappelling lessons were long ago.

The chopper passed several times over the mile-long area of the *kipuka*, identifying where the camouflage-painted roof of the corrugated tin meth lab was located in the center of the "island" of trees: a large building surrounded by smaller ones like a hen and her chicks.

"Nobody visible." Ohale scanned the ground with his binoculars. "Maybe they got out before the lava cut the area off."

"We think Sophie and Jake didn't make it out," Raveaux said, "And that's who I'm here for."

Ohale nodded grimly, not verbalizing the possibility Raveaux was most concerned about—*they hadn't made it out because the meth cookers had done away with them.* Then the criminal gang had decamped, abandoning their jungle lair and leaving it for the lava to claim.

Raveaux and Ohale observed as the pilot, consulting with the National Guard lieutenant in charge, a stocky mixed-Hawaiian man named Wong, chose an area away from the immediate buildings into which to lower the team.

The chopper held steady, rocking only slightly in gusts of wind off the lava plain, as two different ropes deployed off the sides and the Guardsmen rappelled down.

Listening through the comms to the soldiers checking the area to make sure it was clear, verifying that they weren't going to be ambushed, was reassuring. Ohale, going down first, donned a harness. The pilot worked a winch at his dashboard that lowered the big station chief down through the trees.

Soon the harness was trundling back up. Raveaux moved into the empty open area at the back of the chopper. He glanced around the utilitarian space, the walls lined with jump seats whose straps hung empty. An emergency gurney and body basket stowed with first aid supplies was netted securely into the tail area.

"Hopefully we won't need that," he murmured, but he had a bad feeling about what had happened to Sophie and Jake.

That bad feeling fueled his sense of urgency as he leaned out and captured the harness as it swung to the top of the cable beneath the chopper. He pulled it up and examined the straps. Captain Ohale's bulk was greater than Raveaux's whipcord-lean build, so he had to adjust all of the buckles and belts—but soon, wearing a pair of leather gloves that had been stowed in the harness, he was swinging out into space.

Raveaux was grateful he didn't have a problem with heights as he gazed around at the rapidly-approaching, swaying tops of the native ohia and koa trees that came toward him as he was lowered toward the ground. The cable he was attached to bounced and swayed as the helicopter dealt with the breeze off the plain.

The ohia trees were in bloom, decorated by poufs of fragile blossoms made up of delicate filaments, bright red among silvery leaves. A red-orange native bird, an 'i'iwi, to judge from its long, curved beak, hopped from flower to flower on a tree beside him in search of nectar, unfazed by the loud noise of the chopper above, and Raveaux's nearness.

Raveaux dropped into the canopy, and even with the urgency of their mission, he enjoyed the way the branches of a nearby koa tree rose up in graceful candelabra-like shapes, the rough bark of the trunk and branches embellished with lacy, pale green lichens. *If only he could have this experience without the adrenaline of their mission, and the loud noise of the chopper.* He'd listened to the singing of the native birds, and their song was sweet and thrilling in its own way. The Hawaii native forest was not like any he'd ever seen in Europe or anywhere else in the world.

He landed waist-deep in a swath of ferns, and worked quickly with the help of one of the Guardsmen to get out of the harness.

The bundle of straps, with the leather gloves poking out, spun up out of sight. Raveaux followed the soldier, crunching through the ferns and into the cover of the trees.

CHAPTER TWELVE

Connor

IN THE TOPMOST room of the Yām Khûmkạn's temple compound, where the satellite Internet signal was most unimpeded, Connor sat down at his bank of computers. Once the Master had given him access, Connor had re-created the lab in this remote Thai location to match the one at his former Oahu apartment down to the last detail.

He'd supervised the morning drills. He'd made sure Pi had exited the building, and was making his humble way down the jungle road that led away from the compound and into exile. Connor had the day to himself—free to manipulate criminals into killing, maiming, and turning each other in.

So satisfying.

He cracked his knuckles and booted up his rigs. Filled with anticipation, he fired up the Ghost software and checked his caches—there were cases brewing around the world that called for his unique brand of cyber justice.

Connor pulled together threads, researched and planted messages, but interesting as it was, he couldn't settle in, get fully "wired in" to his tasks.

His mind kept circling back to Sophie.

They checked in with each other monthly via their secret chat room. As far as he knew, she was doing well, living in his old apartment, running his former business, Security Solutions, and working active cases when her daughter Momi was with her father on Kaua'i.

But he felt unaccountably restless about her, in need of contact. Maybe it was the stress of dealing with Pi, but he wanted to hear her voice. Giving in to the pull, Connor rang her cell.

It went immediately to voice mail.

She must have her phone off. She always answered for him.

There could be a million reasons for it, but his skin crawled with apprehension—*something was wrong.*

After a short internal debate, Connor opened the surveillance app he had installed on his phone that tracked a microchip Sophie had allowed him to implant under her skin. The chip was satellite-enabled. Within moments, he was able to zero in on her location.

What he saw galvanized him.

Cursing, he reached for his private phone kept plugged in behind the computers, and entered a pre-programmed number he'd never called before.

Kendall Bix had been the director of operations at Security Solutions for years. The unflappable man had proven his trustworthiness through numerous changes in staff and turnover in leadership. In return for allowing him to chip her, Sophie had insisted to Connor that it was necessary to apprise Bix of Connor's status in case of an emergency. Though his company founder identity had been declared legally dead, Sheldon Hamilton was actually living abroad, off the grid. She'd set up a way for them to communicate, should they need to.

Bix answered on the second ring, sounding cautious. "To what do I owe this unexpected honor, Mr. Hamilton?"

"Is Sophie on the Big Island?" Connor had no time for pleasantries. He was half a world away from the woman he loved, and if her location was verified, she was in danger.

"She is." Bix paused, then blew out a breath. "She's working a case with Jake Dunn. A simple snatch and grab of a minor in a remote location. They failed to check in, and I've already deployed an operative to check on their last known coordinates."

"Jake's working the case with her?" He frowned. "Have you been monitoring the geological situation over there?" As he looked at the topographical terrain shown him by the satellite imaging, Connor's belly clenched. Belching ashy emissions from the crater, a fast-moving river of lava was headed for the area where Sophie's GPS appeared. "There is heavy volcanic activity happening in the area where Sophie and Jake are currently located."

"How do you know this?"

"Not relevant right now. I'm leaving immediately, but it'll take me a day or so to get to the Big Island. Liaise me with a rescue chopper and the operative that's looking for them."

"I'm not sure what your role is with this company any longer, Mr. Hamilton." Bix's tone was dry. "But I'm pretty sure you're not giving orders anymore."

"I don't give a shit what you think. Get me what I need, and we can discuss chain of command later." Connor ended the call, already rising from his chair. He opened the door and bellowed into the hall-way. "Nine! Get me the helicopter, now!"

THE HELICOPTER LIFTED and sped away from the compound. Watching the ancient stone temple recede and be swallowed by the surrounding jungle, Connor suppressed worry and doubt.

Pi had been removed. Connor had confirmation that the man had been ejected outside of the walls and the compound was closed to him; but there was no way for Connor to be sure how much influence he still retained among the men. Nine had kept his ear to the ground, but had only been able to confirm that Pi had been working to raise resistance against Connor's leadership for months. It was a vulnerable time to leave the compound.

But Connor had to rescue Sophie. He was the only one who could track her location accurately.

Perhaps, while in flight, he could make contact with the Master. Nine had located the Master on his own private island in the Philippines. He had taken his lover, Sophie's mother, Pim Wat, there to be nursed back to health after he had extracted her from the United States interrogation unit at Guantánamo.

The Master carried a private cell phone, though Connor had never called it. Connor pinged the number on his own satellite-enabled phone as the helicopter headed toward Chiang Mai, where Connor planned to catch a private jet to Hawaii.

"Number One. Why have you disturbed my retreat?" As always, the Master's voice was an instrument that could reach into his very bones and create a connection.

"I'm sorry, Master—it's an emergency. I have had to remove Pi and expel him from the compound. I worry that he has supporters among the men, and now I have to leave the compound to rescue Sophie from volcanic activity on the Big Island. I thought I should contact you, to let you know that the stronghold is vulnerable, and I am not physically present."

A short silence. He could see the Master's severely handsome face in his mind's eye: the sculptured mouth tightened, the elegant lines of his dark brows lowered in disapproval. "Who have you left in charge?"

"My second, Nine, is traveling with me, so I left the three elders who have proved themselves both loyal and capable in charge." Connor gave him their designations.

"You were right to contact me. These are good men, but your absence leaves a void for Pi's poison to work. I told you there would be consequences for sparing his life. I will have to return."

Connor frowned. Soon he would see Sophie, if all went well, and she would want to know news of her pit viper of a mother. "And what of Pim Wat?"

"Pim Wat will come with me to the compound. It was time for us to return, anyway."

"She is well, then?" Pim Wat had been in a self-induced catatonic state following injuries sustained in her capture by the CIA. Connor had hoped she'd die in Guantánamo; the woman was that evil. But the Master had intervened, breaking her out of the prison, proving he could have done so easily at any time.

"Pim Wat is as well as she will become. Contact me when you plan to return. Don't worry about the men; I will return and monitor the situation." The Master ended the call.

As always, when the Master's voice ceased, Connor was left wanting more. He shut his eyes for a moment, meditating on the powerful attraction the man emitted, how he used that to control and influence everyone around him.

The use of voice tones to elicit obedience was something he would study carefully from this day forward. Connor still had so much to learn.

He leaned back against the padded seat, relaxing into his harness as the chopper flew toward their destination. The relief brought by surrendering the tremendous responsibility of the compound's leadership was so great that he immediately fell asleep.

CHAPTER THIRTEEN

Sophie

THE LAST PART of the wall climb alongside the underground pond was particularly grueling. The ledge ran out, and they had to use both hands to maneuver their way along the rough wall, taking turns holding the torch in their mouths, or passing it back and forth.

Finally, they reached the other side. Sophie took the sputtering light from Jake after she made her way off the wall onto solid ground. Once she was out of the way, he leaped off the side of the cliff onto the rocky bank and let out a yodeling yell, pounding his chest. "Tarzan, baby. I'm the ape man."

Sophie grinned. "I don't get it."

"Me Tarzan, you Jane. Classic stories by Edgar Rice Burroughs." He groaned, rubbing his pectoral area. "Dammit, I forgot about my ribs there for a moment. You can look up my literary reference when we get out of here. Meanwhile, I see that bathing pond we were discussing earlier. It's right over there." He pointed.

Sophie turned to look. Jake grabbed the torch out of her hand, and lit his, just as the one she was holding went out. "Whew. Not in a hurry to experience complete darkness again any time soon."

Sophie peered ahead. "There does seem to be some water up ahead. Make sure that new torch is really going."

"It's burning fine, babe, and so is my libido. Now that I'm your 'cootie' I'm going to make a move to seal the deal." He slid an arm around Sophie and leaned in for a kiss, then wrinkled his nose. "Whew. Babe, you stink. I think we better see if we can get clean before any more hanky panky."

"Hanky panky. That's a new one."

"You mean an old one. Popularized in a rock-and-roll song back in the Fifties, but it's really much older than that." They made their way over to a much smaller pool that lapped against the wall. Sophie shrieked as he pretended to push her in. Laughing, he caught her in a parody of how she'd rescued him earlier. "Nah, I can't have you getting your clothes all wet. We need to strip properly and make sure our stuff stays dry." He found a notch in the wall and shoved the torch in carefully. "I'll prep the other torch too. Wouldn't want anything to go out while we're bathing."

Sophie eyed the spring, which seemed to be filling from some underground source; its surface shifted and bubbled. "This does seem separate from the main pond. A different water source, maybe." She tested the pool with a hand, and gave a little gasp. "It's warm! Quite warm, like real bathwater. Maybe it's got a geothermal heat source from the volcano."

"Finally! Something good from Madame Pele." Jake had taken the jar of oil out of his cargo pocket. He peeled up the plastic lid and swizzled the torch they'd used before in the oil, and then put the lid back on, setting the container carefully aside. "The oil's already halfway gone, dammit all." He wedged the unlit torch into a crack in the wall beside the burning one. "In case the first one goes out while unattended."

Jake then stripped off his shirt and draped it over a rock. Standing on one leg, he balanced to pull off his boots and socks one at a time, then draped them to dry over the rocks.

Sophie should have been undressing, but she was too distracted.

His body.

She cursed under her breath as she watched him. Every movement was graceful for such a big man, even when he was injured. How had she forgotten how magnificent his body was? She'd been too busy nursing her grievances to remember it—and what he could do with his fingers. And his tongue. And . . .

Jake emptied his pockets, arranging the lighter and other items in a neat row on a rock beneath the torches. He unbuckled his belt, dropped his pants and boxers, and turned to face her stark naked. His brows rose. "Why are you still dressed?"

"Um. I was taking in the view." Sophie's mouth was dry.

"Oh. Well." Jake stalked toward her like a lion headed for a steak. "Allow me to assist with your clothes. I think I can even help you get properly cleaned up in our handy geothermal hot tub."

"Okay," Sophie said faintly.

Sophie surrendered to the process, enjoying how he took off every stitch of her clothes with evident pleasure in spite of their state, murmuring endearments that melted her even more than the warmth of the spring. They slid into the geothermal waters at the same time, sighing with relief to feel the heated water on their bruised and abused bodies. After swimming and floating, they scrubbed each other with handfuls of pebbles and a bit of coconut husk Sophie had saved. They cleaned away the filth of hardship and struggle, reveling in mineral-rich waters that softened their skin.

And finally, when they were squeaky-clean, they made love.

Being with Jake was all Sophie had missed, longed for, and needed in the more than two years they'd been apart.

CHAPTER FOURTEEN

Raveaux

RAVEAUX PUSHED through the heavy growth of ferns, following after the Guardsman who'd helped him into the sheltering trees. Ohale stood next to the bole of a tall ohia; the native tree's gray, papery bark reminded him of the white birches in France.

"We're going to work our way back to the compound," Ohale said. "The lieutenant wants us to take it slow in case of an ambush."

"Copy that." Raveaux fell in behind the chief as he followed the National Guardsmen. The men spread out, moving forward alertly, with no chatter.

Silence was a relief to Raveaux, and he had his wish: the forest was filled with the sweet, piercing birdsong of the rare native Hawaiian birds. He pushed his helmet back to hang from its strap so that he could hear them better. These are the kinds of things he noticed, the risks he took, that he would never have before Lucie and Gita were taken from him.

Waist high ferns and fallen branches slowed their approach, until suddenly the lieutenant signaled that he'd found a path, and they were to use it. The going had been so slow and noisy through the raw jungle, that Wong must have decided the speed they'd gain was worth the risk of detection. They soon reached a cleared space with a fence that marked the edge of the compound they'd been able to glimpse from the air. The Guardsmen hunkered down, surveying the area, but there was no sign of movement.

The gate, a homemade affair of woven barbed wire, stood ajar. Around the big metal central shed were scattered signs of a hasty departure: an overturned bucket, a plastic bin left open, a jug of water fallen on its side.

"The suspects are probably gone," the lieutenant said, his voice still audible, even with Raveaux's helmet not all the way on. Raveaux flipped it back up and tightened the strap, the better to hear the comm link.

He hung back with the chief next to a fallen log outside the gate. The guardsmen moved forward, their weapons ready, to search the compound.

As he crouched there, Raveaux noticed signs of disturbance in the dead leaves and heavy moss covering the ground. He traced the impression of a boot: *size nine American, with a lug sole.* Sophie wore that size. "I think Sophie and Jake were here, checking out the camp as we are," he told the chief. He pointed out the evidence.

Ohale nodded. "Makes sense."

The commanding officer gave the all clear. The two of them hurried up into the camp. Raveaux was eager to look for any trace of Sophie and Jake in the main building or the huts, which appeared to be crude sleeping areas.

There was no sign of either of them anywhere. The ground outside the main building was disturbed, a maze of crisscrossing boot marks in the muddy soil, but there was no way to tell who had made the marks, or why.

Raveaux discovered the latrine, a foul-smelling shed with a bucket half-filled with feces, close behind one of the huts. A large hole in the ground, screened by ferns, drew him to investigate. An eye-watering stench rose from it—this foul trench was likely their refuse dump.

Raveaux held onto a sapling and peered over the edge into the pit, his heart stuttering with fear at what he might find—but there was nothing to see but a mound of garbage at the bottom.

Raveaux's gaze sharpened—the pile appeared to have been disturbed.

He retrieved his binoculars from inside his vest, and studied the trash carefully.

The top formed a body-sized depression, and there were marks of disturbance around the sides, as if someone had recently been digging in it. He gestured for the chief to come over.

Ohale complied, frowning a bit. "What is it, Raveaux?"

"Either someone lost something in that mess, or Sophie and Jake were tossed in there, probably for safekeeping, and they went through the garbage looking for weapons or something useful."

The chief's eyes gleamed with interest as he surveyed the scene. "That's a lava tube. These things can run for miles. Looks like the ceiling of it caved in to make the hole. Do you think they could still be in there?"

Raveaux squatted at the edge of the pit. He leaned down into the opening. "Sophie!" He called. His voice echoed around the chamber briefly.

No response.

He drew a small, powerful flashlight out of his pants pocket. The chief did the same, and they shone their lights as far as they could around the edges. "It looks like some kind of cavern, but there's no way to tell if they are still inside without going down there," Raveaux said.

He and the chief eyed each other for a moment. "Let's call the lieutenant over and consult with him," Ohale said. "They would have to rappel down into the cavern, and I don't think we brought that kind of equipment."

Just then, the earth shivered.

Raveaux had ridden horseback on his family's farm in France in his youth. He remembered the feeling of when his horse shook its skin to scare off a fly—but now that fly was Raveaux. He fell to his knees, grabbing for the sapling he'd held onto before, but it was out of reach. The quake was strong enough that the edge of the pit began to crumble inward—taking Raveaux with it.

He scrambled back with a cry. Ohale grabbed his vest and yanked him to safety as a large chunk of the cave's lip fell into the refuse pile below.

The two men hurried backward, flattening themselves against the heaving soil. Around them, the trees cracked and groaned. The forest rained leaves and debris down on the rippling ground.

Over in the compound, a man cried out, clearly audible in their comms. A tree fell spectacularly, knifing down through the air to crush one of the huts. The crash of the falling tree, and the splintering sound it made, were all Raveaux could hear for a few moments as he pressed hard into the dirt, his fingers clutching it, his body spread-eagled, as if clinging to the side of that remembered horse's hide.

As suddenly as the shuddering began, it ceased.

The crackling voices of the men filled his helmet as everyone checked in. Raveaux, too, answered to his call sign, and so did the chief next to him. Slowly, the two of them sat up and looked back at the pit. A good six feet of the edge had fallen in, collapsing one whole side of it.

Dread filled Raveaux. "If they're down there, how could they survive that?"

He didn't realize he had spoken aloud until the chief spoke. "Perhaps the interior is more stable. Maybe the perps took them out of the pit. We don't know."

The lieutenant leading the mission trotted up to them. "You two all right?"

Raveaux stood up, dusting dirt off of his clothing. "Fine."

Ohale pointed into the pit. "Right before this collapsed, we discovered that our targets had been in this pit. Would you and the men go in and see if they are still somewhere inside?"

The lieutenant approached carefully, peered into the hole, and shook his head. "Can't take that risk. I almost lost one of my men to that tree. He had barely left the shed when the quake hit. The ground is too unstable for any subterranean rescue attempts right now."

Raveaux was not surprised by this, but nonetheless, disappointment tightened his gut. "What can we do?"

The lieutenant addressed them. "We have verified the camp is clear. We have also verified, now, that your targets were here, and likely captured. The best strategy would be to pursue the meth gang out into the open, since they've fled the *kipuka*. They can't have gotten far, with the lava this active on the plain."

Raveaux felt sick as he waited for the chopper's return. He tried not to look at the pit—because he was almost certain that was where Jake and Sophie had been thrown to die. God knows where they were now—somewhere miles underground, potentially, with a river of lava on its way.

CHAPTER FIFTEEN

Raveaux

RAVEAUX LEANED out of the open side window of the chopper as the team got underway again. Ohale and the lieutenant had spent a little time studying a satellite image of the area, planning a grid to search. "We know they didn't leave via the road they usually used," the lieutenant said. "We need to fly low around the edge of the *kipuka* and look for signs of where they took off across the lava fields. The base camp is well established, so likely they have already planned for an emergency exit in another direction. Once we identify that, hopefully we can catch them before they reconnect with the main road."

The pilot took the chopper even lower, circling around the edge of the forested hump of land, which was well-defined and easy to follow. A clear demarcation existed between the rough, black lava field and the edge of the rise whose elevation had become its own "island."

"There!" Ohale pointed to a break in the trees, his thick arm and beefy hand a solid signpost for Raveaux's binoculars to follow. The pilot circled back in a tight loop, and Raveaux's stomach lifted and tightened uncomfortably.

Sure enough, emerging from a gap in the trees, a faint set of tire tracks had created a noticeable path across the virgin black stone. Now that they'd identified the gang's escape route, the track was fairly easy to follow from above. The chopper pilot increased their speed.

"No telling how long ago they abandoned the camp," Raveaux said into his comm. "What if they're off the lava already?"

"Then we're shit out of luck for this part of the search," Ohale replied. "But we'll up the security at the airports, harbors, and roads —anywhere they might re-enter civilization. I heard there's a new lava flow ahead of us on the plain, though—maybe they're trapped on this side of it. If so, we'll be able to grab them up."

Raveaux glanced back over his shoulder at the Guardsmen in the back of the chopper. They looked tense and serious; some of them were checking their weapons, others closing their eyes to gather inward, tapping into whatever energy resources they could before another lap of tension.

Raveaux had often found police work to be that way—long stretches of waiting and boredom, punctuated by intense danger and stress. Somehow, the combination was addicting—and not just for himself. It felt good to be back in the field in the middle of a dangerous operation. There was no room to think about anything but the immediate moment.

"I see signs of the fresh lava flow," the pilot said. "We are coming up on another *kipuka* just before it."

Raveaux swung his binoculars directly ahead. This wooded mound was much smaller, a mere hillock covered with a few trees and bushes. Directly beyond it, smoke generated by a fast-moving flow of magma made a clear line. An awesome sight, the glowing, molten rock river was more than ten feet wide and had erased everything in its path as it made its way to the sea.

The faint tracks made by the meth gang dead-ended at the edge of the lava river, below the *kipuka*.

The chopper circled around over the area as Ohale, Wong, and

Raveaux scanned the ground. "There's nowhere for them to go," Ohale said. "They must have hidden their vehicles somewhere on the *kipuka*—maybe covered them with branches or something."

"Or, they left earlier than we thought they did and got through before the lava cut off their escape." Raveaux turned to make eye contact with the Guard leader. "Lieutenant, I recommend setting down and checking over the *kipuka* more closely; see if they've found a place to hide."

Ohale shook his head. "Negative on that, Raveaux. We should check the route all the way to wherever it joins a main thoroughfare. We might still find them along the way if they made it through before the flow cut them off."

The Lieutenant nodded. "Let's do both." He told the chopper pilot to follow the track as fast as he could. "If they got trapped, we haven't lost any time. They'll still be stuck behind the lava flow."

Another uncomfortable surge forward hollowed Raveaux's stomach, as the chopper retraced the faint double pair of tire tracks, continuing across the plain. But there was no further sign or interruption until the track swung up to merge with a flat area of Saddle Road.

"End of the line," the pilot said.

"Circle back to the hill near the flow," Lieutenant said. "We'll go in for a look on foot."

Soon, the chopper settled gently on the lava, several football-field lengths from the *kipuka* and the lava flow river. "I don't want to get in trouble in case that flow decides to change direction," the pilot said.

Even though there was no sign of movement on the roughly five-acre hillock of the *kipuka*, the open area between them and their destination made Raveaux nervous—they had no cover whatsoever if the perps decided to start shooting.

"Hopefully they realize there's nowhere for them to go," Ohale was clearly thinking along the same lines. "We're a rescue mission as much as anything."

"Maybe we should communicate that clearly," Raveaux said. "Any of you got a white shirt? A surrender flag?"

"We don't even know if they're there for sure," Ohale said.

"Don't see the harm, and it might reduce the risk for our men," Lieutenant said. "Meanwhile, it's a good sign that no one has taken a potshot at the chopper now that we're down." He turned to his men, clustered near the chopper. "Renfield! A word."

Ohale and Raveaux drew close as one of the men detached himself from the group and came to the Lieutenant's call. "This is Sergeant Chet Renfield, our hostage rescue negotiator. We made sure he was part of our team in case we ended up with some kind of standoff situation. Renfield, what do you think about sending a peaceful message in case we're being monitored?"

"I like that idea." Renfield's expression was obscured by the faceplate of his helmet, but Raveaux glimpsed deep sun lines bracketing intelligent dark eyes. "I brought my negotiation kit; it contains two walkies, and other communication devices, including a reflective white vest and flag. I can put them up and use my bullhorn to communicate. If they aren't hiding out on the *kipuka*, no worries— we'll do a quick sweep and be done. If they are, it might save a kneecap or two."

Raveaux suppressed a shiver inside his combat vest. He'd seen too many men shot in the extremities to find it a joking matter; life could still easily be permanently altered by a non-fatal gunshot wound.

Renfield climbed back into the chopper for his rescue kit. He returned a few minutes later, wearing a white reflective vest over his body armor and carrying a triangular white flag on a thin, flexible pole. "I'll go ahead of the team and leave the walkie near the *kipuka*. If they confirm that they are willing to talk, I'll plant the flag, wait for them to pick up the walkie, and we'll go from there."

Ohale and Lieutenant Wong agreed. The Guardsmen formed up, spreading out to back up and cover Renfield.

Raveaux squatted in the lee of a boulder, feeling apprehensive and useless. He wasn't adding anything to this operation—what was he doing here, when Sophie was still missing? This situation could take hours to investigate and resolve . . . but maybe she was with them. *A hostage.*

If so, why hadn't they shown themselves?

He had to calm down, allow things to unfold, stay calm, look for a chance to help.

Renfield walked steadily forward toward the *kipuka*'s jagged profile of trees, holding the white flag aloft and waving it gently back and forth. He stopped a hundred yards or so from the raised area, and applied his bullhorn to his mouth. "This is the National Guard. We are on a rescue mission, looking for survivors fleeing or trapped by the recent eruption. If you're hiding on the *kipuka,* surrender any weapons and come out; you will not be harmed."

The response was immediate; a gunshot that threw up chips of rock near Renfield, and made all of them jump. The negotiator ducked instinctively, but straightened back up, holding the flag aloft. "Don't shoot. We're here to help. I'm going to leave a walkie here, with the flag, and you can come pick it up so we can talk. You will not be harmed."

Renfield set the walkie down on the rock and turned his back to the *kipuka,* walking unhurriedly back to the chopper. Raveaux felt a vicarious itching between his own shoulder blades; that had to be one of the hardest things in the world to do.

A moment later, movement on the *kipuka.* A man in a red ballcap hurried out onto the lava and took the walkie and the white flag, running back to duck behind a large boulder. "Doesn't look like anyone we need to worry about," Wong said. "Just a meth head punk."

"That's not the reputation Finn O'Brien has," Ohale cautioned. "He has a long record in Ireland, and it includes things like terrorism and murder for hire. He got to Hawaii on a stolen visa and passport, and has been cooking meth and living off the grid for years now—and people keep disappearing around him."

"Where does kidnapping a young girl come into that profile?" Raveaux asked.

Ohale didn't have time to answer that, because the walkie crackled in Renfield's hand. "Hey there, gentlemen." An Irish brogue. "We require assistance in getting away from the lava. We're folks living off the grid, and we came as far as we could on our own. Why all the guns and hostility?" He sounded so genuine that Raveaux's brows rose.

Renfield looked at the Lieutenant. Wong looked at Ohale. Ohale looked at Raveaux. Raveaux shook his head. "We need to know if they have Sophie and Jake," he whispered.

"Well, of course we're happy to help. As to the weapons, you took a pot shot at us first, if you recall. Never know what kind of people you might run into out here," Renfield sounded friendly, too. "Hey, we're looking for a missing couple who were supposed to be hiking out in your area. Names are Jake and Sophie. Have you seen them?"

A short pause. "Never heard of them."

Raveaux's chest tightened and his eyes narrowed as they met Ohale's gaze. The older Hawaiian man looked equally pissed. As they'd suspected, the gang had left Jake and Sophie to die in the pit.

"Wrap it up," Ohale told Renfield. "We have no more time to waste on these lowlifes."

CHAPTER SIXTEEN

Raveaux

RAVEAUX HUNG BACK with the chief as the Guardsmen moved forward to take the meth gang into custody under the protection of the white flag. Negotiations had not taken long, once the team had ascertained that Sophie and Jake were not with the group.

Raveaux stared down at his phone in frustration. "I need to report in to our head of operations and there's no signal out here."

"No problem." Ohale took a heavy-duty satellite phone off his belt and unlocked it for Raveaux. "Give him a call from here."

Raveaux had to look up Bix's private number on his own phone, and enter it manually. A few minutes later the president of operations for Security Solutions picked up. After Raveaux identified himself, Bix said, "About time you checked in."

"We've been a little busy, and there's no signal out here on the lava," Raveaux said. "We're in the middle of a natural disaster, if you've been watching the news. And we've hit a dead end—I hope not a literal one—in finding Jake and Sophie."

"Report," Bix barked.

Raveaux filled Bix in on their progress so far. "The meth crew says they pitched Jake and Sophie into the garbage hole for safekeeping, and abandoned them there when they fled before the oncoming lava reached them."

Bix swore. "Good thing we have an ace in the hole. Get yourself back to Hilo airport ASAP. You're to rendezvous with an associate who is flying in from Thailand to head up the search. He's got a lot of pull in the company, and he'll be coming in on the Security Solutions jet and taking out a chartered chopper to look for them. I've made all the arrangements."

This made no sense. "Our operatives were thrown into a lava tube at a remote *kipuka* that's now cut off from access by an active flow," Raveaux said. "I know where they went in, and it's going to take rappelling and spelunking gear to find them in that hole in the ground. How will some corporate type from overseas be able to do anything more than we've been able to?" He pushed a hand into his hair in agitation and gave it a tug. "I don't know if they could have survived the earthquakes and the escalating amount of lava that's moving." Raveaux's heart was hammering inside his chest as he stared at the group of meth cookers. The group's leader, a man that looked like a stereotype outlaw biker, stared back at him with cold blue eyes. Lia Ayabe, the supposed kidnap victim, clung to the brute until she was pried off and cuffed with the rest of them.

Could his beloved Lucie have grown up to break his heart the way this girl was breaking her father's?

No. Never would have happened. He wouldn't have let it.

Except he'd let her die, instead . . .

"Don't ask questions. Simply do what our associate tells you to. He has tech that can track them that we weren't aware of," Bix said.

"Who is this man? How does he have so much influence in the company?" Operating on not enough intel could be dangerous.

"You can call him Connor, but his name is not important. What he's able to do to find them, is what's relevant here."

Likely this mysterious Connor had planted some sort of tracking device on one of them.

There was nothing to do but agree. "Copy that." Raveaux ended the call with a punch of his finger, and bit back his frustration at the wasted time and effort of the current search and rescue operation. *At least they had Lia Ayabe in custody, and her father would pay the tab for all of this.*

The chopper was heavily loaded, once the perps were secured on board. Comms buzzed with talk as the lieutenant arranged for transport to the jail for their captives, but all of them in the craft fell silent as they flew over a churning river of lava below them.

"Holy shit," the lieutenant said, his voice low with awe.

The liquid rock was moving faster than any of the videos Raveaux had seen of Kilauea's normal eruptions, faster than anything they'd seen thus far. The glowing stone flowed in chunky, red, cresting waves that lifted, formed, collapsed and dissolved, smoking as they melted back into the current of magma. Along the edges of the fast-moving river, fantastical, lacy black formations piled up, only to be pulled back into the stream and disappear.

The color was so intense that it hurt Raveaux's eyes to look at directly, even through his tinted visor.

"How could they survive that?" Ohale said what Raveaux was thinking. His question seemed to echo inside Raveaux's helmet. Raveaux closed his eyes, and did the only thing he knew to do: he prayed for Sophie and Jake.

He didn't believe in God anymore, but still he prayed. *Maybe God still believed in them.*

CHAPTER SEVENTEEN

Jake

EXHAUSTION CAUGHT up with Jake and Sophie after their bath and lovemaking; they'd both been so tired they'd barely been able to keep their eyes open enough to rinse their filthy clothing in the hot spring. Putting the wet garments back on after getting cleaned up had seemed too hideous to contemplate. That left them naked, which wasn't a problem once Sophie discovered a depression in the stone next to the pool that was naturally heated.

"Burying himself in sand and pebbles was how the boy I rescued kept warm while he slept," Sophie told Jake. "We can do the same." They lay in the depression and scooped pebbles and coarse sand from the bottom of the hot spring, using it to cover their bodies as they rested.

They'd decided to put out the torches to save oil while they slept; but the lighter lay right at the edge of their wallow. Jake practiced finding it with his eyes closed several times, before they took the step of dousing the light.

Sophie fell asleep in his arms immediately once they were semi-buried in the warm pebbles, but Jake couldn't seem to.

He kept opening his eyes, which was a mistake. The blackness was absolute and indistinguishable, whether those orbs were open or shut. As he'd experienced before, it was disorienting. He had no sense of direction. His ears seemed to buzz with interior noise, seeking to fill the void of sight, and the edges of his body felt like mere suggestions. He might not actually be present in this particular time and space, but floating in some black amniotic universe of pre-existence.

"These thoughts sound like philosophy," Jake muttered, to hear the sound of his own voice. "Or like something out of the *Lord of the Rings*." He shut his eyes. He had to tune into his other senses, ground himself in this particular moment, tether himself to *now*.

Sophie was in his arms: warm, present, real, breathing softly as she slept. Everything was okay right now, even if his empty belly growled and gnawed at his backbone and the bruises of his beating sent up an ugly chorus. The hunger pangs would subside and come back eventually, but hunger wasn't *pain*. Wasn't any kind of real distress he hadn't been through before. The beating had been bad, but he'd known that kind of pain plenty, and he was healing already.

Nothing kept him down for long, not even being buried alive. He was master of his body, and its discomfort didn't bother him.

Jake stroked gently down Sophie's side, from her shoulder to her thigh. She was wedged against him in the hollow, with pebbles and sand surrounding them in an oddly cozy subterranean blanket.

Warm skin. Soft hollows. Firm muscle. Strong bones. The weight of her head, pillowed on his bicep.

Jake slid his hand down to rest lightly on Sophie's belly. Her soft, quiet breathing lifted and lowered his hand.

Actually, everything was wonderful right now.

Sophie had once needed absolute darkness to sleep at all—a relic of her time living under the cruel hand of Assan Ang, her sadistic ex-husband. She was comfortable in the dark. And if she wasn't afraid of their current situation, if she trusted Jake with her body and her life enough to let go and sleep, then he could relax too. Sophie was wise enough, smart enough, strong enough, and loving enough for both of them.

Gradually Jake's breathing synced with hers. He floated away into a deep, fathomless rest.

THE GROUND VIBRATED.

The blackness whined and creaked.

Jake pulled Sophie beneath him to protect her, curling his body instinctively over and around hers. Small stones struck him, falling from above.

Then the darkness heaved, bucking and groaning and shrieking, the sound of a volcano in labor.

Sophie and Jake both cried out, but their voices were lost in the chaos of sound around them. Hot water splashed over their vulnerable nakedness, burning their skin. Jagged bits of falling rock peppered Jake like shrapnel.

Sophie fought to be free from his tight hold, and they thrashed combatively in their shallow trough.

Consciousness seemed hard to hold onto for Jake.

Was this a nightmare? He couldn't let go of Sophie, wouldn't let her out from under him—protecting her was the only idea he could hold onto, even as he heard the rumble of stone grinding against stone and felt a gush of piping-hot water engulfing their resting place.

Earthquake. Lava tube. Geothermal water filling their cozy trench.

Finally, cognition caught up with disembodied black experience.

He was smothering Sophie.

Jake let go of her at last. Sophie kicked him in the thighs, in the stomach, but thankfully not in the balls, as she thrashed her way out of his arms and up onto the bank of the wallow.

The earth's heaving settled into trembling.

The wails settled into moans.

Falling stone debris turned to a pattering of particles like sharp rain.

Sophie was gone from his touch range, somewhere off to the left, coughing hard.

Jake grasped blindly for the lighter, reaching out to the memorized spot where it had been.

Nothing. *Gone.*

The quake must have dislodged it.

Panic instantly tightened Jake's chest and throat. *But panic was the enemy. Fear led to death.*

He was trained for extreme situations like this.

Jake forced himself to keep his breathing even, to think clearly, to continue to use his hands to search the stone surface of the ledge. He was in control of his mind, body, will, and emotions. He would do whatever was needed to survive and achieve the mission.

But the lighter was definitely AWOL. "Sonofabitch."

Their cozy sleeping spot was now full of water too hot to tolerate as the quake completely subsided. Jake crawled carefully out of the dip, brushing off pebbles, but continued to pat around the edge of the depression for the lighter. "You okay, babe?"

"Fine, my cootie." Sophie's voice was a little hoarse. "Once you stopped crushing me. I located the torch. I hope you have the lighter."

"The earthquake seems to have moved it, but I'm sure I'll find it in a minute." A quick mental picture of the lighter fallen into the water and ruined—*no.* Success came from fixing the mind on a desired scenario and not allowing doubt to creep in.

Jake slowed his breathing and his frantic movements. Ignore pain from falling debris and yesterday's bruises—nothing is terminal or worth attention. Focus on the task at hand—*find the lighter.* He drew himself up into a squat, breathing through his nose, keeping his eyes closed, moving his hands to search out from the edge of the trough in a grid pattern.

Remember the structure of the edge . . . there had been a crack in the rock near the lighter.

Perhaps it had slid into the crevice, and that's why he couldn't feel it.

Jake oriented himself by locating the edge of the wallow and placing his hands carefully there. He felt, hand over hand, over to the crevice, searching slowly along the seam of rock with the tips of his fingers. He felt a smooth obstruction—*the lighter!* He used his pinkie fingertip to pry it out of the notch.

"Got it!" His triumphant cry sounded like a cannon in the thick darkness.

Sophie snorted. "Finally."

Jake heard the rustle of her movements, felt her hand on his knee. He flicked the lighter. It took a couple of tries, but the flame finally caught.

That narrow lick of fire was so bright he was blinded at first, and before his eyes had time to adjust, Sophie had thrust the torch into the flame. The oil flared high with a whoosh.

CHAPTER EIGHTEEN

Sophie

SOPHIE BLINKED, holding steady as she grasped the torch, waiting for her eyes to adjust to the brilliant light after the complete darkness they'd been immersed in for so many hours. Her gaze focused on Jake's face.

His hair was sprinkled with volcanic dust from the recent earthquake. His eyes were tightly shut, his jaw square and clenched, his mouth tight with repressed pain.

She scanned his body for injuries.

He'd climbed out of the trough of water that had been such a warm spot in which to sleep, but now blood ran down his shoulders, back, and side from the pelting he'd taken with sharp pebbles as they fell from the ceiling of the lava tube. Larger chunks littered the area around them. He'd been damn lucky, and so had she, though his protective embrace had been claustrophobic at the time. "You're hurt, my *kun dii*."

"Cootie. I still like it." His eyes opened. He squinted against the light, and shrugged. "Surface damage."

"I should check you over."

"No time, and no way to patch me up, anyway. We need to get moving and figure a way out of here. Who knows if the lava is going to decide to roll down this tube all over again."

"That's a possibility. More likely, a part of the tube might collapse and we could be trapped in here, separated from rescue attempts without a way to communicate," Sophie said.

"Always so cheerful, babe." Jake splashed water over himself to rinse off the oozing blood from his cuts.

Sophie touched the clothing they had rinsed out and laid on the rocks before dousing the torches to rest. The garments were still damp, but a good deal of the moisture had evaporated. As Sophie touched the rocks the fabric rested on, she discovered why.

"Jake. Feel these rocks."

He was kneeling in the trough, rinsing off his bruises and scrapes in the warm water, a distracting sight—*he looked like a gladiator in a ritual bath.* She must be addled by oxytocin; everything he did, everything he was, looked beautiful to her.

He extended a hand to touch the stone wall nearby. "Holy shit! That's hot!"

"Seldom is shit holy, even when extruded by the Dalai Lama." Sophie made an attempt at humor.

Jake glanced at her sharply, then snorted and shook his head. "I see what you're doing. Let's get the hell out of here."

They dressed quickly. There was no way to treat Jake's wounds, so dark patches of blood soon bloomed on his shirt and pants as the abrasions and cuts opened with movement. That Jake had determined not to show any response to his injuries attested to his steely constitution; he was undoubtedly still hurting from the beating the meth gang had given him, too. But she had to trust that he would let her know if anything really was a problem.

Sophie slipped a smooth, warm pebble from the trough they had slept in into her pocket to remember when they'd made love and were truly together again. *Now, if only they could escape alive . . .*

Sophie handed Jake the unlit torch, and held the flaming one aloft. "Grab my belt and let's go."

Jake

SOPHIE LED the way down the tunnel. The space between the walls grew narrower. Lumpy extrusions of smooth, glassy lava reminded him of water frozen in motion. Intermittently, they encountered patches of rough, lightweight, a'a lava, more like pumice. Scratchy and prickly, those areas were harder to navigate. At times they had to turn to the side, sucking in their bellies to squeeze between obstacles. Jake got caught between a carbuncle on one wall and a protrusion from the ceiling. "Whoa, babe."

Sophie turned and held the torch aloft. The buttons on Jake's shirt flew off as he wriggled through the narrow opening. "It's not only getting hotter, it's getting tighter through here. I sure hope we find an exit point soon."

"Me too," Sophie's voice was calm, but he heard suppressed anxiety in it.

They navigated through another narrow area and stumbled on.

The dark tunnel seemed endless. Had they made the right call? Maybe they should turn back to where they at least had water . . .

Sophie turned a corner, Jake close behind, and a chamber opened up before them. "Oh, this is good." Sophie held the torch aloft, but there was already a narrow shaft of light piercing the endless black.

Jake rested his hands on his hips and did a slow survey of the cavern.

The floor was made up of concentric rings of glassy lava, and the ceiling arched above in a bubble-like dome. Fresh air made the torch sputter and bend. A slit of blue sky far above whispered of freedom. Jake walked forward slowly to stand beneath it.

He wasn't excited yet.

His eyes scanned the room, but he could not see an exit.

"I think this is the proverbial end of the line, Jake. A reference to when train tracks were first laid, crossing the United States," Sophie said.

"Extra bonus for knowing not only what the saying meant, but the derivation," Jake said.

She turned to him with a smile. "That's a big word."

"I am not unfamiliar with big words." He pinched her butt. "For instance, right now you're obfuscating the semi-disaster that this chamber is as far as we can go."

"It might not be a disaster if we can get to that opening in the ceiling. It looks wide enough to slip through."

"Big enough for you, maybe." Jake narrowed his eyes, gauging the distance. "I can tell my shoulders and chest are too wide. And how are we going to get up there?"

"There must be a way. You look for that, while I check the perimeter and make sure there are no more exits." She moved off with the torch.

Jake frowned, staring up.

The opening above looked to be about four feet deep, a crack in the bubble that had formed the ceiling of the cavern, covered by a layer of dirt. Ferns and grasses grew around its edges. The crack was probably hardly visible from the ground.

He turned to examine the sides of the cave. The walls were uneven, laddered with stone ledges. Climbing up the sides wouldn't be hard, but even if they reached the ceiling, they'd still be a long way from the actual opening with no way to cross the roof decorated with sharp knuckles of black stone.

It would be a challenging climb, even with proper equipment, and they had nothing.

He fought down a surge of fear.

They were fine. They had a water source a way back, fresh air here. They'd be good here for days, if a little hungry and uncomfortable, until Bix was able to find them—*as long as the lava didn't find them first.*

CHAPTER NINETEEN

Connor

THE PRIVATE JET from Chiang Mai landed at Hilo Airport at last. Connor had slept, worked out, eaten well and meditated for the duration of the flight, gathering and conserving his energy for the challenges ahead. As he'd directed, Bix had arranged for a helicopter to meet them along with an operative from Security Solutions, currently on the island to help with Sophie's case.

Connor descended from the jet, still wearing the white *gi* that was his uniform at the compound. The Security Solutions operative, an elegant blade of a man dressed in tactical gear, raised a brow at his attire, but stepped forward with his hand extended. "Pierre Raveaux. You must be Connor. Bix told me you could help us find Sophie and Jake."

"Good to meet you as well, Inspector Pierre Raveaux." Connor had looked up the man's résumé, and now he tested the strength in Raveaux's cool, dry handshake. "I've read your contractor file. This is my right-hand man. His name is Nine; he speaks only Thai."

Raveaux's dark brown eyes were assessing, but he imitated Nine's reserved bow in his direction. "A pleasure."

"Did you gather the first aid supplies and personnel I requested through Bix?" Connor was already walking toward the sleek multipurpose chopper warming up on the tarmac within sight of their jet. "I assume a flight plan has been filed and all of that."

Raveaux strode to catch up with him. "There have been some problems. All air traffic over the eruption areas has been restricted by the National Guard and the United States Geological Survey. Heat, emissions, and unpredictable explosive events have made any form of viewing of the active lava unsafe at this time."

"We don't care about viewing the freakin' lava." Connor snapped. "Tell me all systems are go."

"Bix took care of hiring the pilot. So far, Mr. Agno has told me he refuses to fly outside of designated areas. But he can get us fairly close to the *kipuka* where Sophie and Jake were abandoned. We may need to go further on foot."

Connor gave a brief nod. That wouldn't be good enough, but he'd deal with that when they came to it.

They reached the Bell Jet Ranger. The pilot was already inside, doing a preflight check. Connor opened the front passenger door and stepped into the craft to sit beside him, while Raveaux took a place with Nine behind them. Connor glanced into the back—the two rear seats had been removed to make a cargo area in the tail. Six canisters of oxygen with plastic masks were netted onto the walls, along with a couple of stretchers and a large first aid kit. *He hoped like hell they didn't have to use any of that.*

Connor greeted the pilot, extending a hand. "Thank you for helping us find and retrieve two of our most valuable personnel. I'm Connor."

"My name's Felipe Agno." The man's eyes gleamed with intelligence and excitement. "I'll certainly try, within the restrictions we're under. This eruption is no joke."

Connor studied the pilot for a moment, reading the man's electrical field as he checked the instruments. *A strong blue, threaded with gray and yellow.* Agno was stubborn and independent. Connor would have to find leverage to get him to go where they'd need to.

Connor donned his helmet and five-point harness, adjusting his seat, as the blades began to whirl. After they completed a brief orientation to the comm units and confirmed their destination, the *kipuka* where Jake and Sophie had last checked in, the chopper rose smoothly into the air.

Connor leaned over, pressing his forehead against the curved Plexiglas window to look below as they left the airport and flew toward the open lava area.

The terrain was barren and rugged as they moved up in elevation, following Saddle Road, an old, well-established route that ran over the lava plains and connected the Big Island's main cities of Hilo and Kona. The two-lane road snaked between them, running between the twin cones of Mauna Loa and Kilauea. Kilauea was the volcano currently erupting, but Mauna Loa, a much higher peak at more than ten thousand feet, was also emitting alarming rumbles and shaking the ground with earthquakes. The United States Geological Survey had sent out alerts that activity might be imminent there as well.

Connor drew his tablet out of the backpack resting between his feet and tapped on the screen, bringing it to life.

The USGS satellite he'd hacked into zeroed in on the location of Sophie's tracking device at his direction. Using his fingertips, Connor was able to zoom in. Nothing useful was visible—only a rugged black plain. Sophie's signal had moved several thousand yards since his last check-in, and he frowned upon seeing that the relative volcanic safety of the *kipuka* itself had been left behind.

She must now be somewhere out on the featureless landscape of the lava plain, where new lava might soon be flowing.

Maybe he could spot them on foot . . . Connor continued using his fingertips to try to narrow the area of focus around the pulsing red beacon of Sophie's GPS chip—but cursed as the picture fragmented into blocky pixels.

The chopper bounced in an updraft, ruining the tracking further.

Agno's voice came over the comm. "I can't go much farther. The USGS has designated this area a no-fly zone. Nothing's visible on the ground yet, but there's volcanic activity under the lava, and it could burst out from any weak point in the crust and nail us."

Connor frowned, tapping the screen to get the GPS coordinates of the beacon to display. "I need you to fly here." He showed the pilot the tablet. "Set your directional program to take us there." He tried to get eye contact with the pilot, to use his voice to command the man as the Master did.

Agno shook his head and kept his eyes on the landscape ahead. "No. I told you when I took this job that I wasn't allowed to fly in any hot spot areas."

"Nine!" Connor growled in Thai. "This man needs to take us to where we want to go."

Nine, seated directly behind the pilot, already had the slender blade he kept on his person ready for action. He applied the tip to the vulnerable nape of the man's neck revealed by the edge of the helmet. Agno yelped, "You can't kill me. You need me to fly this bird. Hijacking is a felony!"

"Nine doesn't have to kill you to make you wish you were dead," Connor said with a humorless smile.

Connor readied himself to disable the Frenchman if he interfered, but Raveaux looked on impassively. There was no sign of surprise or resistance in Raveaux's relaxed but alert posture. His electrical field was a steady green. Clearly, he'd been prepared for the possibility that things would go this way.

Nine applied some pressure; the knife pierced the skin. The pilot winced, his knuckles showing white on the steering collective. "If we get busted, it's all on you." He fed the coordinates Connor showed him into the flight computer.

The helicopter took a new heading, arrowing across featureless lava that probably hid acres of magma activity. Connor stroked the surface of the tablet with his thumb, brushing the pulsing red beacon. "We'll be there soon," he whispered. "Hold on a little longer."

CHAPTER TWENTY

Jake

SOPHIE RETURNED from her circuit around the chamber, her mouth tight with anxiety. "No exits from this room. Not so much as a crack."

"Except directly overhead. Really wish we still had a phone. The ceiling is thin enough here that we might be able to get a signal out." Jake tipped his head back to eye the seductive sliver of blue above them.

"We're in a good position here. It's going to be okay." Sophie seemed confident, in spite of the stress. She wedged the torch into a notch in the wall.

Did she know something he didn't?

"Soph." Jake took hold of Sophie's shoulders, turned her to face him. She was five inches shorter, so those pretty brown eyes were level with his chin, but she refused to look at him. "You got something up your sleeve?"

Sophie frowned, glanced at her arms. Her knit shirt was now laddered with runs and rips. "My sleeves are too tight to conceal anything."

"Figure of speech." He caught her eye. "We have no phones. We're potentially miles from where we went into the tunnel, which is where searchers will go looking for us. How are you so sure that we'll be rescued here?"

"I didn't want to tell you in case you read more into it than there is." Sophie looked down at her feet. Her shoulders slumped under his hands. "Connor monitors me. With a chip. He will find us here with little difficulty since the ceiling is thin. I need to get as close to the opening as possible, and stay there, so the signal is strong."

"He chipped you. Of course, he did. Like you were a dog that might wander off." Old jealousy tightened Jake's gut. "Why am I not surprised?" He let go and walked away, breathing deeply to calm himself. He paced over the uneven ground. "Connor's always here, isn't he? Between us."

"Jake. *You* left *me,* remember?" Sophie followed him, righteous anger raising her voice. "Connor was there for me then. He chipped me because he wanted to make sure I was always safe. He wanted to make sure that he could find me, because of my psycho mother, because of my dangerous job. He has never wavered in his commitment to me, while you—" her voice choked off.

Jake stopped. Turned. *Was she crying?*

Sophie stood still, backlit by the torch, those fine square shoulders of hers still hunched, her hands over her face.

"Gah. I'm such a jealous asshole. I'm sorry." Jake took two long steps back to her, engulfing her in his arms, pressing her rigid body into his. "I'm sorry, I really am. I'm freakin' *glad* that ninja vigilante mastermind tagged you. I might not even punch him out when I finally see him again, if we get out of here alive."

Sophie snuffled against his chest, still covering her face. "You might as well know everything. We tried to—be together. But there wasn't anything but friendship between us. You have to believe that."

"I believe that. Or we would never have gotten this far." Jake kissed her forehead, the scar on her cheek, her lips that tasted of salt and tears.

She pulled back, looked him in the eye. "Connor and I have a bond, and he will always be in my life. He's important to me. I don't want to have stress about him. And you."

"That's fair." Jake clasped her hands. "I also accept Alika. He's Momi's dad, and will always be around, too. You're an unusual woman, and you have unusual relationships. As long as I'm the only guy you sleep with, I'm okay with it." Jake wiggled his brows, trying to make light of needing to hear her make a commitment to him aloud. "Am I your main squeeze, babe?"

Sophie let go of his hands and placed hers on his biceps, kneading them gently with a quality of testing fruit for ripeness. That fleeting dimple appeared in her cheek. "Main squeeze. That must be slang for being my lover. Yes, Jake, you're my lover. My *only* lover." She leaned forward and kissed a scratch beneath his jaw. "My beloved. My *cootie.*"

"I'll take it." Jake drew her in for a kiss. Time became irrelevant. Their surroundings didn't matter. All that mattered was her in his arms.

Suddenly, the ground shuddered and heaved. A terrible groaning filled the cave, a deep roar from somewhere deep, a sound like a thousand demons gathering to drag them to hell.

Another earthquake!

Jake couldn't keep his feet, but he turned as he fell so that Sophie landed on top of him as he hit the bucking, heaving ground—and this time, cracks opened in the floor with a sound like ice breaking on a lake in winter.

Steam hissed out of the cracks, filling the cavern with heat, cutting the visibility, burning their skin.

The torch on the wall went out.

Jake jerked with alarm—*flame needed oxygen, and it wasn't getting any.*

A foul stench filled the air.

Sulfur dioxide smelled horrible. The deadly gas trapped down in the magma usually flushed out before the lava appeared, when an eruption was imminent.

Belching out of the fissures on the cavern's floor with the steam was a shit-ton of awful-smelling sulfur dioxide.

They were about to be gassed like rats, and then burned to a crisp.

Jake didn't even waste breath on cursing. He surged to his feet, staggering as the floor continued to rock n' roll. He evaded a column of swirling mist and sucked in a big breath, running with Sophie along the bouncing, shuddering ground as brittle lava broke loose from above and fell around them. Dirt cascaded through the opening above, peppering the steaming surface of the floor with debris.

They reached the wall and, his lungs already beginning to burn, Jake hoisted himself up onto the lowest ledge. He tugged Sophie's hand and pulled her with him. She climbed after him, her shirt up over her nose and mouth like she'd done before.

He hoped she wasn't breathing—the air was toxic as hell, and a shirt as a mask wasn't going to do a thing.

Jake could taste the sulfur dioxide, the noxious poison of it metallic in his mouth. He climbed desperately, reaching up for the next ledge, swallowing his breath down to make that one gulp last longer, towing Sophie after him as she flagged.

He'd already decided where they would position themselves when he'd assessed the wall—a ledge a couple of feet wide at the top, just beneath the ceiling. They'd be safe there from being parboiled by the superheated steam at the floor, and perhaps the air would be clear enough to breathe because they'd be as close as they could get to the ceiling vent.

In any case, it was their only option.

Sophie gasped and coughed, clawing at him, her eyes frantic— and then she sagged and passed out.

Jake circled an arm under hers and heaved her up against his side. He climbed blindly, hauling her dead weight. Dark spots danced in his vision, narrowing to a tunnel-like circle as he dragged Sophie's limp form, lifted her up, and rolled her onto the highest ledge above him, under the cave's ceiling.

Jake gripped the edge, trying to pull himself up after her, his solar plexus spasming with the need to breathe—and finally, he did.

The air tasted like metal and burned like smoke and gave no relief.

Jake sagged back, collapsing onto a ledge well below Sophie's.

Another breath seared his lungs. He coughed, but it didn't help at all. His whole body shuddered. He pressed his lips into a crack against the wall, sucking the air hiding in it. He was smothering, and it hurt like a mofo.

Agony.

Fade to black.

At least they were together.

CHAPTER TWENTY-ONE

Connor

THE CHOPPER SETTLED onto the lava, rocking slightly on the uneven stone. Connor frowned, scanning the area. "Anybody see any sign of them?" He hadn't been able to spot Sophie or Jake using the satellite imaging, and even though the beacon told him that the craft was virtually on top of her, nothing was visible.

Raveaux was already reaching for the door. "Maybe they're down on the ground. We should search a grid."

"Put on the portable oxy tanks netted onto the wall," Agno said. "I smell sulfur dioxide. It's emitted when lava first breaks out, and it's nasty." He had already torn off his helmet and reached under the seat to grab a plastic breathing mask attached to an oxygen canister.

Nine, discerning what was needed, grabbed three more of the mobile units from their cradles on the wall of the chopper. He put his unit on, keeping his knife at the ready.

"Secure the pilot so he doesn't get any ideas about flying off and leaving us here," Connor told his second in Thai. "Raveaux and I will start searching for them on the ground."

Nine gave a short nod. Connor opened the sliding door of the craft and hopped out.

His rubber-soled sandals didn't seem heavy duty enough for the rugged lava, nor did his thin white *gi* seem like it would withstand much contact with the brutal stone—but there was no help for it. He gestured to his tablet as he spoke to Raveaux. "I had the chopper put down six feet to the left of the beacon, but I'm beginning to wonder if the signal is very accurate. We should see Sophie and Jake already."

Raveaux pointed to the spot Connor indicated. "Did it occur to you they could be below us? I wanted to tell you earlier. Sophie and Jake were dropped into a hole by the meth gang. A lava tube. Some of those go for miles under the surface. If you're picking up the GPS signal here, they are probably below us." The Frenchman scanned the ground. "Since visibility is so poor, we're going to have to walk a grid. Use your tablet to identify the exact spot where the beacon is, and we'll build our grid out from there."

Connor breathed through this shock. *Sophie could be buried out here!* "Sophie! *Sophie!* Answer me!"

He sounded frantic, his voice muffled by the mask, but he didn't care.

No reply.

Dense fog that smelled faintly but distinctively like sulfur swirled around them—this was what hell was going to smell like, most definitely.

But what Raveaux was saying made sense. Connor forced himself to take slow breaths of the oxygen from the mask—it was purer than the usual air, and he could feel it calming him, buoying him.

Embrace that. Use it. You're in control of everything around you.

Connor walked carefully forward, holding the tablet out until he was directly on top of the signal. "This is my best guess for her exact location. But like I said, I don't think this thing can be all that accurate."

Raveaux darted forward suddenly, kneeling on a patch of soil to part some tough-looking grass. "I see steam coming up—*Mon Dieu!* There's a crack here masked by the grass! They could be down below, in a cavern!"

Nine was getting out of the chopper as Connor swiveled back to face him. "We're going to need the pickaxe and shovel. Quickly!"

Nine hurried to fetch the tools.

Connor knelt at the opening beside Raveaux, who was ripping at the tough grass with his bare hands, digging to widen the crack. *"Sophie! Jake!"* The man's voice sounded as frantic as Connor's had been. "We're coming to get you out!"

Soon Nine and Raveaux were both hacking and chopping at the opening with the pickaxe and shovel. The crack, which had begun as a two-foot-long rift, widened under their rapid work.

Connor finally set the tablet aside—the beacon wasn't moving. What did that mean? The fact that she hadn't called out couldn't be good . . .

This kind of thinking wasn't helping. He needed to use his abilities. He sat down cross-legged.

Nine glanced at him with comprehension, but Connor's apparent indolence seemed to push Raveaux over the edge. "You can move some damn dirt and make yourself useful!" Raveaux yelled at him, wild-eyed.

This man cared about Sophie and Jake. Good.

"I am being useful." Connor shut his eyes. He centered himself, tuning into that deep knowing. He opened his inner self to "see."

Two people were below them, one closer to the surface.

The smaller one had to be Sophie. Her energy signature was white, but it was going transparent around the edges as her life force ebbed.

The much larger energy signature beneath her had once been a vibrant orange, but it was darkening fast.

Connor opened his eyes. "I know where they are. Six feet and ten feet down from us, about eight feet to the left. The only way to reach them is to open this crack enough to drop to the bottom of the cavern. They are on the side wall, unconscious—probably from the toxic air."

"*Merde!*" Raveaux redoubled his attack on the ground with the pickaxe. "How do you know this?"

Connor didn't bother to answer. "We're going to be too late," he told Nine. "Unless . . ."

"You can do it, Number One. You've just never tried," Nine guessed what he was thinking as the man often did, while never slowing in spading away the rock and soil that Raveaux loosened with the pickaxe.

Connor shut his eyes again.

Just because he'd never tried it didn't mean it was impossible. He'd only ever slowed *down* time before—*but maybe he could speed it up.* "Anything's possible to those who believe," the Master's resonant voice said in his mind.

Connor went inward.

He pictured Raveaux hitting the ground with the pickaxe as fast as the needle on a sewing machine. Pictured Nine removing the debris, both of them moving a thousand times faster. Every detail was etched in his mind.

He opened his eyes.

His compatriots looked like a film loop set on top speed, dirt flying everywhere. Interesting. He experienced time as normal. Connor stood, hurried to the chopper, and took out the stretcher and the spare O2 tanks, along with a large coil of rope.

When he returned with the rescue equipment, the two men had opened a big enough gap to slip through. Connor slowed time back down, and handed the rope to Nine. "Lower me in."

He carried two extra O2 tanks tucked inside his *gi* and breathed through his mask, oxygenating his lungs, as the men lowered him down the narrow opening into what became a large, dark cavern filled with steam and noxious gas.

Visibility was poor, but he spotted Sophie immediately, sprawled on a stone ledge closest to the ceiling. Her white energy field glowed like moonlight.

Jake lay on a ledge below her. His energy field had gone a deep red. *Jake was close to death.*

The men lowered him to the floor of the chamber. Connor climbed the wall's irregular layers rapidly, reaching Jake first. His former friend's skin was white and clammy and he wasn't breathing —*probably too late to save him.*

"If only I could go back in time," Connor murmured, but from what he could tell so far, he could only affect the moments he currently occupied.

Connor began CPR, sucking O2 from the canister and blowing it into Jake's mouth. He remembered doing this all too well from that other time he'd brought Jake back—*was it worth doing this time?* Jake could be a vegetable already from oxygen deprivation.

Steam thickened around them, and so did the smell of sulfur. The rock walls trembled ominously. *He had to try to save Sophie while there was still time!*

Connor blew one last blast of O2 into Jake's unresponsive mouth and tied the rope around his chest, making a loop under the man's arms. "Pull Jake up! He's not breathing, but I've got the O2 on him. I have to get Sophie out, too. It's getting bad down here!"

The rope, tight with Jake's heavy body, seemed to ascend too slowly. Connor shut his eyes and increased the speed; Jake shot up and out of sight.

The conditions in the cave and the energy he was expending had begun to weaken Connor. He had to concentrate hard on keeping time moving faster as he climbed up to Sophie's rocky ledge.

She lay sprawled face down, unconscious but breathing. Hopefully, she'd been able to get enough oxygen at the top of the chamber, with the air slit nearby. He put the second mask on over her nose and mouth, and turned on the unit.

"Grab the rope!" Raveaux yelled from above as the rope dropped down, swinging back and forth with a rock now tied to the bottom of it.

Connor caught hold after a few tries. He tied the rope under Sophie's armpits, tucked the small tank into the rope loop and yanked on it.

"Pull her up and then get me as soon as you can!" Connor yelled back up to the surface. A yellow indicator light blinked near the control knob of the tank. "My O2 is running low."

"Copy that!" Raveaux called back down. The men hauled Sophie up and out of sight.

Connor sat down on the ledge, suddenly exhausted and dizzy. He tried to speed up the time that the rope came back down to him, but nothing happened. The tunnel above remained stubbornly empty.

Spots circled his vision. He lay down on the ledge, still warm from Sophie's body.

CHAPTER TWENTY-TWO

Raveaux

RAVEAUX HAD MET Jake for the first time a few days before the mission to the Big Island, when Sophie had invited him over to her apartment in the Pendragon Arches for a little party of drink and *pupus*, that Hawaiian word for *hors d'oeuvres*.

She'd had music on, smoky jazz from New Orleans, and the sweet dark sound poured out like molasses as she opened the door. "Glad you could make it, Pierre."

"I am glad as well." Raveaux held out a respectable Beaujolais. "For your wine cabinet."

Sophie smiled. She was wearing something sleek and silver that glimmered to the floor. "I like a recovering alcoholic with the nerve to bring a bottle of wine to a party." She took the offering in its pretty bag. "And knowing your taste, it will be too good for the company."

Raveaux shrugged. "I didn't know what you'd be serving, but of course you can open it now."

"If you say to save it, then I will save it." Her teeth gleamed, a row of harbor lights guiding him in. "Come and meet my friends." She caught his hand to tug him into the dimly-lit room. Raveaux closed the door behind him, letting his eyes adjust to a glow emitted by jars filled with coiled twinkle lights that reminded him of capturing fireflies in bottles in his youth. A small mirror ball in one corner cast spangles over people talking in couples and clusters, some of them dancing. The music surrounded and suffused him.

"Something to hold in your hand is our first order of business." Sophie led him into a geometric corner of the large, open room that marked the kitchen.

More bottles with twinkly lights decorating the area filled one countertop. Sophie reached unerringly in among them and grabbed a green glass bottle. She filled a crystal highball with bubbly water and ice, speared a lime on a plastic sword, and used it to swirl the cubes. She presented the drink to him. "You get one of the only real glasses in the place. Enjoy."

"You remembered my evening Perrier and lime." Raveaux was warmed as he took the glass. "I like the sound of the bubbles and ice cubes, even without the gin."

"I know." Sophie was already turning away to open a cabinet and stow his gift on the top shelf. "For when we need the good stuff," she stage-whispered. "Thank you, Pierre." Her kiss on his cheek sizzled everywhere, and he shut his eyes.

"So, this must be the famous French detective!" The loud male voice interrupting them had to belong to Sophie's boyfriend, Jake.

Raveaux opened his eyes and focused. Jake was backlit and appeared as nothing but a large male shape. "*Bonsoir.* Yes, I am Raveaux. Thank you for inviting me to your evening."

"Any friend of Sophie's is a friend of mine." Jake slid a burly arm around Sophie from behind her, pressing her slender form in its revealing shimmery dress against his body.

The man was as Raveaux had expected, one of those ex-military testosterone-driven types who had to establish dominance with anyone else near his woman. He hadn't warmed to Jake that evening —but even so, he sucked a breath of shock now as he and Nine hauled Jake's heavy form up and out of the pit.

Jake's skin was bright red, as if he'd been parboiled, and where it wasn't bruised, it was stippled with bleeding wounds. His head lolled as the rope dug in under his armpits. The oxygen mask covered his nose and mouth, but his chest didn't seem to be moving.

Nine grabbed the rope and dragged the man up, gesturing toward the chopper and chattering in Thai. "I don't understand what you are saying," Raveaux panted. His hands were raw, his muscles trembling at the strain of pulling Jake up out of the pit. The man was over two hundred pounds of muscle and bone.

Nine made a hand-over-hand gesture, and Raveaux turned to face the pilot, scowling at them through the windshield. "Yes. We need his help to bring Sophie and Connor up, too. I get it."

Nine nodded briskly. He bent down toward Jake, checking his vitals.

The man already looked gone to Raveaux, but they had to try to revive him—and Nine was right. Jake had been so heavy it had taken all their strength to pull him up, and the air coming out of the vent was none too good. He was glad of his small O2 canister as he forced himself to hurry to the chopper. "We need you to help us pull the other two up."

The pilot tugged at plastic zip ties anchoring him to a grip bar at the side of his door. "Then cut me loose."

Raveaux cut the ties with his combat knife. The two of them hurried back.

"He looks bad." The pilot stared down at Jake as Nine did CPR.

Raveaux knelt beside the prone body, preparing to assist, when Nine lifted his mouth from Jake's and grinned suddenly, holding up a finger.

Was Jake's chest rising and falling? It was! Nine swiftly covered the man's nose and mouth with the plastic O2 mask he'd been using. Nine gave him a thumbs-up, and Raveaux nodded, surprised to find himself smiling. "*Très bien.*"

"Where are the other two?" the pilot asked.

"Connor must be trying to revive Sophie." Raveaux's belly was taut with stress. "Why don't you and Nine get Jake on the chopper and secure him on oxygen, and when Connor signals me, I'll start pulling Sophie up. You two can help when you get back." Using hand gestures, he was able to communicate that idea to Nine, and soon the two men were grunting with effort as they carried Jake to the chopper.

Raveaux knelt at the slit, tugging experimentally at the rope they'd dropped back down.

He felt a tug on the rope, and Connor told him to pull Sophie up and that his oxygen was getting low. Raveaux gripped the rope, bracing himself, and pulled.

He did his best to use his back and legs, but his hands burned like fire as the blisters from last time opened and bled. Sophie's weight seemed like half that of Jake, but it was still a lot for someone who'd already used up a lot of his resources. Raveaux dug deep, shutting his eyes, heaving back with his bodyweight, then lunging forward to grab further down the rope, then doing it again.

Relief was sudden as Nine joined in, pulling with him, and the pilot, too. Only a few minutes later, Sophie's short-cropped hair, gray with ash and dirt, appeared in the opening.

They tugged her up onto the lip of the hole. She was as filthy as Jake, but her color was better, and she was breathing regularly from the O2 tank Connor had sent up with her. Nine untied the rope from under her arms as Raveaux checked her pulse.

"She's breathing much more strongly than Jake. Pulse is good, too." He pulled up an eyelid. Her warm brown iris swiveled to look at him, the pupil shrinking rapidly. "She's conscious." He leaned down close to her ear. "Sophie. It's Pierre. Just relax. We're getting you and Jake out of here, and you're on oxygen. Breathe deep and clear your lungs." Her eyelids seemed to flutter in answer; she gave a tiny nod.

"Connor?" Nine pronounced his master's name in an odd way as he knelt at the crumbling slit, calling down into it. "Connor!" The man turned to Raveaux, his eyes white-ringed with panic. He spoke rapidly and gestured—he wanted to go down after his master. "Okay. Let's move Sophie into the chopper and get her settled. That way we can take off as fast as we can after we bring him up," Raveaux gestured to Sophie, then pointing to the helicopter.

Nine looked frustrated, shook his head, indicated the hole.

Raveaux frowned. He felt an urgency about getting their two victims to the hospital as soon as possible. Connor would be all right for a few more minutes.

"Let's move her," he told Agno. "We'll lower Nine back in when she's settled." He gently set the green O2 canister on Sophie's chest, then picked her up under the arms. The pilot picked up her feet, and they carried her toward the chopper.

Nine glared after them, then tied the rope around his waist. He looped it around a large stone, turned and lowered himself out of sight into the hole.

CHAPTER TWENTY-THREE

Raveaux

RAVEAUX AND AGNO pulled on the rope moments later when Nine signaled them, but Connor wasn't coming up—they simply didn't have the strength. "There's a winch on the bird," the pilot panted. "Let me move the chopper closer and we'll use it to haul him up."

"Wish we'd used that from the beginning." Raveaux's lungs were burning, his hands bloody, and his back, legs, and arms trembled. "Let me tie him off on this rock protrusion while you move the helicopter closer to us."

"Gotcha."

Raveaux used his bodyweight and the rope looped around his back to get some leverage, dropping the rope around a knurl of lava and sagging to his knees in relief as the weight came off. The pilot let go of his end of the rope, scrambled to his feet, and ran back to the helicopter. Moments later, he had bunny-hopped the craft to within a few feet of Raveaux. By then, Raveaux had his breath back enough to feed the rope to Agno through the open door and into the floor-mounted winch.

The pilot cranked Connor up within minutes.

The blond man had passed out, but was breathing. His color was good, though his O2 canister appeared to be empty. The pilot brought out another canister and put it on him as Raveaux quickly untied the rope and tossed it back down into the pit. "Nine! Tie this around yourself. We have a winch and we'll get you out in no time!" he hollered into the foul-smelling darkness.

No answer from the enigmatic Thai man.

Sophie, sitting up in the chopper, emitted a hoarse croak at the sight of Connor's body, sprawled on the lip of the pit. Raveaux frowned at her fiercely. "Lie down, before you collapse!" he barked.

Sophie lay back down beside Jake. She took her partner's hand and turned toward him.

Raveaux wrenched his attention back to the current crisis.

Nine had not reappeared.

"Nine!" he bellowed, feeling his heart thunder. "*Merde!*"

There was no help for it—he'd have to go get the man. He spoke to Agno. "I'm going in after Nine. You're going to have to use the winch to lower me, and pull both of us back up at the same time."

"Do it," The pilot said. "Signal me by pulling on the rope when you're ready." Agno glanced at Raveaux's bleeding hands. "Here, take my gloves." He stripped them off and handed them to Raveaux.

"*Merci.*" There were no more O2 cans; they'd have to make do with what Raveaux and Nine were currently using.

Raveaux lashed the rope around his waist and stepped toward the narrow opening. It had been many years since his early training in the French army, but necessity would bring back his skill. His hands were in terrible shape, but at least they were covered now, and they would also do what they needed to.

He took a deep breath of supportive oxygen, and rappelled carefully down into the murk.

Raveaux's eyes stung from the foul gases, but the plastic mask over his nose and mouth kept providing what he needed most to breathe. He braced his feet on the crumbling stone and dirt wall until suddenly it fell away, and he spun downward into a darkness lit by a terrifyingly hot red glow at one edge of the cave—*magma!*

The cavern was filling with lava, bubbling in from a side tunnel in fierce red glowing streams. Raveaux spun gently down as the winch lowered him, and finally spotted Nine.

The man had collapsed on one of the ledges near the ceiling, right where he must have tied the rope onto Connor.

"*Quel désastre,*" Raveaux murmured. "Like a relay race gone bad." He shook his head briefly at the ridiculousness of this deadly adventure—but at least he wore proper clothing and boots, and still had oxygen. Nine and Connor's canisters hadn't been full—they must have been used. And the two had been wearing nothing but martial arts robes and rubber soled sandals, the fools.

The rope dropped him onto a boulder on the floor. Raveaux hurried across the cracked stony surface, jumping over a fingerling of lava, and reached the ledges leading up the side of the cavern. He climbed rapidly to where Nine had passed out and lifted the solidly-built Thai man into his arms. He draped Nine's arms over his shoulders and ran the rope between the man's legs, wrapping his arms around his torso. He tugged on the rope with both hands to signal Agno to pull them up.

Unless he let go of the rope, he wouldn't drop Nine. This modified fireman's carry was the best he could come up with, though bound to be damned uncomfortable by the time they got to the top.

The winch began trundling up, pulling in slack rope that had sagged.

Only then did Raveaux suck a deep breath in, and cover Nine's nose and mouth with his own plastic mask. He pinched Nine on the arm, hard. "Wake up and breathe, man. Breathe," he entreated in French, then English. He shook and joggled Nine in his arms. The man groaned—and breathed. Raveaux quickly moved the mask over his own nose and mouth and drew a breath of the oxygen, then put it back on Nine's face as the man's short, thick eyelashes fluttered. "Breathe," he said again. "Wake up, Nine!"

The rope went taut all of a sudden, lifting Raveaux and Nine off the ledge. The full weight of the other man in his arms and the rough rope running through his torn hands and between their legs hit Raveaux at once. He gave a low cry of agony and made the mistake of inhaling. The foul sulfur gas burned his lungs. He couldn't decide what hurt worse: his hands, his chest where the rope cut in, or his abused throat and streaming eyes.

Suddenly he felt the mask over his face, and he breathed blessed fresh air as Nine held it on him, patting his back in silent thanks. Raveaux kept his eyes shut, but inhaled as deeply as he could without coughing. Seconds later, the mask disappeared as Nine used it to take a breath.

The painful ascent felt endless until they reached the lip. Agno paused the winch, came to the edge, and helped haul the two men up onto level ground. The three of them collapsed for a moment in exhaustion; then Raveaux roused himself.

Raveaux staggered to his feet with Nine in his arms. "Get us out of here!" he yelled to Agno through the plastic mask. "The lava's coming up from below at any minute!"

CHAPTER TWENTY-FOUR

Raveaux

RAVEAUX TURNED his head to look into the back of the chopper as they arrowed at top speed across the desolate lava plain.

Nine and Connor, still out of it, but awake and breathing, sat in the seats behind Raveaux and the pilot. Lying on the floor in the cargo area were Sophie and Jake, covered by emergency thermal blankets and both still on O2. Jake was still unconscious, and though fading, the bright red skin color caused by excessive sulfur dioxide inhalation and hypoxia were worrisome.

The man might have sustained brain damage. *He might never wake up.*

"Stay positive," Connor said in Raveaux's ear through the comm, his voice a thready rasp. Raveaux met the man's sea-blue eyes and nodded briefly—he hadn't realized he'd spoken his fears aloud.

He glanced behind again, and his gaze fastened on Sophie. She was lying on her side facing Jake, stroking his face, his arm. The gesture was filled with longing, with love, with fear.

Raveaux, suddenly nauseous, turned and faced forward. Agno, steady at the controls, glanced at him. "Keep your eyes on the horizon line. Looking down or backward really makes people get airsick fast."

"*Vraiment*," Raveaux murmured. "I am feeling it. Perhaps too much of that bad gas, as well."

"It's amazing you are all doing as well as you are." Agno sounded downright cheerful now that they were headed for the hospital and he'd soon be rid of them. "I've radioed ahead that we have sulfur dioxide inhalation victims to treat. They will want to check all of you out."

"We're on a tight schedule," Connor said. "I'm afraid Nine and I won't be joining Jake and Sophie for medical care."

Nine held up his cruel little blade alongside Agno's sight line. The pilot groaned aloud. "You gotta be shittin' me. Not this again. Put that pig sticker away and I'll take you wherever you want to go —so long as I never have to see any of you again."

Connor's eyes crinkled with humor as he leaned forward between the seats. "Nine and I just need to return to the airport after we let our people off at the hospital. To sweeten the deal and make sure you don't tell anyone about this little adventure, we'll throw in something toward your retirement." He named a figure that made the pilot's eyes widen and his Adam's apple bob.

"That'll do," the man said.

Soon, the chopper was lowering to the parking lot outside the entrance marked Emergency on a big red sign. Raveaux clutched the door's handle, gulping down bile.

Medical personnel ran out to meet them with a gurney; Raveaux flung aside his harness and leaped out of the front seat. "We need two stretchers," he told a nurse as he opened the side door of the helicopter. "The male victim, Jake Dunn, has never regained consciousness, though he's breathing and on oxygen."

The staff fired questions at Raveaux as they loaded Sophie and Jake onto gurneys and hooked up IVs. Connor and Nine stayed seated in the chopper throughout. Moments later, the helicopter was rising in the air, with its roar and blast of stinging prop wash, pushing the medical team to run into the building. Raveaux looked back, and Connor, visible in the side window, raised his hand in goodbye.

Would he ever see that enigmatic man and his Thai sidekick again? No way to tell. He hurried into the building in the wake of the team ferrying Sophie and Jake.

CHAPTER TWENTY-FIVE

Sophie

SOPHIE WOKE up gradually from a terrible dream. It evaded her grasp as such things do, dissipating in a foul-smelling mist that was gone even as she tried to remember it. But as she lay in bed, her eyelids twitching, she tried to bring it back. The dream had felt urgent, important, as if there were some information hidden in it that she needed to act upon.

She moved, and everything hurt. Her lips parted to let out a sound of distress, but no sound came out.

"Easy." Raveaux's accented voice. She felt a straw at her lips. "Drink."

She drank.

Room temperature water tasted like ambrosia and felt like heaven as it flowed across her mouth and down her scratchy, sore throat.

Jake.

Her eyes flew open, searching for him, but all she could see was Raveaux, looking disheveled in the same combat clothing and dark stubble he'd worn for the rescue. He'd pulled his chair close to the bed where he held the plastic cup with its straw, and patted her shoulder awkwardly. "He is being treated. He is alive," Raveaux said. "Drink some more water."

Sophie shut her eyes in relief. They felt gritty and dry as dusty desert stones. She must have been dehydrated, or worse. She drank until she could hold no more, then waved the straw away.

Jake was alive. That's all that mattered.

She slept again.

The next time she woke, it was to feel her father's hand stroking her arm, and hear his deep, resonant voice. "Sophie. My beautiful girl. Wake up, honey."

She opened her eyes. "Dad." Her voice was a croak, but at least she could speak now. "You came."

"Of course, I came." Ambassador Francis Smithson's face looked haggard; there were more white strands than she remembered in his close-cropped hair. "You used up another of your nine lives, my girl."

Sophie lifted a hand to cup his cheek, enjoying the way her golden-brown fingers looked against his darker skin tone. "I love you, Daddy."

"And I love you. I thought you promised never to put me through spending a night next to you in a hospital bed, again."

Sophie rolled her eyes. "I did try. Where's . . ." She looked around. "Raveaux was here."

"He went to get some needed shut-eye and update the folks at Security Solutions when I arrived last night. Haven't seen him today."

"And Jake? How is he?" Her voice trailed off as her father held up the familiar plastic cup and straw. "I can't drink any more until I get to the bathroom. Can you help me?" It suddenly seemed like her bladder was going to burst.

Her father helped her get out of bed and wheel along the IV as she held her gown shut and barely made it to the toilet in time. "They seem to have pumped me full of fluids," she said.

"Making up for all you lost." Frank's expression was serious as he helped her settle back into bed. "I called Alika and Armita to let them know what happened to you. They want to know if they should bring Momi and come."

Sophie's eyes filled, and she shook her head. "No. I don't want Momi to be frightened by seeing me in the hospital. In this kind of shape." She gestured to the bruises and cuts decorating her body.

"When you're home, then. I'll text Armita now, since your phone is missing," her father said.

Sophie took a moment to gather her resources as Frank worked his phone with his thumbs. The nurse entered and took Sophie's blood pressure. "You're looking much better, young lady," she said. "The doctor will want to meet with you in the next few hours and go over a few things, then we plan to discharge you."

"Oh, good. I didn't think there was anything really wrong with me except for inhaling too much of the volcano gas," Sophie said. "But the man I came in with—my partner, Jake Dunn. How is he doing?"

"I can't tell you about that," the nurse said, adjusting the IV drip. "HIPAA regulations. Family only."

"But—" Sophie frowned in frustration. "He's my boyfriend. Ask anyone. I'm the closest thing he has to family in Hawaii."

"I'm sorry. Regulations." The woman adjusted a few more things, made a few more notes. "Your father can help you gather your personal items. We should have you out of here soon."

She left.

Sophie aimed her frustration at her father. "I have to see Jake."

Frank shrugged. "They won't tell me anything either. Maybe Raveaux knows? He brought you two in, had to make a report to your headquarters."

"Where is he?" Sophie scanned the room. "And where is Connor? I could swear he was part of the rescue effort."

"Like I said, I don't know. Who do you want me to call?"

"I don't know Raveaux's number. It's in my phone, and the meth gang took it before they threw us in the pit. I'll have to try to get an update from Bix at Security Solutions." She directed her father on how to find the primary contact number, and soon the phone was ringing through to Bix's office.

Sophie drank more water to lubricate her throat as Bix's crisp voice picked up. "Sophie. I was wondering when I'd hear from you."

"It's hard to communicate without a phone." Sophie coughed. "Or much of a voice. It appears I will be discharged soon—they were treating me for dehydration and gas inhalation. But I can't find out anything about Jake. Is he all right?"

Bix cleared his throat. "I'm sorry to be the one to tell you, but he isn't. He's in a coma and on a ventilator. They're worried about a lack of brain activity that may have to do with being deprived of oxygen for too long."

Sophie's eyes widened and her throat seized up. She tried to speak, but nothing would come out.

Her father snatched the phone and put it on speaker. "Bix? This is Ambassador Smithson. Back up the bus and tell us everything you know."

"I don't know much." Bix's voice had slowed; he sounded genuinely regretful. "I'm sorry, Sophie, and I hope I'm wrong, but the doctor that spoke to me and Raveaux said he'd been deprived of oxygen for too long to recover normally. He was on the ledge four or five feet below you with less oxygen available; and he exerted himself strenuously getting you up onto the shelf above him. He's no longer breathing on his own—that's why they put him on a ventilator. He has not regained consciousness, and he's not expected to."

Sophie gasped, her mouth opening and closing as she tried to breathe, but the air wouldn't come in. *She was smothering.* Her damaged lungs labored and she coughed uncontrollably, curling on her side.

Her father ended the call and pulled Sophie into his arms. "Breathe, honey. Just breathe. It's all you have to do."

But how could she, when Jake couldn't even do that? She coughed and coughed, and then she wept.

CHAPTER TWENTY-SIX

Raveaux

RAVEAUX STARED through the glass window of the Intensive Care Unit at what remained of Jake Dunn. After responding to CPR out in the field, his breathing function had failed, and now he was on a ventilator, propped up in bed. Tubes and wires surrounded him in a nest of beeping, blinking activity, but the man himself lay still. He'd been thoroughly cleaned of the ash and dirt he and Sophie had been so liberally coated in, and the many cuts and abrasions he'd sustained from falling debris were covered with bandages. The red flush had faded from his skin, but his tan was a sickly yellow, and purplish circles hung beneath his puffy eyes, barely visible behind the ventilator's mask.

Jake looked like hell. Close to death.

And he'd probably wish he'd died rather than be a vegetable like this . . . Sophie's heart was going to be broken. Raveaux's belly lurched with compassionate pain.

"Excuse me, sir." A nurse approached. "Are you Pierre Raveaux?"

"I am."

"A patient we are discharging, Sophie Smithson, is asking for you."

"All right." Raveaux sighed heavily. He dreaded breaking the news to her. "Is Jake Dunn's family on their way?"

"Yes. They've been apprised of his condition." The woman turned to look at the broken form on the bed. "Such a shame. He was in the prime of life."

"Yes, he was." Raveaux felt ancient, far from that prime of life—as if he'd always been too old. "I'll go to Sophie's room. No need to show me the way—I know where it is."

He took the stairs instead of the elevator; it was only one flight up to her room, and he needed to get his blood moving. His hands had been professionally bandaged from the damage they'd taken yesterday, but the rest of his body ached like he'd been flogged, and he wheezed as he went up the stairs. "Guess I sucked in a bit of sulfur dioxide, too," he muttered.

At Sophie's floor, he ducked into the men's room for a quick wash and a shave with the plastic disposable he'd picked up in the gift shop. A couple of aspirin and a cup of coffee later, he felt ready to face her—and her intimidating father.

Raveaux walked down the hall and turned into her room. Bright sunlight streamed in over the empty bed. "Sophie?"

She was gone, already.

The cowardly part of him sighed in relief—*someone else would have to tell her about Jake.*

"She left with her father," a nurse told him.

Raveaux hurried down to the lobby, and sure enough, Sophie was sitting in a wheelchair on the sidewalk at the pickup area of the hospital.

He slowed for a moment, just looking at her.

Her short, curly brown hair gleamed in the sunshine. She turned her head, and he sighed a little inside—her profile was as perfect as the statue of Nefertiti in the Metropolitan Museum. She wore a loose purple velvet shirt and black pants that her father had picked up for her.

He reached her side. "Good morning, Sophie."

Sophie looked up. Her eyes were the color of old tea; her lids were swollen, her skin blotchy. The scar stood out on her cheek like a badly stitched seam.

She knew.

Raveaux dropped to one knee beside the wheelchair, taking one of her cold hands in his. "I'm so sorry about Jake."

"Are you?" Her voice was scratchy. "I don't recall your liking him much."

He ignored that. "Jake was a good man, a brave man. It should not go this way for someone like him."

"It should not go this way for anyone. But that's the way things happen sometimes." She stared over Raveaux's shoulder. "My father's coming. I'll be taking a leave of absence from work to recover—from all of this. You can check with Bix for next steps."

"Of course." Raveaux stood back up. He was being dismissed. He squeezed her shoulder. She did not acknowledge it.

A big black Lincoln Continental pulled up. Her father got out and trotted around the front. Frank Smithson was a tall man with an elegant bearing; he moved quickly for someone in his sixties. They'd met briefly at Sophie's bedside the day before, but the ambassador shook his hand. "Pierre Raveaux. Good to see you again. Thanks for all you did for my daughter."

Raveaux felt something small and hard slip into his palm. He slid it into his pocket. "It was nothing. Sophie is a friend."

"Colleague," Sophie said, her eyes still facing front.

"I will be in touch," Raveaux said. "Get well, Sophie."

She did not acknowledge him in any way as she got into the car. Smithson raised a hand to him, though, as they drove away.

Raveaux stared after them for a long moment, then opened his hand to look at what the ambassador had slipped into it.

CHAPTER TWENTY-SEVEN

Sophie
Eighteen hours later

SOPHIE STOOD beside Jake's sister Patty outside of the ICU, gazing through the window at her lover's body on the bed.

"He looks a little better today." Patty's hair roots were coming in, the same dark brown as Jake's hair. Her eyes were gray with a blue ring—*Jake's eyes.* Sophie's heart squeezed in her chest as she met those eyes.

"He's going to wake up any time." Janice Dunn, their mother, stood on the other side of Patty. Her voice sounded shaky. The two women clung to each other, and had since they'd arrived the night before. Patty had been warm toward Sophie, but Janice hadn't spoken to her at all. Sophie could feel hostility coming off the petite woman in waves. Janice Dunn blamed Sophie for Jake's injuries, and she could understand the woman's rage.

And as to Jake looking better, not really. If anything, he looked worse.

The wounds he'd sustained while sheltering her during the quakes inside the tunnel hadn't healed, and he was swathed with bandages. The bruising from the meth gang's beating had spread unpleasantly, and his facial color was yellow and wan.

His head sagged to one side, and Sophie longed to push it back upright against the pillow.

She turned and went to the nurse's station. "Jake's head has fallen sideways. His neck is going to be strained. Can someone go in and check on him?"

The nurse looked down at her monitors and tightened her lips. "He's status quo on his vitals." But her expression softened as she looked up and met Sophie's eyes. "Of course." She picked up the phone and called for Jake's attending nurse.

Jake's mother approached Sophie at the desk. Janice looked haggard, her normally well-groomed ash blonde hair in disarray, her clothes rumpled from sleeping in the waiting room. "Tell us again how you're fine, and Jake has barely survived?" She narrowed quartz-hard gray eyes at Sophie. "I want to hear the whole story. Why is he covered with cuts and bruises, and you're not?"

"Mom!" Patty exclaimed. She'd followed her mother over. "I'm sorry. She needs this to be someone's fault."

"Don't speak about me like I'm not even here," Mrs. Dunn flared. "I want this bitch to give an account."

"I'm covered with cuts and bruises, too." Sophie pushed up her sleeves, showed her black-and-blue, scratched arms. "But it's true that Jake took more damage than I did. He tried to protect me." She met the woman's hard stare. "I love Jake. We had just gotten reunited. I'm devastated that this happened to him."

"Then why did you bring him out to this godforsaken island in the middle of an eruption to do this job?" Mrs. Dunn shrieked. "I wish it were you in there on the bed!"

"I'm so sorry." Sophie covered her face with her hands. Tears filled her eyes. "I wish it were me, too," she whispered.

"Mother!" Patty grabbed her mother's wrists. "That's enough!"

But there was no stopping the hateful words that spewed from the woman's mouth. "Felicia was so much better for him. Sophie's a whore! Having a baby with another guy while she was with Jake. Then getting him shot . . . and *now this!*"

Sophie turned and fled.

She took the stairs down out of the hospital, even though the ICU was eight flights up. Her injured lungs burned and her sobs were harsh in the echoing concrete stairwell as her feet, in new athletic shoes, hurried down and down and down. She could barely see where she was going, but somehow, she made it to the bottom without falling, banging out through the exit into an alley reeking with bagged garbage from the hospital's cafeteria.

Sophie dashed the tears away. She pulled the hood of her sweatshirt up, put her head down, and walked along the sidewalk, heading toward the ocean. She wanted to hear the sound of the sea, smell it. Breathe it. Something briny and clean.

How could tragedy have struck the one she loved a third time? First, grieving through Connor's fake death. Then, Alika losing an arm in a bomb blast. Hurting again when Jake broke up with her, and now—when they'd found each other again, when they'd been so close they could have been one flesh—he was in a coma with possible brain damage? Jake would rather be gone from this world than be brain dead.

And the job of pulling the plug, of making that terrible decision, was going to fall to his angry, bitter, grieving mother. Sophie had no rights to him whatsoever.

She'd been dealt more emotional pain than any one human should have to stand.

Sophie could have retrieved her father's rental car, but she needed to move. She exited the hospital parking lot with its decorative plantings. Heading downhill toward the curve of Hilo Bay, she could smell an occasional whiff of the ocean. She wanted to run, but her lungs were still too damaged to tolerate heavy exercise. Just walking was making her cough.

Her phone buzzed and rang in her pocket. She picked up. "Hello?"

"Sophie, it's Marcella."

"Oh, Marcella." Fresh tears. "I don't know what I'm going to do."

"I heard about Jake. It's the worst, darling, the worst. Where are you?"

Sophie looked around. She was on the main thoroughfare that ran from Hilo Bay to the hospital, which was located up at the top of the town near Rainbow Falls. A light sprinkle cooled her hot cheeks. Cars whisked by. "Walking. Somewhere in Hilo."

"I'm still on Oahu, but I'm trying to get time off to come see you."

The rain increased to a heavy shower and Sophie hurried toward the banyans around Hilo Bay. "Please don't. I can't handle people being nice to me right now. Jake's mother was hateful, and it—felt right somehow. I should have died, too."

"Survivor guilt. You gotta talk to Dr. Wilson."

"I don't have to do anything but put one foot in front of the other." Sophie reached the first of the series of immense banyans that bordered Hilo Bay. Gray and huge as the legs of elephants, the trees rose high overhead and blocked the rain with their thick, rubber-like leaves. She stopped underneath the natural umbrella and shut her eyes. "I think I will wander around for a while. But everywhere I look . . ." She glanced around, choked down a sob. "I see places where we spent time together. We ran and played with the dogs almost every day here in the park when we lived in Hilo. We break-fasted at that restaurant over there." She pointed, as if Marcella could see. "It's like he's already dead, and his ghost is haunting me."

"Oh, Sophie. Gah, I hate this so much. Where are you staying?"

"With my dad. At the Hilo Hilton."

"I'm on my way," Marcella said.

Sophie slid her phone back into her pocket and kept walking.

She went to the waterfront, out onto the jetty that protruded from the park and ran alongside the river. Little old Japanese men lined the outer edges, fishing, as they had for all the years she'd taken a walk there.

If only she could turn back time. Instead of accepting Jake's choice to break up with her and go away with Felicia, she'd have fought it. Tried to win him back. He'd always loved her, even then. *She could have won him back.*

But she'd been hurt too, and absorbed with her new baby, and she'd let him go . . . And they'd lost all that time. Time they could have been together, forging a life.

Sophie stood at the end of the jetty, and watched the wind ruffle over the bay, felt its fingers in her hair. She sat down, cross-legged, on the sun-warmed stone, shut her eyes, and focused on the painful act of breathing.

CHAPTER TWENTY-EIGHT

Sophie
Two days later

SOPHIE SETTLED herself on the leather couch in Dr. Wilson's cozy little office in a small, older plantation home off the campus of the University of Hawaii, Hilo. She looked around the space as the psychologist shuffled some papers at her desk in the corner of the room. The amateurish paintings were still on the walls and the sand garden on the coffee table was neatly raked. "I never expected to be here again."

Dr. Wilson looked up. Her bright blue eyes were prettily set off by a modern-looking blonde shag that fell to her shoulders. "Life has a way of being full of surprises."

"Some surprises are welcome. Some, terrible." Sophie's lips felt numb and tingly; an odd side effect left over from the sulfur dioxide exposure, the doctor had said. She rubbed her cheekbone, where the gunshot scar still gave off similar sensations. She'd worked for years to stop touching that area; today, feeling the rough ridge of tissue under her fingertips was oddly comforting.

"Yes, some surprises are terrible. Lei called me and told me about

Jake." Dr. Wilson picked up her clipboard and came around her desk to seat herself in her puffy recliner across from the couch. "I'm so deeply sorry."

"I'm glad I don't have to be the one to tell you." Sophie met Dr. Wilson's gaze with difficulty. "It was hard enough to make this appointment, and keep it—but Bix said I had to do a stress debrief meeting. Gave me a choice of you, or Dr. Kinoshita."

"I'm glad you chose me," Dr. Wilson smiled. "Now. Where do you want to begin?"

Sophie leaned forward to drag the tiny wooden rake through the smooth surface of the sand in the tray. "It seemed like any other Security Solutions operation when we started out. Jake and I were excited. We hadn't worked with each other closely since we lived together on the Big Island. And we had a lot of relationship excitement mixed in, too, because we hadn't slept together since we reconnected and he broke up with Felicia."

"Oh, interesting. I thought you'd have jumped in the sack first thing."

Sophie shook her head. "No. I wanted to take it slow. Begin again. Clear the past up first. I needed time. Jake wanted to move faster, but he was willing to let me take the lead. So, we'd been dating. Spending time together. We'd kissed a couple of times, but that was all."

"What changed?"

"Jake and I talked honestly once we were trapped in the lava tube. I was still angry with him for leaving me when I was so vulnerable, caring for a newborn, and for not believing me that Connor and I weren't a couple." Sophie sighed, adding a pebble or two from a handy bowl to her design. "I wanted him to prove himself. Show me that he loved me, take time to rebuild the trust between us. . . Not just appear out of nowhere when his girlfriend kicked him out, and jump into my bed. Jake understood that. He told me he accepted that Connor would always be in my life, and so would Alika. But he still reacted jealously when he found out

Connor had chipped me with a GPS, even though that's what ended up saving our lives."

"Whoa! Now I need the story of what happened. All the gritty details."

Sophie told her the sequence of events. "We eventually found a place to clean up and sleep. A geothermal pool."

Dr. Wilson's brows went up. "How perfectly delicious."

Sophie smiled. "We'd said what we needed to say to each other and cleaned up the past. So yes, we made love. It was incredible." Tears pooled in her eyes, and she pressed the backs of her fists against them. "I can't believe the time we lost. That we've lost, now, forever."

Dr. Wilson held up a hand. "Maybe yes, maybe no. He's in a deep coma, that's what I heard."

"Worse than that. They can't find steady brain activity." Sophie looked down—she was holding the little rake hard so that the tines stabbed her in the palm. She opened her fist. "He has an IV to get him the nourishment he needs. He's still on the ventilator, but has a system-wide infection. His mother is in charge of his health care, but according to Patty, his sister, he has a Do Not Resuscitate order in place for a situation like this. He wants the plug to be pulled, and then they can harvest his organs for donation."

"Oh, no, Sophie. I'm so sorry." Dr. Wilson reached for a tissue from the box between them and dabbed her eyes.

"And to make things worse, I'm not allowed to see him." Sophie watched her restlessly moving hands as they made designs with the rake: arcs, swirls, lines. "His mother blames me. Patty, his sister, texts me to keep me informed. They are planning to take him off all life support tomorrow. The organ donation is set to go the minute he dies."

"My God." Dr. Wilson got up, clearly agitated. She went to her little refrigerator in the corner of the room and removed a couple of bottles of water. She handed one to Sophie. "Drink. Please. I need to give you something."

Sophie unscrewed the lid and took a long drink.

She felt numb. Everything was happening around her in a distant way, a mere echo of reality.

At the same time, her conscious mind was alive and well, bargaining like hell for something else to happen for Jake. "It would have been so much better if he and Felicia had never broken up."

"You'd never have taken this job together if that were the case." Dr. Wilson sat down and sipped her water. "What ifs don't serve us."

"And if he'd been with Felicia, likely I'd have taken this job with Raveaux. The outcome would have been different."

"How so?" Dr. Wilson cocked her head. "Tell me about Raveaux."

Sophie wriggled, settling deeper into the cushions. "Raveaux is a good man, a complicated man. I like him. But he is not as big physically as Jake. I passed out early when the sulfur dioxide filled the chamber. Jake carried me up, all the way to the top of the wall, and pushed me onto the ledge nearest the ceiling. I got more good air because of that. Jake ended up where he was, lower than me on the cavern's wall where we were trapped, because he carried me." A giant, gasping sob overtook Sophie. "He gave his life to get me there. And it saved me." She crumpled, folding her arms over her waist and belly, giving way at last to the grief. "I'm alive because he put me above himself, literally."

Dr. Wilson handed her a handful of tissues, and she sobbed into them, great hacking coughing sobs that hurt her lungs and throat.

Dr. Wilson let a good while go by until Sophie had cried herself out. Finally, she straightened up and dabbed her face. She sat back against the cushions.

So did Dr. Wilson. "You said the outcome would have been different if you'd been with Raveaux. Is Raveaux not capable of sacrifice?"

"He is. I know he is." Sophie told Dr. Wilson about the loss of Raveaux's wife and daughter, about his arms, permanently scarred by the fire that had taken their lives. "He's brave. I would trust him with my life in a situation like Jake and I were in. But, as I said, he is a smaller man. We are close in height. I can't see him being physically able to carry me up that wall, push me onto that ledge, like Jake did."

"Then you both would have died." They sat for a moment with the magnitude of what had happened, then Dr. Wilson shook herself visibly. "You can't change the past. We must find a way to deal with what *is*."

"I don't know if I can." Sophie shredded the tissue, looking up into Dr. Wilson's eyes. "I don't know how I will get through tomorrow, and however long it takes for him to die. Without even being able to see him."

"Terrible. Would you like me to try to speak with his relatives on your behalf?"

Sophie shut her eyes, picturing the hatred in Janice Dunn's eyes. "No. It won't help."

"And your daughter? What's going on with Momi?"

"She's fine. She's with Armita and Alika on Kaua`i. They offered to come here to the Big Island, to bring her to me, but I don't have what it takes right now, much as being with her comforts me. Hopefully, by the end of the month, when it's my turn, I will be able to be her mother."

Dr. Wilson shook her head. "You sell yourself short, Sophie. I know you will meet Momi's needs, no matter how you feel in the moment. But what about Connor? He rescued you. Does he know about Jake?"

"I called him. I left a message thanking him, letting him know that Jake was . . . not going to recover. He hasn't called back."

"That seems odd."

"I don't know. He took some inhalation damage too, as did the Thai man with him. Connor told me he keeps the phone charged, but not with him. And as I told you, he couldn't stay or be admitted to the hospital because his Sheldon Hamilton identity's legally dead. I was conscious enough to realize he basically had to hijack the helicopter that rescued us."

"Tell me about that."

"I regained consciousness after they hauled me up from the lava tube and put me on oxygen. I was dazed, but I realized Jake wasn't waking up." Sophie squeezed more tears out of her eyes. "I lay beside him on the helicopter. Touching him. Calling him back to me. I didn't know I was saying goodbye." Sophie met Dr. Wilson's eyes. "How do I get through this? Really. I'm asking sincerely."

"There's no shortcut, my dear. This is the ugly truth of living—death is a part of it. And death is often, more often than people want to acknowledge, not clean or simple. At least Jake's wishes were clear and on record. Wouldn't it be worse to have his mother waiting, and hoping, and keeping him alive, while his body withered away?"

"Yes. That would be worse. Patty agrees. His mother does not, but she cannot overturn his directive." Sophie carefully set the rake down on the side of the sand garden.

Dr. Wilson reached across the table and took Sophie's hands in hers. "All I can do is tell you that I'll be beside you every step of this journey—and reassure you that, though you doubt yourself, you're stronger than you know."

CHAPTER TWENTY-NINE

Raveaux

RAVEAUX LOOKED at his reservations back to Oahu on his phone. He'd called Bix and debriefed remotely. He'd gone to the modest South Hilo Police Department station and given an official statement, for the record, of his experience with the operation to capture Lia Ayabe and the meth making gang—thinking of how that sounded, his mouth almost quirked up. *"That would have made a unique name for a band,"* Gita's voice said in his mind. She loved finding silly band names . . .

He was scheduled to leave Hilo.

But it didn't feel right.

The drama unfolding around Jake's condition was so grave; Sophie might need something, someone. He might be able to help.

Raveaux paced a bit in the musty smelling room of his motel, walking back and forth past the cheap rattan bed stand, the slippery plumeria print coverlet brushing his trouser-clad legs.

Yes, it felt wrong to leave her alone with this crisis to get through —but she wasn't alone. Her friend Marcella had arrived; her father was with her; she was going to therapy with her psychologist, Dr. Wilson, and most clearly: *she wanted nothing to do with him.*

He'd done his best to save Jake's life when he had that opportunity. He'd paid his respects to Jake's mother and sister; he'd said his own secret goodbye through the window of the ICU to the man who held Sophie's heart. No, truly, he had no role here. To continue to stay would only accentuate that, and cause people to wonder—as it caused him to wonder.

Raveaux straightened his shoulders. "Enough," he said aloud. He sent Sophie a text: *"Returning to Oahu. Deeply sorry for all that's happened. Let me know if I can help in any way."*

He picked up his travel duffel and swung his old leather messenger bag, carried to hundreds of crime scenes over the years, up onto his shoulder. He stepped out of the motel room and shut the door, inhaling the briny scent of Hilo Bay, feeling the light breeze on his face, the sun on his hair.

He was alive.

Jake was no longer so, in any meaningful way. It would never be fair; nothing ever was.

And yet, he had to find a way to go on, as he had after Gita and Lucie died. Sophie would have to, as well. Maybe she'd be able to, maybe not. But for now, all he could do was keep going, and be there, when and if she ever needed him.

He called for a rideshare, and soon was on his way to the airport.

OPENING the door of his Waikiki apartment had finally begun to feel a little bit like coming home. The first floor unit with its sliding glass doors that overlooked the concrete trail fronting the hotels and Waikiki beach, was immaculately clean and smelled faintly of disinfectant; his cleaning lady had come while he was gone. The floor-to-ceiling blinds were closed, and the space was cool in the heat of the day, a refuge from the assault of overly cheerful sunshine outside.

He set his keys and wallet in the vintage glass bowl on the corner of the counter leading into the kitchen; hung his messenger bag on the hook on the back of the door, removing his laptop from it. He carried his valise into the bedroom with its tightly made bed, covered in a plain white cotton spread. He plugged the laptop in to recharge at the desk in the corner. And then he reached in his pocket and took out the stick drive that Ambassador Smithson had given him, still wrapped in a thousand-dollar bill.

The money, he understood—a gesture of thanks for helping his daughter. That he'd wrapped the drive in a vintage, out of circulation bill that might be valuable beyond its face value, seemed a classy touch. Raveaux wasn't insulted; he'd have done something similar if a colleague had gone above and beyond to help his child—in fact, no price would have been too great.

These were the moments he was glad he'd had Lucie—to have been a father was an incredible, indescribable human experience that had deepened his joy, his appreciation of the human condition, his wisdom regarding his fellow man. Even if the deepest lesson, in the end, was the depth of pain the loss of a child could cause.

But what was on the stick drive?

Raveaux turned the plain metal plug-in drive over in his hands, feeling a tug of apprehension. There was something here that the Ambassador had wanted him to know, and Sophie not to know.

It was bound to be a sticky wicket, as the Brits said.

Raveaux set the memory stick down on his desk. He returned to the kitchen, fixing himself a snack of slightly stale baguette that reheated nicely in the toaster oven with several slices of a good Gouda and salami. He prepared his favorite Perrier with ice and lime.

Raveaux retracted the blinds, unlocked the slider, and stepped outside onto his sunny lanai. He cranked up the fabric umbrella, and seated himself to enjoy his view of the condo's bit of lawn and the bright white sand and aqua sea of Waikiki Beach. With the sound of gentle waves and laughing children in his ears, he ate his snack and opened his latest paperback.

He was working his way through the Jack Reacher novels by Lee Child, enjoying the spare style of writing, the inferences, the twists and turns. Reacher's stubbornly closed heart continued to seem an unnecessary tragedy—but he understood it all too well.

Finished with his food and his chapter, Raveaux brushed a few crumbs aside for the sparrows. He looked up at the waving palms—who knew that his life would have taken such a turn that this was where he lived, alone?

Ten years ago, he would never even have been able to imagine it. And yet, so it was.

Raveaux lowered the umbrella in case of wind and went back inside. It was too quiet, after the sound of the outdoors. Maybe he should get a small dog or a cat for company—but they weren't allowed in these apartments. He'd have to move.

And maybe, just maybe—he was ready for that.

He went back to the office with the glass of Perrier, sat down, and plugged the stick drive into his computer.

It was encrypted. *"Merde."* Why would the ambassador give him something that he couldn't open? He didn't have the man's number to call and ask.

Maybe it was obvious. He could try a few things, like Sophie's birthday, the name of her dog . . . He cracked his knuckles and went to work.

CHAPTER THIRTY

Raveaux

RAVEAUX BEGAN with the obvious things he knew about Sophie: her name. Her birthday, which he'd gleaned off a glimpse of her license. Momi's name and birthday.

The drive opened for Armita, the name of Momi's nanny.

"Not too secure," Raveaux muttered. "But also, not something just anyone would know. He meant for me to be able to access it."

Raveaux clicked on the folder icon that was the only content listed on the stick drive.

Inside were several sub-folders. He clicked on the one labeled News, and scanned copies of articles detailing the bombing death of Todd Remarkian, the Australian co-owner of Security Solutions, a handsome blond in his mid-thirties who bore a distinct resemblance to Connor, the man who'd hijacked the helicopter to rescue Sophie and Jake.

The back of Raveaux's neck prickled. *Remarkian was supposed to have died in an explosion!*

One of the articles implied that Sheldon Hamilton, the Aussie man's partner and founder of Security Solutions, was wanted for questioning in the incident, but was "overseas indefinitely."

He opened another folder, marked *FBI Case File.*

Atop the case file was a publicity-type portrait of Sheldon Hamilton, a good-looking brunet man who wore a suit well. Hamilton had dark eyes, wore stylish glasses, and sported a small, tidy goatee. As he skimmed the case notes, it appeared that Hamilton was suspected of being an online cyber vigilante whose signature was using tech to pit criminals against one another, usually with lethal results.

More documents dealt with a Security Solutions case gone badly wrong in Thailand. Six men had been killed in an attempt to rescue Sophie Smithson's newborn baby from an inland stronghold run by an organization called the Yām Khûmkạn. Though Sheldon Hamilton's remains had not been recovered, this incident was the last time the Security Solutions owner and CEO had been seen alive.

Pictures of rough jungle graves, one hole containing decomposing bodies and the other containing skulls, attested to death by decapitation.

The photos were watermarked CIA.

A bill of lading—the bodies had been recovered by CIA operatives and shipped back to the United States at Security Solutions' expense.

The families had been paid handsomely from an insurance policy.

An application to have Sheldon Hamilton declared legally dead was the last document in the file—*signed by Sophie.*

How had the ambassador gotten hold of these documents? And why had he given them to Raveaux? He was definitely going to have to have a conversation with Sophie's father.

Raveaux had to get up and go refresh his Perrier and lime. He paced around the small apartment in agitation, swirling ice cubes in his cut crystal glass.

Since he'd been working for Security Solutions, Sophie had been President and CEO of the company, with Kendall Bix as President of

Operations. He'd had no idea there'd been some kind of management shakeup beforehand. How had she ended up where she was? What did he really know about Sophie Smithson?

He sat down and resumed his perusal of the files, this time clicking on a sub-file marked *Internal Security Solutions Docs*.

A copy of a business memo internal document for Security Solutions declared Sophie Smithson owner, President and CEO of the company. It was signed by Sheldon Hamilton.

"So, he appointed her himself," Raveaux said aloud. "But who tried to take Sophie's baby, and why? And how did she get the infant back?" He flipped the pages detailing the retrieval of the bodies from the jungle. "Someone, somewhere, made a deal. The CIA doesn't randomly help out security firms whose operations go wrong." But there was no further information on the baby's recovery, or Sophie's role in it.

Raveaux had made his way through all of the documents in the file, and he was way too agitated to sleep. What he needed was a good long swim. He could think about all of this while he did laps.

Raveaux discharged the stick drive after saving its contents to his secure cloud storage account. He crushed the drive using a meat hammer, and then ran the chip for a moment in the garbage disposal for good measure.

He then changed into a sleek European swim suit paired with a long-sleeved nylon shirt. The water off Waikiki was warm, even at night, but Raveaux was lean, and quickly got chilled in the cool evening air. He picked up his goggles and towel and slipped outside, closing and locking the slider behind him.

The area in front of the hotels and condos was well-lit as usual. Tourists walked along the concrete aisle, talking and laughing. Couples holding hands meandered by. Families, yelling at tired kids, made their way back to their accommodations after restaurant dinners. The air smelled of grilling meat, sunscreen and flowers.

Waikiki was an entirely artificial environment in which to dwell, as if he lived in Disneyland as a part of an exhibit. Yet being here, in this artificially happy bubble, had been good. Everyone around him was on vacation, enjoying their lives, making memories. Raveaux was an observer, not a participant, but that didn't mean that the collective joy of a Hawaiian vacation didn't somehow rub its glow onto him.

He lived here. He never had to go home to a cold, ugly apartment in a city somewhere, or wake up to a job he dreaded. He had left everything known and familiar so as not to be reminded of his losses —and he liked his life, his work, this setting, and his routine.

Even if it was a little lonely now and then.

The sand was still warm on Raveaux's feet as he left the strip of lawn and ornamental plantings on the other side of his deck area. He slipped the door key into his suit's pocket, stowed his towel beside a large white head of coral, and then walked down into the sea.

The beach was a gentle half-moon of sheltered, calm water. The surf was further out, breaking white on an outside barrier reef. Raveaux had wondered about stingrays or crabs underfoot, but a careful snorkeling pass during the daytime had shown nothing but a soft sandy bottom and an occasional lizardfish, poking its camouflaged head up from the sand in hopes of passing prey. Raveaux walked forward boldly, though the water was inky around his legs.

The ocean's surface shifted and gleamed in reflected light from the high-rises, a cool embrace on his skin as he slid on his goggles and sank under. He swam parallel to shore, warming up with a gentle breaststroke, watching the pageantry of the buildings: people on their balconies, people carrying drinks to the beach, people seated on the decks of restaurants and hotels. Everywhere, the mellow sound of Hawaiian music, the chatter of happy voices.

Raveaux moved into freestyle swim. His arms sliced smoothly through the water; he turned his head to breathe on every other stroke.

And he mulled over the file.

Who was the mysterious Connor? Why had he faked his death? And what was his connection to Sheldon Hamilton, the legally dead billionaire CEO of Security Solutions? What was the connection between Connor, and Jake and Sophie? To guess by Nine's ethnicity and their language usage, he and Connor had some connection to Thailand, and likely this Yām Khûmkạn organization.

Raveaux could ask Sophie what the connection was—ask her to explain all of this—but then she would know her father had given him the file. Clearly, Frank Smithson hadn't wanted Sophie to know Raveaux had received it. Why?

No. He couldn't talk to Sophie about it yet. His next step had to be reaching out to the Ambassador, and finding out what the man wanted him to do with the information he'd been given.

One thing he knew for sure: a blond Australian businessman named Todd Remarkian was not actually dead. That man, using an assumed name, had gone to extreme lengths to help rescue Sophie and Jake: and then, to make sure he didn't have to account to anyone for doing so.

CHAPTER THIRTY-ONE

Connor

CONNOR SLEPT HEAVILY on the Learjet back to Thailand, barely waking to eat or drink something that Nine forced upon him. Lying back on his recliner bed after one of these meals, Connor reflected on the events of the last day on the Big Island.

The mission had been a success. He'd gotten in, gotten Sophie and Jake out, and escaped relatively undetected. He'd even gotten away with hijacking Agno's chopper—he'd had the man drop him off directly at the private airstrip, where the Lear had been fueled up and ready to go, and as far as he could tell, Agno had kept quiet about the whole operation.

So why did he feel so drained? His internal resources were depleted to the point that, when he raised a hand to look at it, his energy field, normally a bright glowing gold, had gone a sickly, transparent yellow.

Perhaps it was that he hated to have to leave Sophie—without a word of goodbye, and Jake so close to death.

But Raveaux would look out for her. The Frenchman was already halfway in love with her.

And if the worst happened and Jake died, Connor would bring her to his private island of Phi Ni, which had always been a source of healing and rejuvenation for both of them. She could stay as long as she wanted.

If only Connor could go to Phi Ni now, instead of back to the Yām Khûmkạn compound—but the Master had had to return to the compound to cover for his trip. He would not take kindly to Connor wasting his time.

He also didn't want to do anything that would prompt the Master to uncover his hideout on Phi Ni. It was unlikely that the Master was unaware of Connor's island retreat, but the illusion still stood that his refuge was sacred, and Connor didn't want to endanger that.

If it wasn't leaving Sophie that had so enervated him, it had to be the use of his abilities. He'd pushed that envelope further than ever this time, and must be what had so depleted him.

But that was contrary to the Master's teachings. "When you are in touch with the flow of energy among all things, when you have entered the slipstream of time and matter, you are one with it. The movement of molecules and energy from one place to another is simply a matter of will, not of effort," the Master had said.

Sometimes that was the case.

Other times, like now, Connor's body felt battered by the effort it had expended. His lungs still burned from exposure to sulfur dioxide. And his energy level was so low that even holding his eyelids open was too much work.

THE MULTI-LEGGED journey back to the compound was finally complete as the Yām's private helicopter lowered gently to land on one of the topmost, flat-roofed buildings of the temple. Connor tightened his travel-stained white *gi* and allowed Nine to open his door. He got out of the cockpit and stood for a moment on the sun-warmed stone roof as the chopper's blades cycled down into silence.

He shut his eyes and inhaled the smell of diesel from the transport as it quickly dissipated into the humid air, replaced by the smell of the jungle: mossy damp fecundity with a twist of fermented fruit and tropical flowers.

"You are not looking well." The Master's velvety voice carried all the way from where he stood in the doorway, across the expanse. His leader's rich purple energy field vibrated even with his eyes closed, and Connor sighed with relief: he wasn't alone in these mysteries any longer.

He bowed toward the man silhouetted in the door leading down into the temple. "Master. It is good to see you."

Nine dropped to his knees and put his forehead to the stones in a deep obeisance. "Master," he echoed.

The Master inclined his head in response. "Good to see both of you, as well. Nine, go prepare Number One's chamber for a bath and a visit from the Healer."

"Yes, Master." Nine bounded to his feet and ran off, showing no signs of weariness from their journey.

"You wonder why you are so tired." The Master approached.

"I do." Connor moved to meet him. "But I did things I didn't know were possible to rescue Sophie and Jake. Perhaps it was too much for my current level of ability."

"Come, walk with me in the garden before you go to your chamber."

Connor followed the Master into the cool building. No matter how humidly hot it was outside, or rainy and wet in the monsoon season, the interior of the temple stayed cool and dry. Polished bronze reflectors aimed glowing spots of sunshine here and there to light the dim halls as they moved through the ancient building. Through the slit windows, Connor glimpsed the recruits drilling in the various courtyards—some in rows, performing memorized sequences, others in pairs sparring with various weapons. He was reminded of his rigorous two years as a trainee and the hard muscle and bone he'd developed as a result. "I came back as soon as

Sophie and Jake were admitted to the hospital. No authorities were alerted."

"Good," the Master said. "And it is good that I returned, as well. As soon as I arrived, a group of men loyal to Pi approached me, asking that you be replaced by him as Number One." He paused by one of the deep, narrow windows. "I told them that a challenge to you was a challenge to me."

He moved aside so Connor could see what lay outside.

A row of five heads on spikes decorated the rampart below. They were turned so that they looked down into the courtyard, and the drilling men would face them. Even from behind, Connor recognized Pi's square, blocky head and thick neck.

His stomach lurched. "You didn't need to do that, Master."

The Master narrowed his eyes. "No? You should have killed Pi in combat when I asked you to, and these four men who supported him would not now be dead." He resumed walking. "In any case, Pim Wat needed to wet her blade after her difficult time away. Doing so brought color to her cheeks."

Pim Wat, Sophie's assassin mother and the Master's longtime lover, had been traded by Sophie to the CIA in return for the bodies of the men who'd died on the mission to get Sophie's child back. Pim Wat had gone into a catatonic state for the two years she'd been held captive, until the Master broke her out and took her to his island retreat to recover. And recover she apparently had; Connor shivered at the thought of the woman's blood-soaked blade.

That Sophie, with her brave but gentle spirit, had been born of such a psychopath continued to astound.

And what had he gotten himself into when he so impulsively agreed to train under the Master? The man was a law unto himself.

Connor mentally retraced the steps that had led him to this moment in time as the Master's anointed Number One.

Interpol, the FBI, and the CIA had all wanted to capture Connor to get information about his secret role as an online vigilante known as the Ghost. He'd wanted an escape from the tangled web of deceit, lies, and alternate identities he'd woven, and ultimately, been trapped by. He'd been grieving that Sophie had chosen Jake over him. And in the end, he'd wanted to see if he, too, could harness space, time, and the hearts of followers, the way the Master did. All of that had led to cutting ties with the past and a one hundred percent commitment to the Master and, by extension, the Yām Khûmkạn organization.

The Yām had begun hundreds of years ago as the guardians of the Thai royal family; over the centuries it had evolved into a powerful network of trained ninjas, assassins, and spies whose purpose it was to protect and defend not only the royal family, but the Thai government and the country's interests, as determined by the Yām leadership—most notably, the Master.

Connor was in too deep to get away, ever—and the world was closed to him now that he was a wanted man. *He was where he was.*

They continued down through the various levels, along a passageway past the dining hall, down another flight of stairs, and then emerged out into the garden where Connor had challenged Pi to mount the tiger's eye column.

Tea had been set out for them under the trees. Connor followed the Master across the smooth, soft green grass, past the lotus pond and the banks of flowers, toward the beautiful tea service that awaited them.

The Master seated himself and indicated Connor's chair. "Tell me about the rescue."

Connor told him, leaving nothing out, as he poured fragrant green tea into delicate, handle-less porcelain cups. The Master picked up an almond cookie and bit into it with enjoyment as Connor concluded his tale. "I was not able to speed up time to facilitate my own rescue. I ran out of oxygen and ended up passing out from the gas. Nine got me out, then succumbed as well, and had to be rescued by the Security Solutions operative that was assisting us."

"Not your finest hour," the Master murmured, his purple-black gaze thoughtful as he helped himself to a sesame crisp. "None of that should have happened."

"I agree. I don't understand how I became so weak, how I lost control of my body."

"Your emotions were engaged in the work. You used your own strength, not the universal constant of energy, to perform the time alterations."

Connor shut his eyes, downcast. "I thought I understood the principles. But in the pressure and fear of the moment, I failed."

"You learned your own limits, you mean." The Master picked up the cookie plate. "Have one."

Connor took the cookie; his appetite was gone since he'd glimpsed those severed heads, but he knew better than to refuse. He took a bite.

"Now, drink your tea."

Connor set the cookie aside and picked up the cup and sipped.

"How does it taste?"

"I'm sorry, Master. I'm tired. It tastes—like tea."

"That's where you're wrong." The Master lifted his cup to his lips. "Close your eyes and inhale. Allow the scent receptors in your nose to really take it in. Taste it after that."

Connor shut his eyes. He breathed in the smell. *Jasmine, and something smoky.* As he concentrated, images rolled into his mind: the terraced hillside where the tea had grown in orderly rows and quilt-like patches. Farm folk carefully tended the plants. Drying sheds where the leaves hung or lay, being preserved, filled his inner eye.

A whole world was contained in his cup.

Connor sipped; his eyes still closed.

The taste was like another expression of the smell, a lingering of exotic flowers and smoke on his tongue, the growth of a thousand days in the sun and hundreds of steps of processing, culminating now in a priceless transfer of energy that flowed into his body. "Ahh," he breathed.

"Indeed." The Master set down his cup. "Whenever you are struggling, stop. Open your mind and let a fuller experience come in through your senses. Nothing extra is ever needed for bliss but a moment of perfect awareness."

Connor's phone, in the pocket of his *gi*, chose that moment to ring.

They both ignored the sound until it stopped, and finished the tea and cookies in companionable silence.

CHAPTER THIRTY-TWO

Sophie
Four days after rescue

SOPHIE LAY in bed and stared at the ceiling. The blackout drapes were drawn on another ridiculously beautiful Hilo day. The red beacon of the clock radio beside the bed informed her that it was noon.

Dr. Wilson had exhorted her to count good things in the morning; it wasn't morning here, but it *was*, somewhere else in the world.

One good thing Sophie could think of was that her father had been called back to Washington for some international crisis, and she had their suite at the Hilton to herself.

The second good thing was that Marcella had returned to Oahu; the FBI had only been able to spare her for two days.

The third good thing was that Raveaux was also on Oahu, and was giving Bix a full report. That meant she wouldn't have to.

She was alone, at last, and she could wallow in the oily darkness of depression and grief for as long as it took for Jake to die once he was taken off life support.

And then, she could stay in bed until she had to take charge of Momi again, which wasn't for another ten days.

The emptiness of time stretched before her like a desert with no water in sight.

Sophie glanced at the clock again. Eleven minutes past twelve.

They were unplugging Jake at one p.m., in forty-nine minutes. Janice Dunn had refused to listen to her pleas, or those of his sister Patty, to allow her to be there for her *kun dii*'s last moments.

The cruelty took her breath away; and yet, now that she was a mother, she understood it. Anyone who might cause her daughter harm aroused the deepest antipathy that she was capable of feeling. Janice blamed Sophie for Jake's situation, and though Sophie wasn't responsible for the eruption going on all over the east shore of the Big Island at this moment, she *was* the reason Jake had put himself in harm's way, even to the point of sacrificing himself.

"How do I get through this?" She'd asked Dr. Wilson.

"You'll get through it one second at a time, one minute at a time, one hour at a time, one day at a time," the psychologist had said.

From where she lay, Sophie could see the black case on the vanity in the bathroom where her medications were stored. She had already taken her daily antidepressant, but she had more powerful things for when she had what she and Dr. Wilson now called "an episode." There were sleeping pills and an anxiety reliever.

She could get up and go take the pills she had. Fall asleep, and dream the hours of his death away.

But that was cowardly. Jake deserved more from her—that she endure, with him, what must be endured, even if they were not together in physical space.

Sophie turned on her side and faced the clock, and watched the red numbers slowly merge from one to the next.

She breathed, and she waited. She would go on, because she had to. Because she was a mother, and her daughter needed her.

Sophie shut her eyes, remembered going to an outdoor concert at Ala Moana Beach Park with Armita and Momi, right before the two had left for Alika's custody month on Kaua`i. Sophie had sat on the folding chair with Momi on her lap. Armita sat on her right, next to the "aisle" made by the rows of chairs set under one of the park's spreading banyans.

The ukulele band they were listening to was performing on a little portable stage, backed by the half-moon of placid water where she and Raveaux liked to swim at night. In the late afternoon, a light wind ruffled the turquoise water and bent the leaves of the palms lining the sand, making them sway and dance against the blue sky and white cumulus clouds at the horizon.

Momi had mercifully fallen asleep; she was so active that events like this were usually spent chasing her around and extracting her from trouble. But this time, the concert had fallen during her nap time, and her stubborn daughter had succumbed.

Her chubby legs protruded from under her bright Hawaiian print dress as she straddled Sophie's lap, her plump little feet limp in their sandals. Her face rested on Sophie's chest, lips ajar as she snored, her glossy black curls damp around her face in the tropical heat.

Sophie stroked the little girl's back, comforted by the warm, limp weight that seemed to anchor her to the chair. She'd shut her eyes, breathing in the tender baby smell Momi still had at age two-and-a-half, and had let the Hawaiian music and the beautiful setting lift her mood into something as close to joy as she ever got.

Momi needed her.

Not physically, perhaps, but emotionally. They shared a bond strong enough to endure distance and big enough to hold other people: Armita, her father Alika, her grandmother Esther, and a host of aunties, uncles, cousins on Kaua`i. Even her Uncle Connor and her Grampa Frank, too.

But only Sophie was Momi's mother.

Having endured the wound of Pim Wat's emotional distance as Sophie grew up, she knew for certain that no one could ever take her place in Momi's heart.

Sophie opened her eyes and watched the next ten minutes move by until one p.m. Then, one-oh-five. One-ten. One-fifteen. One-twenty-two.

It had to be done by now. *He was gone.*

Sophie shut her eyes, curling tight around herself in the bed, squeezing her own arms fiercely—but her eyes were dry. She'd cried all the tears she had.

On the nightstand, her phone buzzed. She'd left it on so Patty could check in and tell her how it had gone. Her heart lurched as she saw that it was Patty, as they'd discussed.

Did she want to hear the awful details?

Of course not.

But Sophie wasn't a coward. Today was all about proving that. She picked up the phone. "Hello, Patty." Her voice sounded like her throat had been scrubbed with steel wool.

CHAPTER THIRTY-THREE

Jake
Four days after rescue

JAKE WAS HAVING A WONDERFUL DREAM. His grandmother, a woman with snow-white hair and a soft body that always smelled of talcum powder, was playing cards with him and two of his friends from his Special Forces days—Judah and Henry, men he hadn't seen in years.

His grandfather, a tall, hale and hearty man whom Jake physically resembled, carried a tray loaded with a pitcher of lemonade, glasses, and chocolate cake to where they sat around his grandparents' round, old-fashioned card table.

Lemonade and chocolate cake were two things Jake loved. He grinned at the sight of the treats. "Thanks, Grandpa." The old man grunted, his usual response, but he patted Jake's shoulder.

His friend Henry dealt a fresh hand. "Five card stud," he said. "Ante up."

Jake had imagined heaven would be spectacular. Grander than his grandparents' modest ranch home. Heaven would be filled with streets of gold and palaces of pearl, and there'd be giant angels blowing horns on every street corner.

Instead, he sat in the front parlor of his grandparents' house in Toledo, Ohio, a house he hadn't seen since he was ten years old—where he sat at a table playing cards with dead people.

"Jake, ante up," Henry prompted.

Jake looked down at the stack of Necco candy wafers beside his cards. Perhaps money had no meaning in heaven. That made sense.

Why didn't he have more questions? —but he didn't. He wasn't stressed at all about being dead.

Jake grinned at Henry, who'd died of an aneurysm during their Special Ops training days. He was happy to see Judah, who'd drowned during an underwater search-and-rescue. Kenny, the kid leaning in the doorway, looked like he had when he passed away of a peanut allergy when they were both aged twelve.

"Here, son."

Jake reached out to accept a large, frosty glass of lemonade from Grandpa, gone within six months of Grandma. He didn't remember Grandpa ever pouring him anything, let alone slicing him a piece of rich chocolate cake like he was doing right now. The man had never been without a Marlboro hanging from his lip, and had always been "a mean son-of-a-bitch," according to Jake's father.

"Thanks, Grandpa." Jake sipped the lemonade—cold and sweetly tangy. He smacked his lips. He tossed two Neccos into the pot to ante up, and Henry dealt everyone another card.

Yep, Jake was dead.

He was sure of it. In fact, he remembered the final expenditure of the last bit of energy he had used to push Sophie up onto the ledge above him. He remembered the agony of his last breath, and even his last thought before blessed darkness engulfed him.

This wasn't like the last time he'd died, though, drowned by a torturer in a bucket of water. He hadn't seen anything that time, and it had rocked him. *What if there was no heaven?*

This time, he'd gone to heaven. And yeah, it wasn't what he expected. But cold lemonade, a big slab of chocolate cake, Necco wafers, and some of his favorite people weren't a bad start.

He looked around the room.

Sophie wasn't there.

Did that mean she hadn't died? Or had she gone to some other waiting room in heaven or hell? There was no telling what exactly this place was.

Weirdly, he wasn't all that curious about it.

It was what it was.

He made his play and won the pile of Necco wafers. He scooped them towards him, and hollered, "Kenny!" and tossed his boyhood friend one of the candies. Kenny took a big step forward and caught the wafer on his tongue, and they all cheered.

He tossed more of the Neccos to his Army buddies, and they tried to catch them in their mouths, but most of them missed. Even Grandma tried to catch one, and it landed right on her shelf of cleavage, and they all laughed more than Jake remembered laughing in years.

And then, just that suddenly, the rosy bubble around the parlor burst, and Jake was swimming somewhere deep underwater.

The pressure of the depths squeezed his lungs. He kicked and thrashed, trying to get to the surface, but the water was thick and viscous as oil. His lungs were burning, and the sense of weight was immense. It reminded him of those last horrible moments in the lava tube, but worse somehow—as if his lungs were already filled with fluid and heaving like a bellows, and yet doing nothing to alleviate his terrible need to breathe.

He flopped like a fish onto dry ground, and landed in a bed.

He could feel the sheets, the mattress, the blanket over his legs, the IV in his arm. But he couldn't see, and when he tried to move, nothing happened. He was trapped deep inside his body. Smells of disinfectant and something fake floral assaulted his nose.

He heard the beeping of monitors, and voices.

Familiar voices.

Words sorted out of the sounds hitting his ears like individual pebbles.

His mother: "I don't think he's breathing."

"Give him a minute." An unfamiliar voice—a doctor? "We just took the tube out. The body has to get the message to do it on its own."

"What's that wavy line?" His sister Patty's voice.

"That's brain activity. He had us worried there, for a while, but he seems to be coming back online, as it were."

"Oh, please, Jake. Breathe! Breathe!" His mom pleaded.

Yes, Jake shouted. *Yes, dammit, I'm here, and I'm alive!*

Nothing happened. No one heard him. Even his eyelids refused to obey.

The sense of an anvil sitting on his chest intensified. It hurt, so badly—and then his mouth opened, and he gasped. Air flowed into his damaged lungs as his breathing reflex finally kicked in.

And that hurt like hell, too. His throat felt raw, his lungs bubbled.

"He's breathing!" Patty shrieked. He felt her arms go around him, felt her tears wetting the sheet covering him.

His mother pressed his hand against her cheek. "Jake, Jake—we love you."

Where's Sophie? He screamed. *Sophie!*

They didn't hear him.

CHAPTER THIRTY-FOUR

Sophie

"HE'S ALIVE!" Patty's voice on the phone was a shriek of joy, blasting Sophie's ear drum.

"I don't understand," Sophie said stiffly. She'd been so completely sure he was gone. She hadn't been able to afford hope, not even a teaspoon of it.

"We came in to unplug him as scheduled. The doctor was all excited; he showed us the brain graph, told us that Jake's brain waves had been fluctuating but increasing. We decided to take him off the ventilator, anyway, and he started breathing on his own! Now he's showing signs of waking up!" Sophie heard excited voices in the background, a jumble of exclamations. "He's coming around, Sophie! Get your butt over here. I don't care what our mom says, nothing will bring him back from the dead like having you there!" She told Sophie the room number. "Hurry!"

Sophie lurched up from the bed so quickly that she tripped and fell to her knees on the carpet. "On my way."

Sophie didn't remember leaving the Hilton, getting in the rented Continental, driving to the hospital. She didn't remember parking, walking through the lobby, getting on the elevator, getting off at Jake's floor. She didn't remember finding her way to his room, or even the sight of Janice Dunn's angry face or Patty's smiling one as she walked in and approached the bed.

She only registered Jake.

Her lover was propped up with an IV, and a couple of monitors hooked up to register his vitals. His eyes were shut, but he was breathing on his own, and his cheeks were flushed with color. The ugly bruising of his injuries had faded; the bandages on his wounds were smaller.

He looked like he'd sat down to watch TV and fallen asleep.

"What are you doing here?" Janice snarled.

"That's enough, Mother. Jake wants Sophie here." Patty grabbed Janice by the arm and towed her out of the room.

Sophie sighed with relief to have Jake to herself. She pulled the plastic chair Janice had been sitting on closer to the bed and picked up Jake's hand, holding it in both of her own.

"Jake. My *kun dii*," she whispered. "I love you. I'm here. Please come back to me."

His hand twitched.

No other signs of consciousness.

She scanned the monitors—his heart rate was elevated, and the machine beeped rapidly. The brain activity graph was a tangled mass of intersecting, moving colored lines. His breathing had a wheeze and bubble to it, but his chest rose and fell regularly, a beautiful sight.

"Jake, I know you can hear me. I am by your side. I'm waiting for you for as long as it takes, and I won't leave you if I can help it. But you need to wake up, so you can tell your mother that you want to see me." Sophie kissed the abrasions on his knuckles. "Now I know where you get your temper. And stubbornness!"

Jake's hand moved again. She glanced up. His mouth twitched too.

He was trying to wake up.

She'd give him some incentive. "I see that smile. You're teasing me, Jake. Testing to see if I'll still love you when you're a comatose vegetable. Well, the answer is yes." Sophie blew out a breath. "Furthermore, I want us to get married. I love you so much that I want to do that, even with the charming mother-in-law I'm going to get. So, if that ring your grandmother gave you isn't spoken for yet—I'd like to wear it."

His eyelids fluttered, and opened. His gray irises met her gaze squarely. "Sophie," he croaked. "Yes. I'll marry you."

She'd been wrong. She still had tears to shed for him. Lots of them.

CHAPTER THIRTY-FIVE

Sophie
Afternoon that Jake woke up

SOPHIE PARKED the Continental and went into the Hilton. She stopped at the desk, and asked for a single room—she planned to stay there until Jake was discharged from the hospital, and with her father gone back to Washington, there was no need for the suite. The clerk reassigned her, and she walked to the elevator to pack her things.

She had spent a glorious half hour alone with Jake, quietly sitting together, until Janice and Patty returned and it was Sophie's cue to leave. Janice was crying with joy that Jake had woken, so Sophie decided to save the news of their engagement and let him share it with them. She slipped out, smiling at the sight of him holding his mother's hand as he fell asleep.

Soon she was situated in a new room with a king bed and a balcony that overlooked Hilo Bay, a familiar view from when she and Jake had lived together in a nearby apartment. She made herself a cup of tea and stepped out onto the little balcony, sitting on a lounger to watch the afternoon wind ruffle the water of the Bay and the coconut palms do their hula dance.

There were a lot of people she should call to share the news about Jake: her father. Marcella. Connor. Lei. Alika and Armita. Even Raveaux. But it was all a little sudden and overwhelming to have the tables so completely turn, when she'd been braced for the worst.

She didn't want to call anyone. She wanted to hug this delicious happiness close and savor it all by herself.

Jake had a way to go before he was fully restored to health; the attending physician had warned them that the full extent of any cognitive damage was still undetermined. It was better to wait and see how things unfolded, perhaps wait for him to tell his mother the news of their engagement. Certainly, Sophie didn't want to be the one to do so!

Her phone, resting face down on the little glass table, buzzed in silent mode.

She picked it up and checked the screen: *Pierre Raveaux.* Maybe it was something to do with the case. The thought of speaking with him, telling him the news, felt good. He'd been so kind, so caring about Jake, and now she could tell him that they were engaged—she didn't want Raveaux hoping for things that could never be.

"Hello, Pierre."

"Sophie." She could tell by the surprise in his voice he hadn't thought she'd pick up. "Are you all right?"

"I'm better than all right. Jake woke up from the coma, and we're engaged." Sophie sounded giddy, even to her own ears. She wished she had his grandmother's ring to look at to reassure herself that those magical moments at Jake's bedside had really happened.

A pause.

Clearly, Raveaux needed time for the news to sink in. Sophie rushed to fill the void with words. "His brain activity had been coming and going on the monitors, but his wishes were clear in his health directive, so his mother and sister had the medical team unplug the life support as scheduled. The transplant team was standing by to harvest his organs. But he started breathing on his own, and then . . . he woke up!"

"How wonderful!" Raveaux's voice was sincere. "You love each other and you have another chance at a life together."

"We do. Love each other. And now we're getting married." She glanced down at her hand again, but the fourth finger was still bare. "He's got a way to go to recover, so it will be a while before we have a wedding."

"All in due time," Raveaux said in his measured way. "Congratulations, in any case."

Awkward pause. Why was this so hard? "You must have had a reason for calling?"

"Yes. I'm back on Oahu. I've met with Bix and debriefed about the case, and it occurred to me that I wanted to thank your father for his kindness to me while we were together at the hospital. Can I get his number from you?" Raveaux's voice was perfectly calm and reasonable.

"Dad was especially kind to you?"

"He was."

"And I was not." Her cold behavior toward Raveaux came back to her in an embarrassing rush of images. She'd been so devastated about Jake, so guilty about her attraction to Raveaux, that she'd rejected his simplest gesture. "I'm sorry I was rude, Pierre."

"I took no offense. You were stressed."

"But still—it was ill-done of me. Of course, I'll text you Dad's private number."

"I'd appreciate that."

Another awkward pause. There was so much they weren't saying; so much that could never be said. "I hope you wish us well, Pierre."

"I will always wish every good thing for you, Sophie, especially that you are loved as you deserve. Thank you for the information; I'll see you at the office when you return." Raveaux ended the call.

Sophie listened to the quiet hiss of the severed connection for a long moment, and then set the device aside. She leaned back against the lounger, and hugged her arms around herself as the breeze off the Bay turned cold.

SHE'D FINALLY GONE INSIDE, taken a shower, and was perusing the room service menu. After she ate something, she'd go back to the hospital to sit with Jake.

She had to be next to him, even if he was sleeping. Hopefully he'd spoken with his mother by now . . .

Sophie picked up her phone and answered it when she saw Connor's private number.

"Connor! I'm so glad you called. I have good news about Jake."

"Tell me."

"He came out of the coma. I don't know how much permanent damage he may have sustained, but . . . he was conscious. And we are engaged!" Sophie reflexively looked down at her hand again. *She really wished she had that ring!*

"Wow!" Connor gave a rich chuckle. "But then, I'm getting used to seeing incredible things. Congratulations!" He cleared his throat. "What do you remember about the rescue?"

"I remember that it was you that got us out. Thank you, Connor. We would be dead right now if you hadn't thought of that chip."

"I'm learning to listen to my intuition more and more. In fact, that is how I make all of my decisions these days." A pause. "What's the current situation with Jake?"

Sophie looked around her and sighed. "I don't know. But I was getting ready to go back to the hospital and visit him. I am desperately hoping he's told his mother we're engaged. She blames me for his injuries. It's not fair, but I understand her feelings."

"That must be painful." She could almost see him pinching the bridge of his nose as he switched gears. "I don't expect you to take immediate action on this, but when you have some better idea of his prognosis, I have a favor to ask."

"What is it?"

"Please come to Thailand. To the Yām Khûmkạn compound."

"No." The answer burst out of Sophie forcefully. "I will never willingly visit that place." Sophie had only seen the clandestine organization's temple compound from above, in a helicopter. The series of interlocking buildings, terraces and courtyards built of ancient stone, lined with drilling ranks of ninjas and guarded by RPGs, was not appealing.

"Pim Wat is back. And she wants to see you."

Angry heat flushed the back of Sophie's neck. "I know that the Master rescued her from Guantánamo. But why would I ever want to see that woman again, after she stole my child?"

Pim Wat had taken tiny Momi from Sophie when she was only twelve hours old, setting in motion a series of events that had culminated in the beheading of six good men.

"She wants to reconcile. The Master wants that too. He's invited you to come, and what he asks for, he gets." Connor's voice was resolute. "I serve him, and I have come to trust him. You don't have to. But you can trust *me*. I'll make sure you're safe. You owe me this."

"I owe you my life, but not this. I will not willingly see my mother. Ever again. The answer is no." Sophie ended the call with a punch of her thumb.

Galvanized, she got up and changed.

She needed to see Jake. He was her priority now.

CHAPTER THIRTY-SIX

Sophie

JAKE WAS STILL SLEEPING when she arrived at his hospital room.

Her gaze flew straight to his face, turned toward the door on the white pillows. He was still pale, his visage swollen and marked by bruising, his tan a sickly yellow.

On the other side of the bed sat his mother, Janice.

Her face was as pale as her son's, her hair a mess, and her eyes steely. "What are you doing here?"

Sophie advanced into the room. She still felt hot from her last confrontation; she was in no mood to be pushed around.

"Jake and I are engaged. I have a right to be here."

Janice frowned. She stared pointedly at Sophie's bare hand. "My son told me that you returned our family ring. More than two years ago."

Sophie continued across the room to stand next to Jake. She picked up his hand, squeezing it hard. *Return to me, Jake. I need you!* "He woke up because I called him back."

"What do you mean, Jake woke up? Now?" Jake's sister Monica, a sleek blonde wearing designer clothing, came out of the small bathroom. "We knew he had been conscious, but he has not woken up since you left here earlier."

Sophie abruptly sat down in the empty chair beside Jake's bed. She pressed his big, limp hand between hers. His skin felt hot to the touch, and she placed her palm against his forehead. "He has a fever."

"We know. He's on a cocktail of antibiotics. Those wounds he sustained became infected," Janice said. "Not that you have permission to know any of his medical information."

"You're not wanted here." Monica advanced to stand beside her mother. "Get out of this room before we call security."

"Where's Patty?" Sophie looked around frantically. Jake's favorite sister had always been her advocate, had even become a budding friend.

"Patty had to go back to California. Her kid was sick. But that's not your concern, either," Monica said, hands on her hips. "You need to leave."

"No. I'm staying." Sophie squeezed Jake's hand between hers, pressed it against her cheek. She leaned down to whisper in his ear. "Jake, I know you're not well, but I need you. Please wake up."

Monica picked up the phone. "Hi. This is Jake Dunn's sister, Monica Dunn. There's a woman in our room who is not authorized to be here. She's not family. We need security to come remove her."

"Don't do this. He needs me." Sophie wrapped her arms around Jake's upper body and laid her head on his chest. His heart thumped irregularly beneath her cheek. His chest rose and fell with rasping breaths. Heat rose from his body, and an invisible tremor shook him. She turned her head to look at the brain activity monitor, but it was turned off. "Why isn't that monitor hooked up?"

"We fired that quack doctor who's been overseeing his care. We are having a neurologist from New York flown in to evaluate him and oversee his case," Monica said. "Though it's none of your business."

Sophie shut her eyes, drawing inward as she focused on the

sound of Jake's laboring heart. "Something is very wrong with him. You need to call the doctor *now*."

Monica's bright red lips drew into a thin line. "He's going to be fine. But you need to get gone. You're the reason he's in this bed in the first place."

Tears welled in Sophie's eyes. "He chose this line of work. He chose to push me to safety," she whispered hoarsely. "I would have happily traded places with him."

Two pairs of gray eyes glared at her across Jake's broad chest as she lay her cheek over his heart. *At least they knew better than to try to touch her; that would not have ended well.*

The door opened. Two bulky men in security uniforms entered. "You need to come with us, miss."

Sophie turned her head to assess them. She could take these doughy rental cops out, no problem. It wouldn't take five minutes to knock them out of commission. Her mind ran through the punches, jabs, and flips she could use.

But then what? The police would be called. She would eventually be overpowered and end up in jail. And how could she help Jake from there?

Sophie turned her head and applied her mouth to Jake's in a deep kiss.

His lips felt flaccid beneath hers; the vital spark that was such a part of him was missing. But his skin was so hot . . .

And she couldn't hear his heartbeat any longer.

The security guards grabbed her arms and bodily lifted her off of her fiancé. Sophie struggled with the urge to fight but went limp in their arms instead, sliding to the floor so that they had to physically drag her out of the room.

"Something is wrong," she called. "Jake, I love you."

Jake's vitals alarm went off suddenly; a loud, terrible beeping. The security guards dragged Sophie into the hall as Monica and Janice shrieked for help.

The medical response team rushed into Jake's room from their stations.

Sophie couldn't let herself be hauled off and not even know what was happening.

She burst up from the floor and broke the guards' hold in an arc of pure, powerful movement, and rushed back to the doorway.

But she couldn't approach the bed, because even Monica and Janice had been forced out into the hall as Jake's team assessed the situation.

The three women stood with their faces plastered to the window that offered a view of the life-and-death battle taking place in the room.

With a DNR order in place, there was nothing the team could do for him. The grim-faced doctor faced a hysterical Janice as she screamed at them to resuscitate him. "Jake's wishes were made clear in legally binding terms. He was on a ventilator for four days, but with little brain activity. With that support removed, he fell back into a coma with the complication of this secondary infection, which has invaded his organs. There's no way to bring him back from this. I'm very sorry, but you must accept the fact that he's gone."

At 8:05 p.m. Hawaii time, Jacob Sean Overstreet Dunn was pronounced dead.

Sophie stared at her fiancé's lifeless body as his mother and sister clung to each other, sobbing, and his medical team slowly and soberly cleared up equipment.

Jake probably wouldn't even be able to be an organ donor with that infection.

He'd have been so disappointed about that.

Jake's heart had stopped beating even before the alarms on the monitors went off.

Thoughts blew across her mind in irrelevant bubbles. Everything seemed very far away. *Sophie had been the one closest to him when he took his final breath.*

She wrapped her arms around herself, holding onto that thought.

The security guards, who had been standing back from the drama, approached Sophie. "Miss, you need to come with us. It's all over now. He's in a better place," one of them said.

"Are you sure about that better place?" Sophie cocked her head and squinted her eyes at the man thoughtfully. "I hope so, because Jake believed in that."

"I'm sure it's true," the man said. "Our bodies die, but our spirits live on."

Sophie turned back to stare through the window. Jake's skin looked almost translucent and his mouth hung slack. He was gone and had left an empty husk posed on the bed.

"Come with us, miss." The security guard touched her arm.

But Sophie didn't move. She couldn't. It was too hard to take in.

Janice lifted her streaming face from Monica's shoulder. Her visage was contorted with grief, her eyes wild. "Get out of here!" She screamed. "You're the reason he's dead! You killed my son!"

It was time to go.

"Goodbye, my *kun dii*." Sophie whispered.

She turned and walked woodenly down the hall, a security guard on either side.

CHAPTER THIRTY-SEVEN

Sophie
Two weeks later

THREE DAYS after arriving on Phi Ni, Sophie woke in her familiar bed in the guest suite she used at Connor's house. She lay still on the silky white sheets, staring up at the thick teak beams and woven matting that lined the interior of the roof. A brightly colored green gecko with red spots on its tail ran across the ceiling, chirping cheerfully.

For a long moment in that gray space between asleep and awake, Sophie savored the sensations of the soft bed and top quality sheets. This was her favorite place in the world to be. Why did she feel so achy and exhausted?

She stretched her arms and legs. *Was she injured?*

Oh. Yes.

Jake was dead.

She treasured those few moments when she first woke up, before her body, with its bone deep sorrow, reminded her of her loss. The grief lived in her flesh, weighing it down, sapping her vitality. It owned her physical self, while her mind couldn't seem to hold onto the fact that Jake was gone, even though she'd attended his memorial with all of their mutual friends.

Every minute of that beautiful, bittersweet gathering was etched on her brain, much as she longed to forget or deny it. Janice had tried to bar Sophie's attendance, but Patty had taken Sophie's side and sat with her through the brief, moving service at Ala Moana Beach Park under one of the banyan trees.

She'd found a little comfort in hearing from Patty that several of Jake's vital organs had been infection free, and had been donated.

"He was adamant that anything useful left of his body be given to someone who might need it," Patty had said at the memorial. The sweet blonde woman had shaken her head. "Jake never believed he'd live to be a ripe old age."

Maybe, given how he had made his living, that had once been true. But in those precious moments Sophie had shared in his arms underground, she knew that they'd both hoped for much more than they'd been given.

After the memorial, Connor had urged her to go to Phi Ni. With Momi and Armita back with Sophie for her custody month, unable to sleep or eat, Sophie had packed up her household and taken the Security Solutions jet to Thailand for the month, hoping the island paradise could work its healing magic one more time.

The gecko skittered away. The chatter of mynahs came in through the wooden louvers that shaded the room from Thailand's heat during the day. In the three days they'd been on the island, Sophie could already feel peace beginning to massage her battered soul.

Momi loved Phi Ni, playing all day with Sophie and Armita on the pristine half-moon of beach below Connor's clifftop mansion, paddling in the calm turquoise water, and building sandcastles.

Another day without Jake stretched before her, but Momi deserved her full attention and Sophie would do what she had to, keeping to their simple daily routine. Sophie tossed the light coverlet aside and sat up. She stretched her arms overhead, and then opened the louvers further. Sunlight poured in like honey.

Ginger and Anubis raised their heads from their dog beds across the room, their ears pricked. "Hey, pups. It's good to be with you again." The two got up and padded over; they knew better than to get on the bed with her, but she took a moment to pet Ginger's silky head and play with her soft ears, and scratch dignified Anubis's chest.

Momi poked her curly head up from the trundle bed beside Sophie's. "Mama!" Her large, light brown eyes sparkled up at Sophie. "Momi come up!"

"Of course, darling." Sophie caught the toddler under the armpits and lifted her onto the bed. Momi, at two and a half, had become aware of herself as a separate person from her parents or Armita this month. She declared her intentions loudly in the third person, and "no" was currently her favorite word.

With her daughter around, there was little time for Sophie to get deep into sadness. Not only was Momi lively, energetic, and good-natured, she was demanding.

Her daughter was the very antidote to grief and depression, but even so, Sophie had increased her dose of medication. No matter how down she got, she would not allow a low mood to color the relationship with her child, as her mother Pim Wat had done with her.

That didn't mean being upbeat was easy.

"Peek-a-boo!" Momi yelled, lifting up Sophie's cover and ducking under it.

Sophie snapped the coverlet up and down, hiding intermittently, as Momi shrieked and giggled with delight at her favorite game.

Armita appeared in the doorway, a smile on her face. Sophie's favorite childhood nanny provided the consistency that Momi needed in moving between two different households on a monthly basis. "Little Bean, your breakfast is ready. Time to come with Auntie Armita."

"No!" Momi said.

"Would you like eggs, or fruit?" Armita advanced calmly, and plucked Momi out of the bedclothes. Momi kicked her plump legs and shrieked "No!" but Armita continued on down the hall with the toddler tucked under her arm.

Sophie was left in blessed peace. She collapsed back onto the bed and picked up her phone on the side table. She set an alarm for five minutes.

Five minutes a day was all the time she gave herself to grieve for Jake.

To cry for how much she had loved him, and he her.

To weep over how much time they had lost to pride and stubbornness.

To wail for the future they would never have together.

Sophie let go of all of the emotions she'd held locked down. She buried her face in her pillow and howled, beating it with her fists. She choked with sobs, blew her nose on a fistful of tissues, and cried some more, until her throat was raw and her eyes puffed up into slits.

Thank God for Armita. She and the nanny had discussed how to handle things going forward; Armita had suggested that five minutes of unrestrained crying would help Sophie get through the days without being derailed too often.

When the phone alarm went off, Sophie hit the button, got up, made her bed, and went into the bathroom to take a shower. She cried a little more under the fall of water, but it was okay because her tears washed away as soon as they fell.

Sophie was dressed and heading for the dining room where Connor's houseman Nam served them breakfast, when she heard the thrum of a helicopter approaching.

"Connor!" Her numb heart gave its first bump of excitement since Jake's death. She hurried down the hallway. One wall was made of glass panels that looked out at a courtyard with a statue of Kuan Yin, a fountain, and exotic flowers and plants. The flagstone floor was cool on Sophie's bare feet as she opened one side of the large double doors in front, and stepped out onto the top step with its exotic bronze dragons flanking massive teak doors.

The chopper settled gently onto the helipad directly in front of the barn that doubled as a garage and storage area. Sophie held up a hand to shield her eyes from the strong breeze generated by the rotors, and her lightweight dress plastered back against her body.

The rotors slowed, the door slid back, and Connor jumped out and walked toward her. His blond hair and aqua eyes contrasted with a tan that spoke of hours of drilling practice in the hot Thai sun. He did not smile, and neither did Sophie, as she descended the steps to meet him.

Connor's arms encircled her in a powerful hug. One of his hands caressed the back of her head, encouraging her to lay its weight on his shoulder. "I'm so sorry, Sophie. Jake was a good man. The best."

Sophie nodded, shutting her eyes against the sting of quick tears. "That he was."

The other door of the chopper slid open and banged shut, but she didn't raise her head. She clung to Connor, drawing strength from the man who had been both lover and friend.

"I'm sorry. I had to bring them. I hope you will forgive me," Connor whispered in her ear. "Keep an open mind. This could be a good thing."

Sophie stiffened and pulled back.

Standing behind Connor, compellingly handsome in his white *gi*, stood the Master. Beside him, dwarfed by his height, was Sophie's tiny, deadly mother, Pim Wat.

CHAPTER THIRTY-EIGHT

Sophie

PIM WAT'S arms and legs reminded Sophie of those of a starving child. Her once-beautiful face, a face that had opened doors worldwide to do her deadly work as an assassin, was distorted: one cheekbone was higher than the other, and one eye was half-hidden by a droopy lid. Her long, black, silky hair, once her pride and joy, had gone completely white. Shorn tufts surrounded her skull like dandelion fluff.

Sophie switched her gaze to the Master. The leader of Thailand's clandestine national security organization had not changed a bit. Tall for a Thai man, he stood straight as bamboo in a snowy white martial arts outfit, his deep purple eyes a dark mystery in his amber-skinned face.

"What do you want?" Sophie saw no point in social niceties.

Pim Wat stepped forward. "I forgive you. And I want you to forgive me. I want peace between us."

"I don't care what you want." Anger was armor. Releasing its hot power felt good, energizing. *Anything to break the numbness.*

The Master turned to Pim Wat. "You asked for this meeting,

Beautiful One. Now you have it. Number One will show me his house while you speak to your daughter." The man walked toward the mansion with unhurried grace as Connor strode to catch up.

Sophie clenched her fists. Connor had told her his house on Phi Ni was his refuge, that he had done his best to hide its existence from the Master. She had felt safe here; she'd thought he did too. Clearly, all of that had been an illusion. The Master had probably known about it for years.

Sophie redirected her gaze to her mother. "You stole my child from me when she was twelve hours old. You then beheaded six good men, including Thom, a man Connor and I cared for greatly. You tried to strangle your own sister right in front of me. And we won't even get into the kind of mother you were when I was growing up, something that hurts even more now that I'm a mother myself. Those are only the beginning of your crimes."

"I expected you would want to have your say."

"This will achieve nothing," Sophie said. "I hate the very sight of you."

Pim Wat turned and walked down the drive, entering the grounds surrounding the house. The mansion was built in a beautiful combination of eastern and western styles, cantilevered out over a hundred-foot limestone cliff. Sophie trailed after her mother—she didn't want to speak to Connor or the Master, either. She hoped like hell Armita had the sense to hide away with Momi.

Pim Wat paused next to one of the neatly trimmed coconut trees. Its fronds waved overhead in the soft, gentle breeze. They had reached the edge of the property. Decorative ornamental plants and shrubs marked the edges of the lawn along the sides, but the sheer cliff that overlooked the half-moon of beach below was bordered only by a wire fence erected as a precaution against Momi's wanderings.

Nam had placed a wooden bench there, and Pim Wat walked over and seated herself on one end of it. "I want us to work things out. I want to see my granddaughter."

"When hell freezes over. You may not see my daughter, nor Armita. You cannot be trusted with either of them." Sophie made an effort to calm her racing heart, to lower her voice; visible anger only showed Pim Wat that she still had emotional power over Sophie.

Armita had served Pim Wat for more than twenty years, suffering abuse as her handmaiden. Armita was the one who had taken Momi back to Sophie. If the nanny had not done that, Sophie might never have seen her daughter again, and Pim Wat had sworn to kill Armita for it.

Pim Wat turned her ravaged face toward Sophie, facing her unflinchingly. "If it's an apology you want, then I'm sorry. I've had ample time to reflect on my choices while in Guantánamo. Thanks to you." Her gaze pierced Sophie. "Let's not forget who put me there for years, to be tortured for information about the Yām Khûmkạn."

"No more than you deserved."

"And the push down the stairs that ruined my face?"

"You threw yourself down those steps, and you know it." Sophie turned away to look out at the view. It was breathtaking to gaze over that cliff. "You can't make me feel guilty about what happened at our old house. I won't let you."

"I acknowledge that. I wanted you to feel guilty. I'm sorry for that, too." Pim Wat's voice was small. "I was wrong. About so many things."

Sheer limestone in soft shades of buff and pale yellow fell away below them. Gentle, translucent turquoise waves lapped against the white beach far below. Atolls crowned in tropical plants studded the bay like chess pieces. Far out on the horizon, cumulus clouds floated by in the shape of fantastical creatures, riding the light breezes like something out of a reverie.

Time went by.

They didn't speak. What was there to say?

The gulf between Sophie and her mother seemed unbridgeable and beyond repairing.

And yet . . .

Pim Wat was here. Alive, and apologizing. Anyone could die, even the strongest among them, at any time. Sophie had never known that truth in such a deep way as she had since Jake's passing. All of this was a choice. She could make peace with her mother, or she could live with a sword of rage stabbed through her own heart.

She turned to her mother. "I don't trust you, and I never will. You don't deserve forgiveness, and you never will. But because you're my mother, and because I want to live in harmony, for my own health and for the sake of my daughter, I accept your apology."

Sophie extended an open hand, resting it on the bench between them. Pim Wat set hers in Sophie's, a light and brittle bundle of twigs. "Thank you."

Sophie held her mother's hand on the bench. They gazed down at the view together, in silence.

"I'm so sad for you about Jake," Pim Wat said. "I know you loved him."

Sophie shut her eyes against a memory of the near-drowning Jake had endured at her mother's hands. *She had to keep letting go; she wanted no part of bitterness.* "I did love him. So much."

Gentle swishing in the lush grass announced the arrival of Connor and the Master. "It's time to go, my Beautiful One."

The Master's hypnotic voice brought Pim Wat to her feet. She touched Sophie on the shoulder with a skeletal hand as she passed by, heading for the helicopter. "Be well, my daughter. I love you."

For the first time in her life, Sophie felt those words penetrate. Her mother had said them before, but Sophie had never believed it.

What had shifted?

Why, in this moment and during this strange encounter, did she finally, really feel her mother's love?

Maybe it was Sophie who had changed.

Maybe it was she whose heart could finally receive what little the flawed, twisted person who had given birth to her was able to give.

But Sophie didn't turn her head to watch them go. She watched the view, instead. A white tern spun like a snowflake through the currents of wind far below, as the helicopter's engine roared. She shut her eyes and let the prop wash blow over her as it flew away.

Connor joined her on the bench.

Sophie turned tear-swollen eyes to glare at her dearest friend, her staunchest supporter, a man she would have sworn would give his life for her. "How could you?"

"I obey the Master." Connor shook his head. "He's impossible to resist. You know that. And he really seems to love your mother."

Sophie looked out at the ocean. "Are you staying?"

"He's given me leave to be with you as long as you're here."

She met Connor's sea-blue gaze. "I can't trust you anymore. You know that, don't you?"

"I should have asked if it was okay to bring them, but I knew what you'd say, and I was afraid you would leave. The Master insisted Pim Wat have a chance to speak to you." Connor gazed down at his hands, brown and calloused from weapons practice. "I'm sorry."

"I guess I must keep practicing forgiveness." Sophie sighed. "I've decided bitterness and anger are luxuries I can't afford. Momi will be so excited to see you. Let's go take her to the beach."

And so they did.

CHAPTER THIRTY-NINE

Raveaux
Two weeks into Sophie's stay on Phi Ni

RAVEAUX SLID into the leather booth of the refined restaurant in downtown Honolulu's exclusive civic club. Ambassador Smithson was already seated. Even wearing casual golf clothes, Sophie's father had a distinguished appearance. White wings marked his close-cropped black hair, and when he turned, Raveaux recognized the profile he shared with Sophie. "Thank you for meeting me so soon after my return from Washington."

"Of course. You made sure I would." Raveaux smiled to take any sting from his words. He slid the one thousand dollar note that had wrapped the stick drive across the table to the ambassador. "While I appreciate seeing this unusual vintage bill, I won't accept anything for helping your daughter."

Smithson's dark brown eyes were thoughtful and assessing, another expression Raveaux recognized from Sophie's face, as he removed the money from the table and slid it into his pocket. "Good to know."

Raveaux looked around the place, taking in the dim chandeliers, the heavy koa tables, the padded leather booths built for privacy and confidential conversations. "I take it you come here often. A very exclusive club."

"Old guys like me like to have our little comfort zones."

The waitress arrived with large menus mounted on wooden boards, and a pot of tea already made for the ambassador. Raveaux ordered an espresso, and then considered the menu. "What's good? If Sophie were here, she would warn you that I'm a bit of a food snob."

Smithson smiled. "I could tell by looking at you."

Raveaux glanced down at his tailored silk shirt, tie, and dress slacks over casual Italian loafers. "It's not every day that you get to meet with a U.S. ambassador at his club."

"But still. It's nice to see a man who dresses well here in Hawaii, Monsieur Raveaux." The ambassador sipped his tea. "Or may I call you Pierre?"

"Pierre is fine. We are of an age."

"Hardly. You're a youngster compared to me—but do call me Frank."

The ambassador poured more tea. All of his motions reminded Raveaux of Sophie. What had her mother been like? She must have been lovely, but all he knew about Pim Wat was that she'd been a Thai aristocrat. The shape of Sophie's head might have been her father's, but her features had come from a beautiful woman.

"Tell me about yourself, Pierre." The ambassador fiddled with his teaspoon.

"I won't insult you, Frank, by refusing to answer. But after reading the file you gave me, I'm not naïve enough to think you haven't checked me out thoroughly, already."

Smithson chuckled. "I read a report on you, yes, but I always like to hear what a person has to say about himself."

The waitress returned with Raveaux's espresso, ready to take their order. The ambassador recommended the eggs Benedict; he, however, ordered a stack of pancakes, bacon, and scrambled eggs. Raveaux went with Smithson's recommendation.

After the server had left, Raveaux sat back. "Why did you give me that file?"

The ambassador tilted his head to the side. "Not until you've told me about yourself."

Raveaux wrapped both hands around the espresso cup, drawing heat from the beverage. "I imagine you want to know more about why I came to Hawaii. I moved here after I retired as an investigator because I needed a change after my wife and daughter were killed. What you may not have read in the file is that I lost myself in the bottle for two years after they were gone; I blamed myself, you see, and I was haunted—not just by my loss, but how it happened. I saw the car explode, and I couldn't save them." Raveaux unbuttoned his sleeves, rolled them back to the elbows. The ambassador sucked in a gasp at the vivid, shiny, ropy scarring that distorted the skin of his hands and arms. "I needed a fresh start with no reminders, because for a long time, I wanted to join my family."

Smithson cleared his throat. "I appreciate your honesty. And how are you doing now?"

Raveaux shrugged. "*Comme ci, comme ça.* I no longer drink, and that's something."

They both sipped their beverages in surprisingly companionable silence.

The ambassador spoke at last. "I gave you that file because I'm worried about my daughter. Especially now, with the loss she's suffered. And unless I miss my guess—you care about her."

Raveaux's gaze hardened, and he straightened in his seat. Perhaps Raveaux's emotions had shown in the hospital, as he was watching over Sophie in her bed. "Of course, I care about your daughter. She is the CEO of Security Solutions and a brilliant and talented woman I'm proud to work for."

The ambassador smiled. "That's not what I meant, and you know it. But don't worry, I won't say anything to her. She's too raw to ever believe there could be another, and I understand that." He sighed. "I liked Jake, but I never thought he was the one for her." Smithson poured himself more tea.

What was the man implying? Raveaux's pulse thumped, but he kept his expression neutral as he finished his espresso.

The ambassador went on. "Sophie's vulnerable in ways you may not be aware. She suffers from depression, and with this blow she's taken, I worry she'll be sucked into a dark place I never want to see her return to." He told Raveaux a story of how Sophie had self-isolated out on a lava plain during one of her cases, and almost died. "Her mother also suffered from depression. But Pim Wat—that's a tale for another day."

Their breakfast arrived. Raveaux was pleasantly surprised by the smooth lightness and tang of the Hollandaise sauce and the perfect consistency of the poached eggs. "This is excellent, Frank. Perhaps the best breakfast I've had since I moved to Hawaii."

"Now you see why I belong to this club." Smithson's teeth were white and perfect against his dark complexion; he was as charismatic as his daughter.

"Tell me more about why you gave me the file—and you haven't answered why you're worried about Sophie, besides her depression. How does that relate to the man detailed in the records you gave me?"

"Something that isn't in the records, a link that hasn't been proven, is that the blond man who helped rescue Sophie and Jake, the man who calls himself Connor, is also Sheldon Hamilton."

Raveaux's brows rose. "What? I saw nothing about that in the file."

The ambassador nodded. "That's because no one's been able to find an actual link. I was the one to make the connection. I know my daughter. She's loyal to a fault." Smithson forked up a mouthful of pancake and chewed thoughtfully. "I've taken a backseat to her love life shenanigans up until now, and kept my mouth shut—as hard as it's been. Sophie had been through enough with her first marriage to deserve a chance at love, so I kept quiet as she seemed to make one mistake after the next in her relationships, the worst of them being her ongoing involvement with this Connor character."

"I met him. I found him quite impressive." Raveaux swirled the last of his egg, ham and muffin in the delicious sauce. "He was extraordinarily brave, and seemed to have some paranormal ability. He was able to tell where Jake and Sophie were, underground—and not only by using the chip he'd implanted on her."

"What do you mean, paranormal ability?" The ambassador's level brows drew together. "Tell me in detail what happened with the rescue, and how that man got clean away."

"He basically hijacked the pilot and his chopper. I knew some extraordinary measures would need to be taken to travel through restricted airspace to rescue them, so I didn't object." Raveaux explained the series of events ending with Sophie and Jake's drop off at the hospital. "Whoever this man really is, Kendall Bix has some idea. He directed me to meet Connor and his Thai partner at the airport. He didn't say who Connor was, only that he was important and had a role with Security Solutions." Raveaux set his plate aside and steepled his fingers. "If, as you say, Connor played dual roles as Todd Remarkian and Sheldon Hamilton, founding partners at Security Solutions, it would make sense that Sophie and Bix would both be aware of his continued existence. What I don't understand, and hope you can help me with, is how Sophie ended up as CEO of Security Solutions—and why."

"Ah yes." The ambassador gestured for more hot water in his teapot. "I mentioned my daughter's romantic stumbles, didn't I? Well, she dated Todd/Sheldon and uncovered not only his dual identity, but his secret life as an online vigilante. They were lovers."

That shouldn't have surprised Raveaux—why else would that enigmatic blond man have planted a chip on her? But it still hit him like a body blow. "I see." But he didn't. Not really. "And where does Momi come in?"

"She was the surprise result of Sophie's relationship with Alika Wolcott."

"And who is he?" Raveaux frowned. "What kind of timeline are we covering for all of these 'relationship stumbles'?" He made air quotes with his fingers.

"Approximately eight years. Sophie escaped from her first husband at age twenty-four after marrying at nineteen. She used to do MMA fighting, and Alika was her friend and coach. He was her first relationship after her divorce. Then Todd/Sheldon. Then Jake."

"Help me understand." Raveaux ordered another espresso when the hot water came for the ambassador's tea. "How is it that Alika fathered Momi, then?"

"An accident during one of her cases." Smithson shook his head. "A happy one, it turns out. I wouldn't trade my granddaughter for anything. Sophie was between relationships at the time Momi was conceived."

"Who is Sophie involved with romantically, then?"

"Jake. It's been only Jake since before Momi was born."

"And everyone knows about everyone else? And is—okay with it?"

"After Momi and Sophie were reunited and Jake was freed from captivity in Thailand two years ago—that was all in the file—he broke up with Sophie. He started his own business with another woman, Felicia, for two years." The ambassador pushed his plate aside. "I suspect there was some crossover with the vigilante Connor that caused the breakup, because that man stayed in Thailand with the Yām Khûmkạn, an organization that's closely monitored by the CIA." Smithson gestured for their plates to be cleared. "It's a regular soap opera. Sophie was finally getting over Jake when they reunited, right after your case in San Francisco."

"I understand now," Raveaux murmured. That's why Sophie'd been open to a relationship with him during that case—there'd been a brief time, before Jake came back into her life, when Raveaux could swear she'd been attracted to him, too. "But I still don't get why you wanted me to know all of this."

The ambassador's mouth tightened and his brows drew down.

"Because, Pierre, I want you to take down the Ghost. I want that man who calls himself Connor out of my daughter's life. Him, and those criminals in Thailand that he works with."

Raveaux reeled, pushing back from the table at this bombshell. "I am a private citizen, sir, from another country. A retired investigator, no longer associated with any agency." A timely interruption gave a measure of relief as the waitress brought Raveaux his fresh espresso. He accepted the small thick cup, and she cleared the rest of their breakfast clutter. When she'd gone, Raveaux continued. "How do you have all of this information?"

"The file you received was collected by the Secret Service. They, along with the FBI, Interpol, NSA, and CIA, have decided that the Ghost, the man who calls himself Connor, is a threat to our national security. They've formed a multi-agency task force to bring him in. We'd like you to be a part of it, and we're not taking 'no' for an answer."

Raveaux raised his brows. "I do not respond well to bullying, sir." He slid to the side of the booth and stood up. "This matter is none of my business."

"We'll make it your business."

Raveaux took out his wallet. He peeled off a fifty-dollar bill, tucking it under the salt shaker. "*Au revoir*, sir. Breakfast is on me."

He could feel Ambassador Smithson's gaze burning a hole in his back as he walked away.

CHAPTER FORTY

Raveaux
One day later, evening

RAVEAUX FINISHED his solitary and excellent meal, a top-quality pork chop with sautéed scallions, half a baguette slathered with butter from a nearby bakery, and a generous portion of baked summer squash drizzled with honey. He was proud of the progress he'd made in allowing himself little indulgences, and he'd been reflecting on that when the doorbell sounded an unfamiliar chime.

Raveaux had no visitors and expected none. He grabbed his loaded gun from the slot in the side table where he kept it handy, and peered over to check the spyhole.

Two men in leisurewear with concealed sidearms darkened his doorstep. One of them looked familiar.

Not good.

There was nothing to be done but brazen it out. Raveaux put his weapon away and opened the door.

He immediately recognized Stefan Voise of Interpol, even before Voise held up his identification. "Stefan! What brings you to this corner of the world?"

Voise stepped forward. They slapped each other's backs amiably, though this could not possibly be a social visit. The man had a five o'clock shadow no matter the time of day, and he rubbed his chin with a scraping sound that sawed at Raveaux's nerves as he indicated his partner. "Meet my colleague. Karl Beckett of the CIA."

"Ah. A gathering of cops and spies." Raveaux tried for good humor. "To what do I owe the pleasure?"

His comment fell flat in the face of Beckett's chilly stare. "May we come in?"

"Of course." Raveaux swept the door wide. "Welcome to my humble abode."

The men entered, refused beverages, sat on the couch, and proceeded to grill Raveaux, questioning him about his work with Security Solutions, his relationship with Sophie, and finally, every detail he remembered about the blond man who called himself Connor and "his Thai sidekick" during the recent rescue on the lava plain.

Raveaux eventually sat back in his Danish slingback chair and raised his hands in surrender. "Gentlemen. Really. I need to know what this is about."

"You were briefed by Ambassador Smithson," Beckett said. "As he must have told you, this is a multi-agency investigation, including the FBI, into the man who calls himself Connor, an international criminal who poses a danger to our national security."

"Isn't the FBI supposed to conduct investigations on US soil?" Raveaux cocked his head. He was pretty sure these men were legitimate, not least because he knew one of them, but how the roles were being applied was interesting.

"The FBI is a part of our task force, but the two of us came to talk with you, Pierre, to emphasize the international nature of this case," Voise said. "As Ambassador Smithson must have told you, our task force includes the Secret Service, CIA, NSA, FBI, and Interpol."

"So many agencies for one little fugitive," Raveaux said.

Beckett leaned forward from Raveaux's low, modern leather sofa.

"Let's cut to the chase. We have the full cooperation of the Immigration and Naturalization Service, too. You will be deported back to France with a stop at Guantánamo for interrogation, to face obstruction of justice charges—if you don't cooperate fully in helping us capture this man and his associates."

Raveaux had been braced for that. He didn't react. He'd never believed all this effort and manpower were being deployed to capture only Connor, no matter how effective a cyber vigilante he was. "Who are the associates you're after?"

"That's classified," Beckett said.

Voise softened the CIA man's comment with an affable shrug. "Suffice to say, Connor is a big fish, but we're after even bigger ones."

Raveaux sat forward and placed his wrists together in a 'you got me' gesture. "What do you want me to do?"

They proposed that Raveaux lure Sophie back to the United States with an excuse, so that they could track where she was hiding and likely "consorting" (according to Beckett) with Connor at a hidden location in Thailand. "She visits him at that location and uses the Security Solutions jet on her trips. All we need are the coordinates, verification that the man's there, and we can scoop him up. Our contact in Thailand has already agreed to his extradition."

"Extradition where?" Raveaux's brows raised.

"Where we take all traitors like him. Guantánamo, of course."

"All right." Raveaux had no choice but to agree in this moment. "But I can't contact Sophie for at least a full month since she went on leave. She won't come in before then. She has her daughter with her, and she's grieving. If I push too hard, she'll check with Bix at Security Solutions, find out it's a hoax, and this whole trap will fall apart."

They'd agreed, reluctantly, to push back their timetable.

At last Raveaux was left in peace. He shut the door and locked it behind them, a vain gesture. He had to try to work out some kind of plan—but at least, for the moment, he'd bought a couple of weeks' time.

Raveaux hurried to change and go for a swim so he could sort through this latest challenge.

He dove into the cool dark water. His goggles protected his eyes, but there was no point in opening them—the moon hadn't risen, and there was nothing to see but the reflected lights of the hotels dancing on the waves and faint starlight overhead. He breathed on every other stroke as his arms scythed through the water in a smooth over-hand crawl, his feet kicking up a foamy wake.

Raveaux's heart rate, jacked up by the unwelcome visit to his apartment, finally began to calm as he swam—but the toehold he had on his new life had never felt more tenuous.

He reached the end of the curve of Waikiki Beach, marked by a stone jetty. He executed a flip turn before he reached the rocky area and headed back, mulling over the events of the evening.

He was trapped. His apartment had to be bugged. Everything he did was likely under surveillance, and as a foreign citizen on a work visa, he had few rights.

Raveaux paused, taking a moment to tread water and rest. He put his goggles atop his head and tipped it back to gaze at the starry sky. A few silvery wisps of cloud floated by; off in the distance he heard a plane approaching the nearby airport. But when he submerged his ears, all he heard was the swish of water, and off in the distance, the haunting song of whales.

If he called Sophie back to Hawaii with the trumped-up story they'd given him to tell her, he'd be betraying her in the worst way, and for what? There were elements in play of which he had little idea, such as this clandestine Yām Khûmkạn organization.

The ambassador probably thought he was protecting his daughter by cooperating with law enforcement on this operation—but there were larger forces at work. Sophie and Armita could too easily become collateral damage in a clash between the "criminal associates" and the international agencies—or handy scapegoats if things didn't go as planned and someone had to take the fall.

Raveaux slid his goggles back down over his eyes, turned, and resumed his crawl stroke. He swam and swam through the dark water, wrestling with the situation, trying to find a way out—for himself, and for Sophie.

CHAPTER FORTY-ONE

Sophie
Two weeks after Raveaux's visit from the agents

SOPHIE'S CUSTODY month with Momi on the island had passed, one week blending into the next like a dream. Each day, Sophie slept a little better, ate a little more, and cried a little less. Long walks on the beach, teaching Momi to swim, picking flowers, playing in the sand, and chasing the active toddler around the island seemed to be working their healing magic.

On one of her daughter's daily video calls, she asked to speak to Momi's father.

"How are you doing?" Alika asked, his brows drawn together in concern. Their longtime friendship had only been strengthened by co-parenting Momi.

"One day at a time, as they say." Sophie ran her fingers through her daughter's ringlets as Momi played nearby on the floor with her favorite truck, making rumbling noises as she pushed it back and forth. "I hate to ask this of you, and I never have since she was born, but . . . can I keep Little Bean for another month? I don't know how

I'm going to do without her once she leaves." Sophie bit her lip. "I'm holding off the depression, but—Momi is a wonderful distraction."

"Sure. I understand. I'll miss her, but if Sandy had died, I'd be asking for the same thing." Alika had married the physical therapist who'd helped him adjust to having only one arm, and they seemed very happy together. "We both know Momi's pure joy to be around —with a few temper tantrums thrown in." He smiled fondly at his daughter across the miles.

"Thanks, Alika. I'm on leave from work, and this island is a healing place for me."

"Keep me posted on how things are going, how you're doing. Are you working out?"

"Not much, actually." Sophie shook her head. "Dr. Wilson calls it anhedonia—loss of interest in activities you usually enjoy. I've been lying around, playing with Momi, or taking swims in the ocean. The water's even warmer and calmer here than Hawaii."

"Speaking as your former coach here—I think you need to hit the weights and add cardio to your routine. I know you, Sophie, and if you aren't getting those endorphins, the depression could get worse."

"At this point, I can't tell how much of feeling so lethargic is grief, or depression. Maybe they're the same right now." Sophie's smile was forced. "But thanks for the encouragement. I'll give it a try, because as usual, I know you're right." She told Momi to say goodbye to her daddy, and they ended the call.

Armita came to the door, waving a towel in each hand. "It's bath time, Little Bean. You get the red towel, or the blue one. Which do you want?"

"No bath! No towel!" shrieked Momi, jumping up to run away. Armita made growling noises and flapped the towels like wings, and Momi's temper turned to giggles as they ran toward the bathroom.

Sophie remained where she sat, cross-legged on the woven matting that covered the teak floor.

She had her daughter for another month. *A reprieve.*

She stood up and swayed at the rush of blood from her head. She grabbed the edge of the dresser until the wooziness passed. Even as it did, she continued to cling to the dresser, needing its support.

"No," she said aloud. "No, it can't be." But the last time she remembered feeling faint was when she was pregnant with Momi. "No," she said again, and fumbled over to the bed to collapse upon it, throwing an arm over her eyes. "Oh, no."

She had to force herself to think the situation through and count the weeks backward.

She and Jake had made love in that lava tube close to eight weeks ago. She'd begun to take a pill prior to that, but it must not have been up to effective strength, and she'd been so distracted by grief she hadn't noticed missing her period.

Sophie slid her hands up her flat belly to cup her breasts. They were plump and tender to the touch, even though she'd had no appetite and lost weight since Jake died.

She didn't need a pregnancy test to know—all the signs were there.

"How could this have happened to me?" Sophie whispered aloud, speaking to the spotted gecko who really liked the beam above her bed. "I can't have another child with no partner." Her cheeks heated at the shame—*two children by different men, and no ring on her finger!*

And yet.

This was Jake's child. He would have been so happy. He would have been ecstatic.

Her hand slid down to rest over the apple-sized hardness of her uterus, resting in the cradle of her pelvis. She palpated the area gently, closing her eyes.

She could almost feel Jake's arms around her, his tender kiss on that spot where the baby grew. He'd lavished kisses on Momi, there too, while Sophie was pregnant; once he decided she was his, she *had been*—in all but name.

And if this baby lived, something more of Jake than a few organs donated to strangers would remain. The child would always remind her of her *kun dii*, and of the love and passion they'd shared. He or she would be a living epitaph.

That Jake wasn't alive to share this moment with her made tears rush to Sophie's eyes.

She wrapped both arms over her face to stifle them. "Five minutes. That's all I get. Five minutes," she muttered. She breathed through the urge to cry, and uncovered her face.

Connor came to the door. He frowned at the sight of her lying flat on the bed. "It's dinnertime and Nam has some great stir fry going. You feeling okay?"

Sophie sat up quickly, hiding her dizziness at the abrupt motion. "Yes. I hope you don't mind having us for longer—Alika said it's okay for me to keep Momi another month."

A grin broke across Connor's tanned face. Unlike Sophie, he spent long hours working out in his gym, running around the island, meditating in precipitous locations, and drilling with his collection of weapons. He was as hard and chiseled as he'd been the day he joined her from the compound. "I can't promise I'll be able to stay the whole time, but I hope so. I could get used to this relaxed life."

"Ha! You? Relaxed?" Sophie slid an arm through Connor's as she walked toward the dining room, firmly shutting a mental door on the thought of her pregnancy. "I'm going to join you in the gym tomorrow."

CHAPTER FORTY-TWO

Sophie

SOPHIE LAY on the bench and pushed a barbell loaded with half of her usual weight. She was shocked by how much muscle tone she'd lost, between the ordeal in the lava tube and a couple of months of wallowing in grief. But Sophie'd meant what she said to Connor the day before; pregnant or not, she was getting back in shape.

Across from her, Connor pistoned his body up and down on a pullup bar set in the doorway of the open-air gym, a space she was very familiar with from the time she'd spent in it more than two years ago, getting fit after Momi's birth and preparing to retrieve her from her mother.

Sophie's ears were covered by a pair of cordless headphones, and the heavy beat of rock music kept her moving even as her arms trembled with strain. Finally, she dropped the bar back into its cradle, and took her time sitting back up. She lifted a water bottle to drink, though it made her queasy. Staying hydrated was important.

She hadn't wanted to get up that morning at all. The days ahead had seemed entirely overwhelming when she'd woken up and remembered that, not only was Jake dead, she was pregnant with his baby.

But then Momi had climbed up for her wake-up game of peek-a-boo, and Sophie had suddenly seen how it could be: two little heads popping up beside her bed, instead of one. Two pairs of arms to hug, two little bodies to hold, two little people to love.

And one of them she'd have with her all the time, and not have to share with anyone.

But she'd still needed every one of her five minutes of cry time to vent her self-pity over this new mountain to climb, alone, when she wasn't in shape for it on any level—until Connor had shown up at the door with a handful of spandex, and told her it was time to work out.

"Want to spar later?" Connor's voice was fuzzy with her headphones on.

Sophie turned the music off to hear his question repeated as he walked over to her, sweat gleaming on his tanned muscles, wearing only a pair of nylon shorts. Sophie eyed him up and down—he'd always been in good shape, but he was at a whole new level since he became the Master's Number One. Handsome as he was, she felt nothing for him but friendship—and broken trust. He'd demonstrated where his loyalties lay, and she couldn't forget it.

"I'll pass on that for now. As you can see, I've got a way to go to get back in shape." Sophie set the water bottle down. Her phone beeped, a loud toning in her headphones. She got so few calls here that she hit the Receive button automatically. "This is Sophie."

"Sophie? It's Pierre Raveaux." The Frenchman's voice was smooth as a good cognac.

She'd always liked his voice—but she didn't want to like it.

"Hello, Pierre," Sophie said coolly. "I'm on leave. What's so urgent that you had to call me at my private residence?" No, she didn't want to hear this man's voice. Or speak to him. Or see him, especially now that she knew about the baby. Maybe she could get away with never seeing him again . . .

"I'm sorry to disturb you, Sophie. But the girl we brought in—Lia Ayabe, remember her? She is suing Security Solutions for wrongful action. Emotional and physical pain and suffering."

"What?" Sophie stood up too fast and had to grab the weight bench for support. "She's a minor with no resources. How can she do that?"

"We didn't know when we got the case that she had declared herself an emancipated minor, and apparently, she's quite wealthy. Her mother left her money, and Mr. Ayabe neglected to tell us that." Sophie could almost see Raveaux's Gallic shrug. "I'm sure this will eventually resolve in our favor, but the Security Solutions lawyers are asking you to come back to Hawaii to give a deposition. A formal statement in question and answer form about your activities on the case."

"I know what a deposition is. *Maggots crawling on a scurvy corpse,*" Sophie swore. She began to pace. "Just when I was getting back into the gym."

"Excuses, excuses," Connor teased. He lay down on a slant board and began sit-ups.

"I don't see why I have to come all the way back for the deposition," Sophie complained to Raveaux. "Can't we record my statement remotely?"

"Unfortunately, they insist it has to be done in person." Raveaux was getting tired of her testiness; she could tell by his extra calm, deliberate tone. "Everyone regrets disturbing you in your time of grief."

"*Son of a two-headed dog,*" Sophie snapped. "Tell Bix he should be the one to call me for this kind of thing in the future, and tell him to send the corporate jet ASAP."

"Send the jet where?" The inquiry hung in the air. "Are you even in the United States? Bix is on vacation."

"Fine. I'll call for the plane." Sophie hit the End button.

"Wow, you're salty." Connor swiveled around and mopped his streaming face with a thin cotton towel. "Who was that?"

"Raveaux. Summoning me back to the office on Oahu for a deposition." Sophie got on the elliptical trainer in the corner of the room. "Is it okay to leave Momi and Armita here with you for a few days? I won't be gone long. But I want you to stay here and make sure they're safe."

"Of course." Connor smiled. "Don't worry. I've got your back."

Sophie narrowed her eyes at him. "Of course I worry. The Master and my mother know where my daughter and her nanny are, and you're the one that led them here."

Connor narrowed his eyes right back at her. "Do you really think they didn't know about this place all along? Given that, if they wanted to take Momi and Armita, they already would have done so."

Sophie had no answer for that. She pumped her arms and circled her legs, quickly getting out of breath on the elliptical.

"Your mother wants to bury the hatchet," Connor said, getting on a bike alongside her.

"I'm not familiar with that phrase."

"It means make peace. End the warfare. It comes from a Native American custom dating back several centuries."

"I accepted her apology. Doesn't mean I plan to let her get any closer to me or mine."

"Fair enough—but don't lose sleep over Pim Wat making some kind of move on Momi. You saw the woman; she's a wreck."

"I know who and what she is. What she's capable of. I'll never trust her around my child. Or Armita, given their history. Period."

Connor nodded. "And I agree. But I trust the Master, and I don't believe he'd let her do you any harm."

"I hope you're right." Sophie got off the elliptical. "And now I have to go get ready to fly back to Honolulu. Just watch over them, will you?"

"You know I will." Connor leaned over and gave her a kiss on the cheek. "Like they were my own."

CHAPTER FORTY-THREE

Sophie
Twenty-four hours later

SOPHIE WALKED to her office at Security Solutions after greeting Paula, her assistant, who'd been reassigned to man the front desk in her absence.

Sophie'd slept for most of the thirteen-hour flight from Phi Ni to Honolulu. She then had taken the time to shop for food. At her Pendragon Arches apartment, she showered, dressed carefully, and put on makeup, keeping an eye on the time—and she'd arrived at the Security Solutions building early. Time enough to review her email, and see if anything required her immediate attention before the deposition was scheduled.

Her underlying grief and the pregnancy continued to sap her energy, and she looked forward to a few minutes alone as she pressed down the door handle of her office—and found it unlocked.

Sophie frowned as she pushed the portal open and stepped inside.

Seated in a chair in front of her desk, an ankle propped on a knee and a paperback open in his hands in his characteristic pose, was Raveaux.

"Pierre." She blew out a breath of both annoyance and relief. "I told you not to come into my office without permission."

"As Hippocrates is believed to have said, 'desperate times call for desperate measures.'" Raveaux waved his book at her. "I wanted to be sure to let you know the schedule as soon as you arrived."

Sophie narrowed her eyes—a note was taped inside the open pages of his Jack Reacher novel. Written in bold block letters was, *"THIS OFFICE IS BUGGED WITH VISUAL AND AUDIO. SO AM I. I HAVE AN IMPORTANT MESSAGE FOR YOU."*

Raveaux closed the book and set it on her desk. "The deposition is set up in a conference room downstairs. Do you want to go over your statement with me, first?" His dark eyes telegraphed worry, concern—and urgency.

Sophie kept her face neutral, wearing the blank mask she'd learned years ago at the hands of her sadistic ex-husband. She'd stepped off the plane into something major, and she had no idea what it was. *She needed that message from Raveaux.*

How long did she have before someone, from some government agency, knocked down the door and took her, or Raveaux, in for questioning? Brazening this out and pretending to detect the bugs according to their normal security procedures seemed the best way to go.

"I haven't been in this office for a while and I always do a security check when I come back from a trip." Sophie removed a surveillance detection wand from the front drawer of her desk. "Let me make sure we're clear before we get started." She stood up and walked around the room in a familiar pattern—and if she'd been observed for long, they would know that she checked her office at least monthly.

Beeps went off in the light beside her desk and a node across the room near the curtains. "This is not good, Raveaux," she said. "I'll have to put off our talk until I can notify Paula of a security breach and order a full check of the premises. Where's Bix?"

"He's still on vacation until next week." Raveaux lowered his brows. A finger subtly pointed to one of the plain gold cufflinks holding closed the sleeve of his dark blue shirt. *That's where he was bugged.*

"That's unfortunate. I prefer him to have to deal with things like this." Sophie sat back down at her desk and hit the intercom button. "Paula, there's been a security breach. We need a level three sweep of the building, beginning with my office."

"Right away, Sophie." Paula's voice sounded as cheerful as if she'd called to ask for a coffee.

Sophie hadn't used the device in ages, but she had a signal jammer in the tool bag she kept in her desk. That would work to temporarily disable the equipment, including whatever was on Raveaux. She had to work fast in case her detection of the surveillance triggered a raid.

Sophie took her keys out of her pocket, found her desk's cabinet key and unlocked it, quickly pulling out a small zippered holdall she stored there. She unzipped the black nylon bag and grabbed the jammer, flicking it on.

An indicator light went green and pulsed. Sophie held the jammer aloft but put a finger to her lips, catching Raveaux's eye—she had to make sure everything that could be used to listen in on them was off.

She held out her hand for Raveaux's phone. "Turn it off, please."

Raveaux did so, and handed it over. "This seems a little extreme, Ms. Smithson."

He was still playacting for the button mike! Whoever was making Raveaux do this had a lot of power over him. Who could it be?

"We share and keep a lot of confidential information in our offices." Sophie got up from her desk and pulled the cord to close heavy blackout drapes over the large, plate-glass window, in case of long-distance equipment monitoring them. "I would hate for any of our clients' data to fall into the wrong hands. That's why I'm glad I kept the computers off, in case they've been breached or programmed to send a signal to some other unit." Sophie indicated the three monitors that decorated her desk. Amara, Jinjai, and Ying were heavily encrypted, even if they could have been activated without her fob, which, as far as she knew, was impossible.

Still, she had to test that the jammer was working.

Sophie reached into her carryall and took out a small surveillance cam about the size of a dime. She activated it by pressing the button on the back, then set it on her desk. She took out her phone and scrolled to an app, activated it. "Testing, one, two. Testing," she said into the node.

The monitoring window on her phone remained a staticky white box; if the device was transmitting, she'd have had both audio and video. "Good. Signals are blocked."

Finally, Sophie turned off her own phone. She popped out the sim cards of both hers and Raveaux's and set them down on the desk. She activated the desktop fan on the corner of her work area and leaned into the breeze, her hair, now past her ears, tossing in the wind. "Finally. I think you're safe to tell me what you need to if you keep your mouth in the air stream."

Just then a knock came from the door.

They both moved away from the fan. Raveaux, who was closer, stood up and opened it. Two men Sophie recognized from the tech department entered. With little conversation or fanfare, they removed the audio/video surveillance devices and wanded the room again for good measure. Sophie noted how Raveaux slid his hand deep into his pocket, concealing the device he wore, and moved away from the security team so it wouldn't be detected.

Raveaux couldn't afford for his handlers to know his bug had been discovered. Fear spiked Sophie's heart rate. He was taking some kind of tremendous personal risk in giving her whatever message he carried.

Finally, the tech team left.

Sophie locked the door behind them and, pressing her back

against it, turned to face Raveaux. "This will buy us a few more minutes if there's someone on the way to detain me."

"That's not what's happening right now, but it could." Raveaux's olive skin had gone white around his lips with stress, but his intelligent dark eyes were determined. He gestured for her to come forward into the fan's air space again. "In case we missed anything."

Sophie rolled her office chair out from behind the desk and sat down in it, facing him. The blades of the old-fashioned metal fan blew a stream of air between them. Their knees were close enough to touch. Sophie moved restlessly in her chair, uncomfortable with Raveaux's intent gaze. "Hurry. What is it you have to tell me?"

CHAPTER FORTY-FOUR

Raveaux

RAVEAUX REACHED into his pocket and pulled out a paper-wrapped, cylindrical object. He held it out to Sophie. "For you."

Her honey-brown eyes were wary and her golden tan paler than it should have been, given a month on a Thailand beach, but her hands were steady as she took the package. "What is this?"

"Open it. You'll need it." The plain brown paper bag wrapping the spare burner phone Raveaux had brought Sophie annoyed him with its crudity, but it was all he'd had in his apartment to hide the device he'd fortunately had stowed away in case of needing to place any confidential calls—he was sure he was under surveillance in his apartment. Retrieving the phone from a side pocket in his suitcase, concealing it and wrapping it had been a feat of ingenuity involving hiding in the shower. "We've made a window to talk here, but make no mistake. We're both under a microscope."

Sophie uncovered the phone. "This a burner?"

"Yes. Unused and charged."

Her gaze flicked up to his. "Who is doing this to you? To us?"

"A multi-agency task force made up of CIA, FBI, NSA, Interpol, and the Secret Service. I'm not entirely sure who's waiting for you down in the conference room, but in case you didn't realize it—there's no deposition today." He drew a calming breath and shut his eyes, sorting his thoughts as he leaned forward into the flow of air from the fan. "I was given a file loaded with information about a cyber vigilante called the Ghost, aka Sheldon Hamilton, aka Todd Remarkian. Who he is. Where he is. What he's been up to."

"Oh no." Sophie swayed and grabbed the desk for support. He was glad she was already sitting down.

"Yes. These agencies have collected a tremendous amount of information, most of it not provable in a court of law—and until recently, they'd been content to have driven him out of the United States to operate out of that camp in Thailand, or wherever he is. Now, they've decided that he's a threat to national security, and they want him. Badly." Raveaux had spent many a sleepless night after his meeting with the ambassador until finally, he'd come up with this plan to warn Sophie—leaving out the part about her father's involvement. He didn't want to hit her with that unless he had to—she was already dealing with enough. "I was visited by a two-man team consisting of an Interpol agent I knew from my detective days in France, along with a CIA agent. They threatened me with deportation and worse if I didn't get you back here with an excuse, and use that to help capture Connor."

"I know why they've decided he's a threat, but I need to warn him right away. How are they planning to capture him?" Sophie's eyes had gone wide.

"Download the flight plan from the Security Solutions jet and make a raid on wherever you've been hiding," Raveaux said. "They wanted to verify that he's there first, though, hence my bringing you a burner you can use to warn him. You said you know why they decided he was a threat—why is that?"

"It involves my mother." Sophie smiled humorlessly. "She's an assassin and a spy, and she was recently extracted from Guantánamo. I'm sure they suspect Connor's involvement, and Pim Wat is public enemy number one. They won't be happy that she got away."

Raveaux's mouth hung open at this revelation. Frank Smithson hadn't said a word about Pim Wat, but the woman was his ex-wife. The ambassador had to have known much more than he'd chosen to share with Raveaux. *What were his real motives?*

"Pierre. Thank you. You took a huge risk in telling me, and you didn't have to." Sophie gazed at Raveaux, and he felt her eyes moving over each of his features, warm as a touch. "Give me a moment alone with the fan. I need to use the phone you brought me for an important call."

"Of course. I'll go to the restroom." Raveaux's whole body felt lit up from her gratitude, her trust. He exited the office, waved to efficient Paula at her station in the lobby area, and entered the men's room.

This room probably wasn't bugged, but he still was, and Voise, who'd been chosen to be his handler, would be wanting a report on his meeting with Sophie. He moved a potted plant in front of the door to slow down anyone entering, and went into one of the stalls.

The cufflink at his wrist was audio only, thank God. He spoke into the tiny hole that marked the receiver. "Subject is on high alert after routine sweep for bugs in her office yielded two discoveries. She turned on a jammer at her desk, quote, "until we go through the whole building with a level three sweep," and she closed the curtains, as I'm sure you noticed. I stayed on point and helped her review her statement for the deposition. You didn't miss anything. She should be down to the conference room shortly; I will make sure of it."

Raveaux flushed the toilet, exited the stall, and washed his hands, wishing he could drown the damn cufflink under the water—but he was "skating on thin ice" as the Americans said, and if Sophie didn't show up at the conference room, he was going to be in deep trouble.

But he wasn't going to make her go there alone. He'd find a way to get the meeting stopped if it got out of hand . . .

Raveaux headed back to Sophie's office, but when he opened the door, she was gone.

His stomach plummeted.

He'd be going to Guantánamo for sure if she'd made a run for it.

Raveaux turned off the fan and replaced it on the corner of Sophie's desk. He opened the curtains. Everything had to seem normal.

He returned to the reception area. Paula looked lovely, as usual, with a plumeria pinned behind her ear and a fitted floral sheath dress that made the most of her buxom figure. "Paula, excuse me. I was expecting to continue my meeting with Ms. Smithson. It's a matter of some urgency. Do you know where she went?"

"Oh, you two must have had a misunderstanding. She went down to the conference room for her deposition already. I'm sure you can meet after that. Do you want me to pencil you in on her schedule?"

The "deposition" was almost certainly going to result in Sophie being taken into custody until Connor was captured, but he forced himself to smile. "Yes, please. Have her call me when she's available. Thanks so much."

He turned and took the stairs, walking deliberately, considering his next moves.

He could ditch the surveillance device and make a run for it. Try to stay off the grid and out of sight until all of this blew over. But he didn't have the resources and connections here in Honolulu that he did in France, to pull off invisibility for more than a day or two.

That left him with having to continue to play his part, and hope that the team believed he was complying with their plan.

But he didn't have to do that entirely.

If Sophie really had followed through with walking into whatever waited for her in the conference room, things were going to be unpleasant for her, and get worse from there. He had to try to head that off.

Raveaux exited the stairwell on the third floor and walked confidently into a maze of cubicles and offices until he reached an empty room with the door ajar. He slipped inside, shut the door, and locked it. He grabbed a jacket hanging on the back of a chair and wrapped it quickly around his wrist, covering the cufflink, and pressed it tight against his side. He then stood in the flow of the tall floor fan, and hit an outside line on the desk phone. He called the main number for Sophie's office.

"Security Solutions. Paula speaking."

"Paula? It's Pierre Raveaux. I couldn't speak freely because of being bugged. Call your on-site security team to come help Sophie in the conference room. The men interviewing her are not lawyers. They're hostile agents, and she's in trouble."

"Right away, Mr. Raveaux." The phone went dead.

He hung up the receiver.

He'd done what he could—and it might cost him everything.

He unwrapped his wrist, draped the jacket back over the chair, and slipped out, closing the door. None of the people working in their offices so much as looked at him.

He stepped back into the stairwell, and soon reached the bottom of the stairs. He straightened his sleeves, touching the cufflink. The tiny gold piece of tech felt as heavy as an anchor on his wrist. He longed to try to go dark and disappear.

Instead, he spoke aloud into the cufflink. "Returning to my apartment. Available for debrief when the team is ready."

His fate lay in Sophie's hands, now.

CHAPTER FORTY-FIVE

Sophie

SOPHIE TOOK a moment to visit the women's restroom to prepare, before heading into the conference room for whoever waited for her there.

After a nervous pee, she hid the burner phone by taping it to the back of one of the toilet wells. She then went to the sink area, washed her hands, and touched up her makeup from a little zippered bag inside her business tote.

She brushed down her black, easy movement dress slacks and plum-red silk blouse, making sure they were immaculate. She then chose a lipstick that matched the blouse and dabbed it on her full lips. A whisk of mascara, a whiff of perfume, and her favorite Tahitian pearl earrings completed her ensemble.

Thankfully, Sophie had been able to reach Connor on the burner Raveaux had given her; he'd promised to leave Phi Ni for the Yām compound immediately. Hopefully, he got out before they raided the island—she'd done all she could to ensure that.

Sophie stood back and assessed herself in the mirror. She looked smart, powerful, well put together, and in control. Gone were the days of wearing yoga pants and carrying a knapsack filled with tech equipment; Sophie was a female CEO in the male-dominated world of private security, and she needed to look professional—especially today.

Sophie walked into the lower level conference room with the long stride of a confident woman in a hurry, her head up and her expression annoyed. "Agent McDonald," she exclaimed. "What are you doing here?"

She did not have to do much acting to seem surprised. McDonald, a portly man prone to loud aloha wear with the reddened nose of a drinker, had been her handler at the CIA during their attempt to recruit her some years ago. She'd neither seen nor heard from him since.

"We're here to interview you on a matter of national security. "McDonald gestured to another man seated next to him. "This is Special Agent Pillman of the FBI."

"I know who you are," she said, as Pillman, gray-haired and pale-eyed, held up a credential wallet. She disliked the agent heartily. He'd worked for Internal Affairs when she'd been with the FBI, and he'd been particularly rough on her friend Lei Texeira during an investigation. "More importantly, what are you two doing in my building? I'm supposed to be giving a deposition."

McDonald leaned back in his chair and interlaced his fingers, with their short, bitten nails, over his belly. "Ah. That, my dear, was a fabrication. We needed you to come back to the states on a matter of national security."

"So you say." Sophie had to keep an upper hand as long as she could; the men's relatively relaxed demeanor told her that Raveaux's warning to her had not yet been detected. *She could add to his credibility with them.* "That bastard Raveaux must be your plant. Remind me to fire him on your way out."

"Don't blame the man too much; he's a guest in our country and wants to stay here." McDonald hadn't brushed his teeth after lunch, and a bit of parsley set off his grin.

"I will be recording these proceedings." Sophie took her phone out of her pocket.

Agent Pillman stood up, and, faster than she would have believed, reached across the table and plucked it out of her fingers. He tossed it to McDonald. "Still unlocked. You can check her last calls."

"Hey!" Sophie exclaimed, even as Pillman twisted an arm behind her back and forced her, face down, over the table. He frisked her one-handed, efficient and harsh.

"She's clean." Still keeping Sophie's arm twisted up, he moved her over to sit down on a chair, and then zip-tied her hands behind it.

"I'll scream for help," Sophie said. "This is a security firm. You'd be taken down in minutes."

"No you won't call out," McDonald said. "Because we have your daughter and your nanny, and they won't like where we put them if you don't cooperate."

Bile surged up Sophie's throat. "No."

Her mind scrabbled to make sense of this. She'd just called the island; had spoken to Connor and Armita, both. There hadn't been time for anyone to be captured. These men were bluffing.

But they'd tipped their hand that they planned to grab Armita and Momi to guarantee her cooperation, and Sophie hadn't planned for that. "I feel sick."

"Lean over and puke if you have to. You've got a cleaning service." Pillman walked over and locked the door. "We've already checked for bugs in here—nothing but ours."

"How dare you," Sophie growled.

"Drop the princess act, Sophie." McDonald poured himself some water from the carafe Paula had helpfully left on the table. "Your daddy can't help you now. You're being investigated for aiding and abetting an international fugitive."

"I don't know what you're talking about."

"Connor, that's who we're talking about. The cyber vigilante who calls himself the Ghost, and several other names, all of whom are now 'deceased.'" McDonald made air quotes. "We want to know all you can tell us about him and his operation."

"I can't tell you anything, because I don't know what you're talking about."

"Come on, Sophie. We know you were lovers. We know all about the Todd Remarkian/Sheldon Hamilton switcheroo. Don't play coy with me. This guy is bad news, almost as bad as your mother."

"Now that's just rude," Sophie said. "I want a lawyer." She pursed her lips and set her chin, glaring at both of them.

"I'm sure you've heard of the Patriot Act," Pillman said. "You don't get a lawyer, sweet cheeks."

Thank God Raveaux had warned her. *Thank God, and thank you, Pierre Raveaux!* Walking into this trap unaware would have been even worse than walking into it knowing she was in for a rough time.

The door blew open with no warning, banging back to hit the wall with a boom. Two burly men in black Security Solutions uniforms held a door cannon, while another two moved in, weapons drawn.

Pillman and McDonald reached for their handguns.

"Hands up!" The Security Solutions section leader, an experienced ex-military officer named, Janner, barked out.

"FBI! Stand down!" Pillman put his hands up as he responded. "This is a law enforcement interview, and you are disturbing the proceedings!"

"Hell it is! That's our CEO you've got tied to the chair, and that's illegal last time I checked," Janner replied.

"Let us show you our identifications," Pillman insisted. "Or I'll slap you all with an obstruction charge."

Sophie rocked her chair back and forth. "Cut my restraints, please, Mr. Janner." Janner darted forward and slashed Sophie's zip ties with a combat knife. "Thanks." Sophie didn't want to stay and be caught up in the pissing match that would follow, and end with her being taken into custody. She had to get out *now*. "Mr. Janner, remove their weapons and keep these gentlemen here—they're pretending to be agents. Take their credential wallets, and call their agencies to check on their identifications. I have some phone calls to make."

"Absolutely, Ms. Smithson."

"Don't let her out of here!" McDonald howled as Janner moved forward to take their weapons and IDs.

Sophie darted out of the room. She headed for the restroom to retrieve the burner phone.

The process of figuring out who was who would take a while, and hopefully she'd be in the air and on her way to Thailand before it was sorted out.

CHAPTER FORTY-SIX

Sophie

SOPHIE SLEPT for most of the thirteen-hour flight to Phi Ni, but when she wasn't sleeping, she was on her satellite-enabled laptop—hunting for Connor, Armita, and Momi.

The house at Phi Ni was as safe from digital incursions as anywhere could be. Connor had never granted her access to his server except when she was using his equipment in the house. Even using her best programs on the laptop, Sophie was unable to breach his security to tap into the video surveillance camera at the house, which might have allowed her to see what was going on there.

She sent Connor an encrypted email to their secret chatroom telling him about the interview with the agents. *"I hope you have my daughter and nanny, even if that means they're at the compound. I can deal with just about anything, but not threats against them."* She signed with her old screen ID, MMAFighter.

She stared down at the small green cursor pulsing against the black DOS background, and hit Send.

The pilot came on the intercom, announcing that he was descending into Phi Ni. Sophie watched the brilliant turquoise ocean come closer and closer, the beach and palm trees whiz by, the smooth black tarmac rise to meet them in landing.

They taxied over to the large metal hangar. Sophie let herself out of the jet, lowering the stairs and hurrying down them. Usually, Nam or his wife met them at the hangar with their utilitarian pickup truck, but no one was there. She approached the hangar, and stopped at the sight that met her.

The side door had been marked in a big X with bright red plastic NO TRESPASSING tape. More tape crisscrossed the windows. A notice was taped to one side of the entrance.

Sophie approached to read it.

NOTICE OF SEIZURE BY THE DEPARTMENT OF JUSTICE:

This Property is Forfeit in a Criminal Proceeding as a Result of Felonious Activities that Violate Statutes. . .

Sophie read on into legalese citing the statutes under which the property was forfeit, namely ***Crimes of a Felonious Nature Against the Citizens of the United States.***

Her heart beat with heavy thuds. *They'd executed their raid, and confiscated Connor's property.*

But she had to see what, or who, might still be up at the house.

Sophie returned to the jet and told the pilot team to wait to hear from her before leaving. "I'm going up to the house to see what's going on. I hope to be back soon with my daughter and her nanny."

She had the key to the hangar on her fob; she broke the tape and opened the small side door to the huge steel barn. She retracted the rolling garage style doors so the team could make sure the jet had everything it needed for the return trip.

The estate's quad all-terrain vehicle was right where she remembered it, keys in the ignition. Sophie fired it up and took off up the winding, crushed coral road to the house.

Warm late afternoon wind blew in Sophie's face, and she squinted behind her sunglasses as the ATV roared between her thighs. The road to the house was always longer than she remembered. She hit a pothole and lurched up from the seat—*and rougher, too.*

Likely Connor had taken Armita and Momi with him. All three of them were probably at the remote compound in Thailand, out of cell phone reach.

But Nam would be at the house. He would know what was going on; he would fill her in. Nam, a quiet, dignified, graceful Thai man, had become one of Sophie's favorite people.

As she zoomed uphill, past the turnoff to the boathouse with its abandoned coconut plantation, past the turnoff to Nam and his wife's separate cottage and garden, and finally up to the mansion, Sophie tried to calm her racing heart.

But what she saw when she pulled up in front of the grand entrance was not reassuring.

The double door handles had been looped together by a chain and a large padlock. Crude boards had been nailed across the entrance, increasing the locked-down effect. More crimson plastic NO TRES-PASSING tape crisscrossed the windows and side doors. A notice that looked the same as the one she'd already read was taped to one side of the entrance.

Sophie turned to look at the barn; it was similarly sealed.

"Nam?" She put her hands around her mouth and called again. "Nam! It's Sophie!"

No answer. The place appeared deserted.

Sophie walked up the stone steps. Her hand caressed the shiny spot she often rubbed on one of the dragons' heads as she checked that the notice on the door was what she'd already read.

It was. Everything of Connor's, the whole island, had been seized.

"Son of a two-headed goat." She hurried around the outside of the entire building. Every window and door was boarded up, sealed, and marked with the tape.

Surveillance cameras were probably tracking her every move right now.

Sophie battled a wave of nausea as she headed back to the quad. "It's going to be okay," she said aloud, but in her mind, she heard the reassurance spoken in Jake's distinctive voice.

Jake was gone. He would never be at her side again, helping her, supporting her, loving her.

Sophie staggered over to an ornamental bush and vomited up the little she'd eaten on the plane.

Standing back up, wiping her mouth, her knees shaky, Sophie took a long look around at the beautiful house and grounds. *She might never see this place again.* She walked over to the bench where she'd made peace with her mother and gazed out at the incredible view, drawing some deep breaths to combat the last of the nausea. "Goodbye, Phi Ni. Thank you for being so good to me. I hope I can see you again someday."

She got on the ATV and drove down to Nam's house.

The same tape and notice marked the door of Nam's cottage. The place appeared deserted, and the couple's lush garden was already wilting in the tropical sun.

A new spike of terror hit Sophie's bloodstream.

What if they'd been taken into custody, to be used against her? She searched around the couple's house to no avail. There was no clue where they might have gone.

Fear reached a new level as she suddenly wondered if the pilot might have taken off without her, marooning her here. What if they had received directions from the Department of Justice? She had to assume the agents on the case knew she was trespassing on the premises, and she couldn't blame the pilots for following orders.

There was nothing for her here, and nothing to learn except that the agents had followed through on their threats.

Sophie ran to the quad, jumped on, and sped back down the mountain.

CHAPTER FORTY-SEVEN

Sophie

THE JET WAS STILL PARKED on the tarmac. The pilot and his copilot were pumping fuel from the underground tank that Connor kept filled.

Sophie blew out a breath of relief as she drove the ATV into the huge, dim, cool hangar. She parked the quad in the corner where it was typically stored.

Her mind ground restlessly through her options. No one was answering his phone; either the phones were out of range, had been disabled, or had been confiscated, as hers had been.

She could stay in Thailand, and try to look for Armita and Momi, hoping that they had taken shelter on the mainland, or were at the Yām Khûmkạn compound with Connor.

But she had made her feelings about the compound clear to him. If Connor had moved to take care of Armita and Momi as she hoped he had, he would not have taken them there—he would have sent them back to Hawaii, where they would be safe from her mother.

Connor might have taken Nam and his wife to the compound, though. They would be cared for, perhaps even given jobs.

It was possible they'd all been taken into custody, but Connor was usually miles ahead of law enforcement. She could only trust that her warning had set in motion a series of events that would ensure not only Connor's safety, but that of those dearest to her. Yes, he'd betrayed her trust by bringing Pim Wat and the Master to a place she'd imagined was safe; but as he had pointed out, that always had been an illusion.

Her best option was to return to her apartment, contact her father, and enlist all the help and protection she could get against the DOJ probe. From there, she would hope to hear from Armita, wherever she was hiding with Momi, once things were safe.

Armita would contact her. She had in the past; she was the one who had taken Momi away from Pim Wat and brought the baby to Sophie, at the risk of her own life.

Sophie closed and locked the doors of the hangar, re-sealing the tape, and hurried to meet the pilots. "Everyone is gone, and the houses are marked, too. Wheels up as soon as you can get us in the air. We're going back to Hawaii."

THEY LANDED in Honolulu twelve hours later. Sophie wasted no time collecting her things and calling for a rideshare to her apartment.

She could be walking right into a Department of Justice trap by heading back there, but she had to see if Armita had left her a message via her landline or computers.

The rideshare vehicle wove through busy downtown Honolulu traffic, headed for the Pendragon Arches building. She took out the burner and called her father.

The ambassador picked up right away. "Sophie! Why didn't you call me back?"

"I left you this number, Dad. Why didn't *you* call *me* back?"

"I tried, but none of the calls would hook up."

Sophie frowned in annoyance. "I should have been able to

retrieve a message, but I have been flying for the last thirty or so hours." Maybe the lack of communication had been the cheap phone —at a time when her sanity depended on it, technology had failed. "What's going on with the DOJ investigation, Dad? Have you been able to find anything out?"

Her father cleared his throat. "I spoke to my Secret Service contact about the situation. There's a full-blown multi-agency investigation going on into this Connor character, Sophie."

"I know. That's what I told you. Two men, one from the CIA and one from the FBI, restrained me in my own building to force me to tell them where he was. I don't know what is going on." She shut her eyes and pinched the bridge of her nose—*there was so much she couldn't tell him!* "Can you help me deal with these people, Dad?"

"I hired a top-notch criminal defense attorney for you. He told me to advise you to stay close to home. Don't do anything suspicious. I'll text you his info; you should call him right away about next steps."

"Don't do anything suspicious, like fly to a private island in Thailand?" Sophie forced a laugh. "That's fine, Dad. I'm back now, and not planning on going anywhere else."

"Can we get together? I'd like to talk further." She heard a current of anxiety behind her father's words. *Maybe he had more to tell her but didn't want to talk on the phone.*

"I'll call you tomorrow. Right now, I'm so hungry I could eat a whole donkey." After her nausea and fatigue, her appetite had come raging back—and she remembered that, too, from her first trimester with Momi.

"You mean, 'eat a horse.'" Her father chuckled, but it sounded forced. *Someone was definitely listening in.* "Get some rest and we'll talk tomorrow. Love you, Sophie. I'm glad you're home."

Sophie put the phone away and stared out the vehicle's window. Cars honked, bikers whizzed by, kids on skateboards and dogs on leashes filled the sidewalks. Palm trees reflected in windows. Colors were bright and sounds loud, but Sophie hardly registered any of it, not even the massive shade trees that sheltered the area from the brilliant sun and heat of downtown, as they turned into her neighborhood.

The web of lies she'd become a part of, woven around protecting Connor's identity, was tightening around her—and she had no idea how to get free of it.

But that wasn't what she was really worried about now.

Where were Armita and Momi? And the dogs?

She was going to have to call Alika, and tell him they were missing. The thought made her belly clench. Sophie glanced down at the stubbornly silent phone and tried Armita's number one more time.

"Here you are," the driver said, pulling up in front of the elegant, well-appointed Pendragon Arches building, where Security Solutions owned several units, including the one she lived in. Sophie thanked the driver and exited the vehicle.

She pushed through the glass doors and greeted the elderly security officer at his desk as she carried her travel backpack through the beautifully decorated lobby, spangles of light from the chandeliers falling on her like drops of sunshine.

Once on the elevator, Sophie dictated a list of chores into the phone's voice memo: *order takeout. That call to Alika. Contact the lawyer. Talk to Paula and Bix at Security Solutions about whatever ended up happening with leaving those agents in the conference room. Make an appointment with OB/GYN.*

The elevator dinged, and opened.

She walked down the hall to the door of her unit, stuck her key in —and a dog barked on the other side of the door.

Ginger.

And then, the patter of running feet, and a stream of giggles.

Momi.

Sophie's heart soared—there was no other way to describe the expansive feeling of joy that lifted her chest and filled her eyes with tears. She turned the key and pushed the door gently inward.

"Mama!" Momi shrieked. "You're home!"

Ginger reached Sophie first, thrusting her nose into Sophie's crotch and lashing her legs with a thick tail. Momi embraced her legs and snuggled into Sophie with her silky head. Anubis hung back, whining, and behind him, petite Armita clapped her hands. "Sophie! Oh, thank God! I thought they'd taken you in!"

"I need a hug. From all of you." Sophie dropped to her knees and opened her arms wide enough to hold two dogs, a toddler, and a ninja nanny—and they engulfed her right back with their love.

EPILOGUE

Five days later

Sophie ushered Dr. Wilson into her office at Security Solutions. "I can't tell you how grateful I am, Dr. Wilson, that you came all the way from the Big Island to meet with me."

"Oh, don't worry about that." Dr. Wilson looked younger than her years in a flowered wrap dress and low-heeled nude sandals that made the most of her athletic legs. "I was glad to get off the island for a few days. The eruption over there is causing a lot of damage, and everyone is on edge."

"I believe it. I've been screening the news so as not to get too stressed, myself." Sophie embraced Dr. Wilson in a welcoming hug.

The psychologist smelled of something lemony that reminded Sophie of Jake's favorite citrus aftershave. *Another painful memory.* When would they stop coming?

"I'm always happy to work with you, Sophie, and don't feel too bad about the extra travel. I've promised myself a little shopping trip at Ala Moana Center when we're done." Dr. Wilson looked around Sophie's spacious office with its bank of windows, solid executive desk area topped by computer monitors, round work table with chairs, and stylish seating corner. "Where would you like us to sit?"

"Let's get comfortable over here on the couch. It's hard for me to switch to therapy mode in this work setting." Sophie went behind her desk and closed the sheer drape layer to cut down the sunlight streaming through the windows—and to block the view of anyone trying to spy on them.

The furniture pieces in the corner area were done in soft, buttery chocolate leather, and faced a low coffee table in native koa hardwood. Dr. Wilson settled herself in a trim armchair facing the couch. She took out a tablet, one of the new, modern ones that converted handwriting to text. "You're right about changing gears. Environmental cues create expectations that can help open the door to an effective session. But I know you have a lot to talk about, and the choice to do appropriate self-care here is as good as entering my office."

"How do you like that device you're using?" Sophie had fetched a square cardboard package from her desk, and she set the small box in front of her. They made conversation for a few moments as Sophie settled herself, making sure that tissues were handy.

Dr. Wilson pointed her stylus at the box. "What's that?" The cardboard package was open at the top, its sealing tape cut. A hand-written address with Sophie's name and a plethora of postage marked its exterior.

"I opened it, saw what it might be, and that's as far as I got before I called you. It's from Patty, Jake's sister. But I couldn't bear to open it any further to see what's inside."

Dr. Wilson didn't try to comfort Sophie, to rush in with platitudes as someone else might have. She simply sat and waited; her intelligent blue eyes compassionate. "What do you think it might be?"

"Something that belonged to Jake." Sophie twisted her fingers together. "I didn't feel strong enough to look."

"Do you feel ready to open it now?"

"With you here to give me courage, yes." Sophie leaned forward.

She opened the flaps of the cardboard box. Inside, a sealed envelope with Sophie's name on it lay on top of a small, black velvet bag of the type used for jewelry. Sophie removed the missive and opened the envelope. A dove flying on the front of a simple card brought a prickle of tears to her eyes, and she opened it to see feminine looping handwriting.

She read the card aloud.

"DEAR SOPHIE:

Words cannot express how sorry I am for my mother's and sister's behavior toward you during Jake's death and memorial. Even if you hadn't been engaged, as I believe you were, they never should have treated you so poorly. These ashes are a part of my portion from the funeral home. I want you to have them for whatever ceremony feels right to you in remembering him.

You would have been a wonderful sister, and that's why I'm sending you our family ring, too. Jake mailed it to me for safekeeping more than two years ago. I know he wanted you to wear it; you'd have it on right now if he'd had more time on this earth. I hope this gesture makes up a little for the cruelty you experienced.

I, more than anyone, know how much Jake loved you.

Your sister, Patty."

DR. WILSON REACHED for the tissues at the same time as Sophie. Their fingers collided, and Sophie pulled out a handful and passed it to Dr. Wilson. They both chuckled a little, as they wiped their eyes.

"I don't know if I can do this," Sophie whispered.

"You can. Open the pouch."

Sophie took the black bag out of the box. She opened the cord with trembling fingers, and upended it into her palm. The familiar cushion cut diamond ring in its antique white gold setting landed in her palm, along with a walnut-sized Ziploc bag filled with a gray, grainy substance—*Jake's ashes.*

The juxtaposition was too much.

Sophie sobbed aloud, her hand curled into a fist around the precious items. When the storm had passed, she wiped her eyes. "I love Patty."

"I love her, too. What a woman. Now, what is this cruelty she is referring to?"

Sophie told Dr. Wilson about the events at the hospital, and the ongoing bitterness that Janice and Monica had demonstrated toward her at Jake's memorial. "To have these items from Patty is priceless. Especially now." Sophie's hand slid down to rest on her abdomen. She'd worn a comfortable, body-skimming dress; her skin already felt tender and easily irritated by tight clothing. "I'm pregnant with Jake's baby."

Dr. Wilson's eyes flew open, and her mouth opened in surprise. "Oh my! What an adventure you're having!"

"What an adventure, indeed." Sophie laughed through her tears. "You always know the right thing to say, Dr. Wilson."

"And this is the very best thing that could have happened after the tragedy of Jake's death."

Sophie's eyes felt so hot and swollen that it was hard to meet Dr. Wilson's honest blue gaze. "Do you really think so? Because it's pretty daunting to have a second child with no ring on my finger."

"But you do have a ring." Dr. Wilson pointed to the antique diamond, now resting on the table beside the tiny bag of ashes. "Something you might not know is that I'm a licensed officiant for weddings. By the power vested in me by the state of Hawaii, I pronounce you and Jake legally engaged."

Sophie's mouth quirked up in a smile as she slid the ring onto the fourth finger of her left hand—a perfect fit, just what she'd been missing since the day she and Jake exchanged promises at his hospital bed. "I don't think that counts for anything, Dr. Wilson, but thank you."

"Wait and see. I bet it does. Jake will have left a life insurance policy, something from his army retirement, his Social Security benefits. You might not need the money, but his child is entitled to it. I'll swear to your engagement's legal standing in any court of law."

Sophie leaned over to hug the psychologist. "Thank you."

Dr. Wilson cleared her throat. "This is huge, but there are still a lot of loose ends to the situation you've been dealing with. Let's process that, now, because with any luck at all, what we discussed is only going to get bigger." Dr. Wilson glanced meaningfully at Sophie's waistline.

Sophie filled Dr. Wilson in on the call she had gotten from Raveaux on Phi Ni, bringing her back to Honolulu, and the trap that had been set for Connor. Thanks to Raveaux, she'd warned Connor, who'd moved quickly to get Momi, Armita and the dogs on a plane back to Hawaii. He'd then taken his houseman, Nam, and his wife Kupa, back to the compound in Thailand.

"By the time the agents raided the island, the place was deserted. I flew back there looking for Momi and Armita, and found that everything had been seized by the Department of Justice. It was a shock at the time—but my new lawyer says it was an illegal seizure. Sheldon Hamilton, the owner of Phi Ni, had deeded it over to me before his death, and the island didn't actually belong to him anymore. We're fighting the seizure in court. Ultimately, I expect to win." Sophie got up and walked over to the credenza against one wall. "Would you like a cup of tea?"

"Can't think of anything I'd like more."

Paula kept the tea service stocked, and Sophie poured instant hot water from the electric kettle into a pot. She added loose leaf jasmine tea and carried the tray of tea things over to the low table.

"What's the status of the multi-agency investigation now? Are you concerned about it, since those two agents tried to interview you here at Security Solutions?"

"My father got me an excellent defense lawyer, as I said. He's challenging every move that team makes as far as involving me in the case. So far, I've only had to go to one interview with Agent Pillman down at my old FBI headquarters. I took the lawyer with me, and it went exactly nowhere for the FBI." Sophie poured the tea into their cups through a strainer. "I'm being closely monitored, though. I sweep this office and my house every day for surveillance devices, and still, they keep trying to bug me."

Dr. Wilson picked up a cup and blew on the surface of the tea. "What about this character, Raveaux? He seems to have been instrumental in all of this."

"Pierre took a tremendous risk in warning me about the raid. He's also under constant surveillance, and has been threatened with deportation—and worse. I have engaged Security Solutions' legal team to come up with a plan to try to protect him." Sophie picked up her teacup, holding the delicate handle, and admired the play of light on the vintage diamond on her finger. "Thankfully, Connor is safe with Nam and his wife at the Yām Khûmkạn compound. I've seen its fortifications, and nothing short of an act of war would be able to pry him, the Master, or Pim Wat out of there."

Sophie's tea was finally cool enough for her to take a sip, and she lifted the fragrant beverage to her lips. Her enhanced sense of smell made the flowery scent and taste impossibly sweet and delicious. She met Dr. Wilson's eyes. "Pim Wat and the Master are the ones the Justice Department is really after. This is far from over, but you could say we won the first skirmish, if not the battle."

"Tell me more about Pim Wat and the Master. Last time we talked, Connor had told you they were off somewhere, and the Master was trying to heal Pim Wat from what she suffered at Guantánamo."

"Yes, but while I was on the island, Connor brought them to visit. We 'buried the hatchet' at Pim Wat's request."

"Given your mother's profession, I'm not sure that's an appropriate idiom," Dr. Wilson said dryly.

Sophie shocked herself by laughing. Maybe it was all too much, but she laughed and laughed, tipping over sideways on the couch—

until the laughter turned to tears. Eventually she sat up and mopped her face with more tissues. "Whew. This is exhausting. I need a nap."

"First trimester is hard on the body. Tiredness and mood swings are as common as morning sickness."

"I know. This isn't my first rodeo, as the saying goes." Sophie straightened up. "My charming mother looked awful. She was completely changed." Sophie described the scene: Pim Wat's frailty and changed appearance, even the break of trust with Connor. "He defended himself that the Master had known about the island for years, that it was never the refuge we hoped it was. But the fact remains that he didn't warn me that he was bringing them. He gave me no choice in the matter. I told him after they left, that I could never trust him the same way. Basically, he's shown where his loyalties lie."

"And let's not forget that he let you believe he'd died, when he killed his Todd Remarkian identity," Dr. Wilson said. "You grieved for him deeply, and it was all a lie. I know you love Connor, but I have always had concerns about him. Remembering that he serves the Master's agenda might be an important thing to keep in mind going forward. Perhaps Connor is changing in a way that no longer fits with your lifestyle as a working mother."

"Trust you, Dr. Wilson, to put your finger on it exactly. But I owe my life to Connor. If he hadn't put that chip in me, I'd be dead, along with Jake." Sophie unconsciously fingered where the chip lay, in the soft skin under her arm.

"Do you still want the chip? Do you want to be someone that this wanted fugitive can find, anywhere in the world, at the touch of a button?" Dr. Wilson's elegant eyebrows had risen. "Maybe that's something you should think about." She pointed to the small bag. "What are you going to do with the ashes?"

"I don't know yet." Sophie slid the little Ziploc back into the velvet pouch and put it in the hidden pocket of her dress. She wanted it close to her, on her body—like the ring.

"I've worked with a lot of grieving people, and here's a bit of advice: don't hold onto those ashes too long." Dr. Wilson set down her empty teacup and stood up.

Across from her, Sophie did the same.

"We've covered a lot of ground today. I'm going to be on the island for a couple more days, if you want to meet again. But now I'm off to the mall, to buy myself a few new dresses."

Sophie smiled. "If you don't mind, I'll come with you. I need a few new dresses too—from the maternity store."

⁂

HOURS LATER, Sophie pulled into the parking lot at Waikiki Beach. She was tired, but in a good way, wrung out from laughing and crying and shopping.

She and Dr. Wilson had enjoyed their time at the mall. Buying maternity clothes and a few tiny baby things had made her pregnancy feel more real. But she wasn't yet ready to go home to the evening routine with Armita, Momi, and the dogs.

She was going to take Dr. Wilson's advice—it had served her well in the past.

Sophie made sure her shopping bags in the back seat were covered by a beach towel. Break-ins were common in this area. She got out of the SUV her father had bought her so long ago, after her FBI Academy graduation, and locked it. The floaty dress she had worn that day felt soft and comfortable, blowing around her body as she walked down onto the sand of the beloved beach she had run on and swum at for so many years.

She and Jake hadn't visited it often. The bulk of the time they'd spent as a couple had been in Hilo. But this was a special place to her, and always would be. She wanted to think of Jake when she was here with her babies, teaching them to swim in the gentle waves and running with her dogs on the sand.

Sophie walked down to the water's edge. The ocean purled softly over her feet. Sunset glazed the waves with the colors of fire and lava. Palm trees fluttered their fronds in the breeze. This was paradise—and it was home.

Sophie reached into her pocket and took out the small black velvet pouch. She pulled the cord that opened it, revealing the miniature bag inside, filled with a handful of ash.

All that was left of her *kun dii.*

"Cootie, you mean," his voice said in her mind. "Get it right, babe."

She smiled.

Because that wasn't all that was left of Jake. She carried him in her body, in the DNA of her child, and he would live on. *Such a divine mystery.*

Sophie opened the tiny Ziploc and scattered the bit of ashes on the next wave that moved in to caress her toes.

She shut her eyes—and almost, almost—could feel him kiss her goodbye.

Turn the page for a sneak peek of, *Wired Strong*, Paradise Crime Thrillers book 12.

SNEAK PEEK
WIRED STRONG, PARADISE CRIME THRILLERS BOOK 12

Pim Wat
Same timeframe as the end of Wired Ghost

Pɪᴍ Wᴀᴛ sᴛᴀʀᴇᴅ at her reflection in the mirror.

She was supposed to be meditating. The Master wanted her to learn to manage her emotions, her mind, her body.

And technically, she *was* meditating—on the ruin of her once beautiful face.

Scar tissue twisted across her skin like a snake. One eye was higher than the other, because a broken cheekbone hadn't been set. The other eye wouldn't open all the way—the lid had been torn and resewn poorly, giving her the look of a drunkard. And her jaw had been broken and not reset, causing a droop to her mouth and ruining her bite. Eating was painful and speech difficult.

The dandelion fluff covering her skull, gone white from suffering, she could grow out and dye.

But her face?

Pim Wat was a gargoyle now, a travesty. She had no intention of mastering her emotions about that.

She picked up the heavy, expensive bottle of perfume

resting on her vanity, and hurled it at the mirror. The flask broke with a satisfying crash that flung shards of crystal and glass all over the luxurious chamber, filling her hair and peppering her skin with painful shrapnel that reeked of jasmine and roses.

Pim Wat welcomed the searing of a thousand tiny cuts. She smiled through the pain, letting the shards impale her where they would.

Pain was her friend. Pain woke her up; it was a spur in her side, driving her to greatness. She was done being a malleable doll that the Master could mold into someone loving, forgiving, passive. She'd never been those things, and this outward ugliness didn't suit her, either.

The Master called her "my beautiful one," and "my deadly viper."

Pim Wat wasn't, now, but she would be again.

She'd rise from these ashes like a phoenix to strike terror into her enemies; she'd rain death on those who'd stolen years of her life—beginning with that disloyal whore who'd handed her over to the torturers.

She'd enjoyed the masquerade of asking Sophie's forgiveness. Now her daughter wouldn't see vengeance coming.

A knock at the door. "Madam? Are you all right?" The quavering voice of Pim Wat's attendant was muffled by the heavy wooden portal. The woman was a peasant, wife of Number One's houseman Nam. The couple had recently been brought to the Yām Khûmkạn compound as refugees, hiding from the raid that the U.S. Department of Justice had made on their home. Kupa should be grateful to be allowed to serve Pim Wat, but the woman continually needed discipline.

"Bring a feather duster, broom, and pan, Kupa," Pim Wat said. "There's been an accident."

"Right away, my lady." The maid's footsteps hurried away.

Pim Wat finally shut her eyes.

She could meditate now, sitting in outward stillness, and plan her escape.

Marcella
Four weeks after Wired Ghost

MARCELLA SHUT the door of the office at Fight Club, and turned to face her friend. "Did you wand the room for bugs?"

"I did." Sophie rose from the chair behind the battered metal desk, a relic from a time when the now prosperous gym had been small and struggling. She held a device in her hand as she approached Marcella. "Extend your arms, please."

Marcella rolled her eyes. "Really? There's no room in this outfit for anything but my tits." She extended her arms and allowed Sophie to sweep the palm-sized device over the exercise bra and tight workout shorts she wore. "I can't believe we've come to this."

Sophie switched off the handheld detector. "I don't think you'd intentionally try to entrap me, but there are agents in your office who'd do anything to take me down."

"Special Agent Pillman of Internal Affairs, you mean." Marcella made a rude Italian hand gesture. "That man's a menace, and that's on a good day."

Sophie gestured to the leather couch against the wall. "Let's get comfortable. It's been too long since we caught up, and we have a lot to talk about."

"I know. I'm the one who asked you to meet me." Marcella put her hands on her hips, and ran an eyeball over her friend.

Sophie wasn't looking half bad, considering she'd lost her fiancé, Jake Dunn, in a volcano-related tragedy only three months before. Prone to depression, Sophie had been known to take to her bed without eating for days at a time. Marcella had feared that Jake's death, coupled with the departure of Sophie's daughter and nanny to

Kaua'i for their custody month with the child's father, might have brought on such an episode.

Instead, Sophie's usually short hair was nearly touching her shoulders in a riot of thick brown ringlets. Her tawny skin glowed, and though there were bags under her eyes, an unfamiliar roundness filled out Sophie's cheeks, breasts, and hips. "Are you ready for a little sparring? You look like you're getting soft."

"Not today." Sophie sat down on the couch and patted the open area beside her. "Now that we've made sure the area is secure, you need to tell me what is going on with this investigation into Connor."

"Okay, I'll tell you what I can, but it isn't much. They won't let me anywhere near the case." Marcella flopped onto the old leather couch, smoothing her sleek ponytail. "I've heard whispers around the office indicating there's an FBI faction that wants to take you into custody in order to bring in Connor—by using you as a combo of hostage and bait. I had to listen at Waxman's door to get this—and thankfully, he wasn't in favor."

Sophie's honey-brown eyes were concerned. "Who was in the meeting?"

"Pillman and Gundersohn. I'm sure you already know there's a full-on multi-agency task force out to get the Ghost. With Interpol and the CIA on board, Pillman argued that they could let those guys do the dirty work of picking you up and storing you somewhere, and pretend not to be involved." Marcella laid a hand on Sophie's arm, squeezing it to impress Sophie of her worry. "I'm not sure even your dad's influence is going to be enough to keep you safe. You have to go somewhere. Hide."

Sophie shook her head. "No. I can't hide. I've lawyered up, as they say. And so far, Bennie Fernandez is worth every penny I'm paying him."

"That awful little man!" Marcella tossed her head back and laughed, picturing the defense lawyer's cherubic, Santa Claus appearance and wicked legal aptitude. "Never thought I'd be on the same side as him, but he's kicked our ass in court a half dozen times. I'm a little less worried about you now."

"Ever since Connor came out of hiding to rescue Jake and me from the volcano, that task force has been relentless. We've been through two full searches of the Security Solutions building. Subpoenas of our records and computers. They're trying to squeeze Connor by seizing his property and any assets they can find; but he saw that coming a long time ago, and transferred ownership to me. Now I'm the one dealing with all the pressure." Sophie shook her head. "I wish they'd give it up. He's untouchable at the Yām Khûmkạn compound in Thailand, and he doesn't care about any of this anymore."

"I'll be honest, Sophie." Marcella leaned forward and made eye contact with her best friend. "I don't trust that man, whatever name he's currently going by, as far as I can throw him. The more time that goes by, and the longer he's involved with that weird-ass Thai organization, the less I think he has your best interests at heart."

Sophie looked down. She rubbed the back of her arm. "I know you mean well, Marcella, but Connor and I have a bond. I owe him my life. He'd never betray me or let them take me."

Marcella bit her lip to keep from responding. *She didn't believe that for a minute.* The man who called himself Connor had many names, and many other loyalties. He always had—or he'd have protected Sophie better than just dumping everything, including his dog, on her. "I felt duty-bound, because of our friendship, to warn you. What if the CIA just grabs you, lawyers be damned, and whisks you off? Threatens to torture you, forces you to communicate with Connor so he comes to get you?"

Sophie was still rubbing the back of her arm, an odd habit. "I've thought of that. And I do need to do something to deal with that possibility. But hiding isn't the answer—these organizations work in the shadows. No, I need to stay in the light to stay safe, even though it goes against my natural inclinations."

Marcella got up in agitation. She stalked over to the water cooler and filled a plastic cup with filtered water for each of them. She handed one to Sophie, eyeing the lovely antique engagement ring her friend wore in memory of Jake. "What does 'staying in the light' mean, exactly?"

"Instead of hiding, I need to be even more visible. Involved with the workings of Security Solutions. Surrounded by a security team at home and at the office, 24/7. Going to events on my father's arm as his plus-one. Occupying an untouchable position by being a United States Ambassador's daughter. I need to be seen—even in my current condition." Sophie smoothed her left hand, decorated with that sparkler of a diamond, over her waist. "You're right that I'm going soft, Marcella. I'm twelve weeks pregnant, and it's Jake's."

"What? No—seriously? Again?" Marcella's eyes flew open, and she clapped a hand over her mouth, wishing she could take back the words. "I didn't mean that the way it sounded. I only meant—how hard it already is for you, as a single mom. Jake's baby too—oh my gosh, you—you must be . . ."

But Marcella couldn't imagine Sophie's situation—not really, and she knew it. She was happily married to the love of her life, Honolulu Police Department detective Marcus Kamuela. Someday they hoped to be parents. She'd never want to have to deal with a pregnancy and a child alone—not only once, but twice.

Jake's death seemed even more tragic now.

Sophie's full lips drew into a tight line and her expression closed down. "I expect that kind of response from a lot of people, Marcella, but I didn't expect it from you."

"Gah! I'm sorry, darling. If you're happy, I'm happy." Marcella lifted her hands in a "surrender" gesture. "Jake's baby. Oh my. His family must be ecstatic."

"They don't know. No one knows but Dr. Wilson. And now you." Sophie's hand still rested over her abdomen. "This baby is all I have of Jake. All I'll ever have." Her eyes filled. "And I can't help but believe that it's meant to be, because of that. No matter how challenging the situation is."

"Oh, honey, of course." Marcella reached out to hug her friend, but Sophie pushed her away and stood up.

"I think you'd better go. I told Alika I'd check out his computer system and the bookkeeping here at his office." Sophie's gaze was already on the computer resting on the desk. Sophie's ex, Alika, her daughter Momi's father, owned the gym. Sophie and Alika seemed to be solid friends as they co-parented their two-and-a-half-year-old with the help of Armita, Momi's dedicated nanny. "Let me know if you hear anything new at the FBI."

"I'm sorry I didn't respond the way you wanted me to about your news, Soph, but I'm here for you. I'll help however I can." Marcella made a tossing gesture. "Maybe you've got spaghetti cravings? I make a mean pasta primavera."

"That won't be necessary. Everything's handled." Sophie walked behind the desk and sat down, turning on the computer. "Have a good workout."

Marcella stood still for a long moment, but Sophie didn't look up.

Marcella's shoulders sagged. She walked to the door and shut it gently behind her.

She wanted to leave—to run away from this echoing, smelly gym with all its memories, and meet Marcus at home. She'd get a hug, maybe make love—just so she could reassure herself that they were alive and together. That Sophie's tragedy wasn't hers.

Her whole being lit up at the thought of being in Marcus's arms. Safe. Treasured. Passionately desired.

But what kind of friend did that make her?

She'd given Sophie an uncensored negative response when she was the first person other than Sophie's therapist trusted with the news of her pregnancy. Sheer selfishness to run to her husband for comfort when Sophie had no one.

No. Marcella wasn't perfect, but she was a better friend than that. She'd stay at the gym, do her workout, and see if Sophie wanted to talk after she was done in the office.

Marcella went over to one of the exercise bikes, got on, and set it for a rigorous mountain climb, keeping one eye on the door. Then weights, still watching for Sophie.

Ninety minutes passed, and eventually Marcella's Catholic guilt was assuaged by the sweaty workout—but when she finally went to the office and tried the door, it was locked.

The blinds were closed. No light showed in the crack under the portal.

Sophie had left, alone.

Continue reading *Wired Strong*: tobyneal.net/WSwb

ACKNOWLEDGMENTS

Dear Readers!

Heavy sigh. *Sniff* Whew.

I honestly didn't see that coming.

And then...it happened on the page, and it was. . . what was meant to be.

I was on a deadline to finish Wired Ghost, but lost my laptop at the airport on the way to visit family in Hawaii. I lost ten days of work until I returned and could retrieve that laptop! I had to finish the book—and so I stopped trying to plan, and I let the characters dictate the story.

What happened next, from the chapter when the volcanic eruption reached the chamber where Sophie and Jake were trapped, until that very last scene on the beach—was written as the characters themselves revealed it. I laughed, I cried, I jumped with excitement, I shed tears at the end no matter how many times I read it.

It was perfect.

Why was it perfect?

Because this was how Jake wanted his story to end.

Jake was someone who appeared on the paper as a minor character in *Wired Rogue #2*. I had no great plans for this rude, crude dude, except that he be a foil for Sophie and provide some comic relief. He started out two dimensional, almost a cliché—but his character grew, and changed, and he eventually became his very best self, someone worthy of Sophie's love.

I came to like him very much, flaws and all— even love him a little bit.

And when I let go of the steering wheel of this story, Jake chose a true hero's death for himself—which was always his highest aspiration.

Jake will live on. In flashbacks, memories, stories told between friends and family—and in the child he left with Sophie.

I hope you won't grieve, but will press on with Sophie as she continues to grow into her best self too, and we discover who that is in *Wired Strong*, #12.

Until next time, I'll be writing. Much aloha and love,

FREE BOOKS

Join my mystery and romance lists and receive free, full-length, award-winning ebooks of *Torch Ginger* & *Somewhere on St. Thomas* as welcome gifts: tobyneal.net/TNNews

TOBY'S BOOKSHELF

PARADISE CRIME SERIES

Paradise Crime Mysteries
Blood Orchids

Torch Ginger

Black Jasmine

Broken Ferns

Twisted Vine

Shattered Palms

Dark Lava

Fire Beach

Rip Tides

Bone Hook

Red Rain

Bitter Feast

Razor Rocks

Wrong Turn

Shark Cove

Coming 2021

Paradise Crime Mysteries Novella
Clipped Wings

Paradise Crime Mystery
Special Agent Marcella Scott
Stolen in Paradise

Paradise Crime Suspense Mysteries
Unsound

Paradise Crime Thrillers
Wired In

Wired Rogue

Wired Hard

Wired Dark

Wired Dawn

Wired Justice

Wired Secret

Wired Fear

Wired Courage

Wired Truth

Wired Ghost

Wired Strong

Wired Revenge

Coming 2021

ROMANCES
Toby Jane

The Somewhere Series
Somewhere on St. Thomas

Somewhere in the City

Somewhere in California

The Somewhere Series
Secret Billionaire Romance
Somewhere in Wine Country
Somewhere in Montana
Date TBA
Somewhere in San Francisco
Date TBA

A Second Chance Hawaii Romance
Somewhere on Maui

Co-Authored Romance Thrillers
The Scorch Series
Scorch Road
Cinder Road
Smoke Road
Burnt Road
Flame Road
Smolder Road

YOUNG ADULT

Standalone
Island Fire

NONFICTION
TW Neal

Memoir
Freckled
Open Road

ABOUT THE AUTHOR

Kirkus Reviews calls Neal's writing, *"persistently riveting. Masterly."*

Award-winning, USA Today bestselling social worker turned author Toby Neal grew up on the island of Kaua`i in Hawaii. Neal is a mental health therapist, a career that has informed the depth and complexity of the characters in her stories. Neal's mysteries and thrillers explore the crimes and issues of Hawaii from the bottom of the ocean to the top of volcanoes. Fans call her stories, *"Immersive, addicting, and the next best thing to being there."*

Neal also pens romance and romantic thrillers as Toby Jane and writes memoir/nonfiction under TW Neal.

Visit tobyneal.net for more ways to stay in touch!
or
Join my Facebook readers group, *Friends Who Like Toby Neal Books,* for special giveaways and perks.

Made in the USA
Las Vegas, NV
19 April 2022